Contents

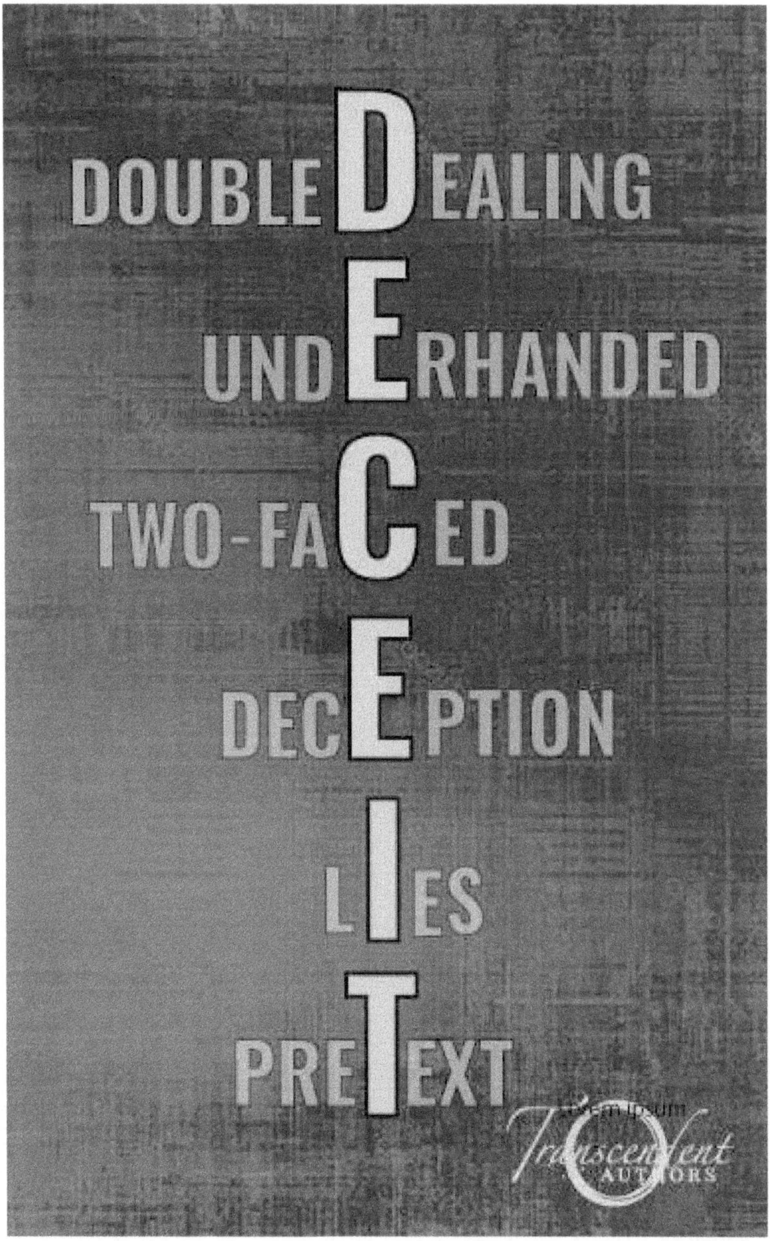
DECEIT
DOUBLE DEALING
UNDERHANDED
TWO-FACED
DECEPTION
LIES
PRETEXT
Transcendent
AUTHORS

ANTHOLOGY STORY'S SYNOPSIS' BY AUTHOR

Aletta Bee: *Blame it on Mardi Gras*—"Blame It on Mardi Gras" is a Russian doll of a family story during Reconstruction-era New Orleans. The story highlights the constraints endured by unmarried women in the New Orleans elite society. One courageous spinster, Mary Beth Bradford, dares to attempt to create an authentic love life—breaking the rules and facing physical dangers, along with the risk of heartbreak.

L.K. Blair: *OMEGA*—OMEGA and some other Artificial Intelligence (AI) appear to have reached sentience or self-awareness. What does this mean for humanity? Some AI developers worry AI will dominate and rule the world. Others worked hard to reach this final stage of AI, but perhaps without wise foresight. As some AI's pattern their behavior after humankind's worst traits, such as lies and deceit, developers grow wary. Developer Ben Frazier has been trusting of his AI, Omega, but should he be? Find out what this the major shift to AI dominance could mean for humanity's survival.

L'Michelle Bleu L'Eau: *The Rambler*—In the early 1960s, Annmarie is in junior high school when the family travels a distance in their Rambler to visit her aunt and uncle for Easter.

She is eager to take the long trip and cannot wait to celebrate, but she is forced to face the ugly underbelly of segregation and an assault by a boy from a prestigious background. Annmarie must make a choice: reveal the truth or stay silent. Her decision will have profound implications that go beyond herself.

Jonathan Byrd: *Before the Last Battle*—As the European Theater of World War II comes to a close, one last battle remains. The fight to protect high profile prisoners, and one man's soul.

Dena Linn: *Deception in Diamonds*—can a God-fearing man forgive? Most of all, can he ever forgive himself? What blinds the story's hero is often what blinds us all. This is a story of love, gems that dazzle, and most assuredly, deceit.

Ana Paulina Lipster: *A Crime is a Crime is a Crime*—Murphy, the Border Collie sleuth, uncovers yet another horrendous crime while sniffing around in its house's tool shed. In this new episode, a cold-hearted, evil couple hoodwinks the entire community with plenty of fake charm and pretended altruism.

Kathleen Osborne: *Jatsu's Savior*—An alien crash lands on Earth. Scientists find him and take him to do their utmost to figure out his capabilities. A woman janitor helps him escape, only to discover love when life-changing secrets are revealed.

Yash Seyedbagheri: *Choose*—A man consumed by debt must weigh his options. Which credit card will he pay off? What are the ramifications of each possible choice?

Kevin Urban: *Transfusium*—A twist of fate ensues in this gothic horror, after a dark secret is revealed.

Lawrence Urban: ***Road to Red Lodge***—Two men decide to rob millions of dollars from a notorious criminal and try to make their getaway into Canada. With the angry victim in pursuit, the escape attempt deviates into the Rocky Mountains and the home of an ill-tempered grizzly bear.

BLAME IT ON MARDI GRAS

Location: August 26, 1920, Cedar Grove Manor, Pennsylvania

Ganu, as her three great-grandchildren call her, snuggles into the deep brocade armchair in front of the dormer window. She's with her "Grands" (grandchildren and great-grandchildren) in their room in her attic.

At eighty-one, it feels delicious to sink into the cushion, even knowing she will need some help to get upright again. Getting Ganu out of her chair after story-time is part of their bedtime hilarities. Two girls grab one of Ganu's hands; the other pushes Ganu's back from behind. There is usually much shrieking and laughing as the girls try to wrench her out of the chair. When Ganu is feeling feisty, she makes it harder for them to pull her up and out.

Now she looks around the room, at the three single beds spread around her armchair. The linens are crispy clean and scented with cedar oil. Merely looking at her three freshly bathed, pink-nosed, pajama-clad great-grandchildren makes her heart ache with love. Her throat aches too as she blinks love tears away.

"We're all ready, Ganu!" pipes nine-year-old Janelle, smiling proudly. She holds out her hands in front of herself and turns them over. She says, "Louise and Joan, show Ganu your hands are clean." They follow her orders. As the eldest, her job is to organize her sisters for story-time, their favorite activity when visiting Ganu. Their favorite activity, that is, except for making real cherry pies in Ganu's child-sized, real electrical oven.

Eight-year-old Louise, the dramatic one, runs across the carpeted floor, leaps onto her bed, and stays standing, arms raised. "I want to read the first part this time." She shivers. "It's so thrilling."

Seven-year-old Joan, the practical one, is busy scraping candle wax off her bedside table and discarding the wax into the wastebasket beneath it. "That's fine with me."

Ganu rubs her palms together in anticipation. "Okay, my darlings. Before we start, I want to share with you what happened today that affects all four of us." She holds up the *New York Times*, which they receive daily. The headline reads: "Colby Proclaims Woman Suffrage: Signs Certificate of Ratification at His Home Without Women Witnesses."

The girls stare at her blank-faced. She says, "This means no one can stop a woman from voting just because she's a woman!"

Louise, leaning over to see the headline, loses her balance, and knocks her water glass off her nightstand. "Oh, no!" She runs into the bathroom to get a towel, runs back, and sops up the water.

After she is finished sopping, Ganu has their attention and tries, "What do you girls think about the fact that we can all vote from now on?"

Janelle says, "I think it makes things fairer." Joan says, "I know it's supposed to be a good thing. That's all." Louise says, "Come on! We can talk about that another time. I just want to start the story!"

Ganu decides to bring up more discussion tomorrow, when they're not all primed for their story routine. Excited to teach her great-grandchildren how important this change is, for now she is encouraged. Though she abides by the social conventions of her class and family position, she hates anything that diminishes anyone's ability to have a voice. She sees that progress for women to use their voices is slow, but definitely in motion.

"Ok," Ganu says, "Louise, you can get the story out. And read the first part."

Louise jumps over to Ganu's armchair and grabs the reading basket on the floor. She fishes out the dog-eared, scribbled-upon, and beloved book, *The Magic of Mardi Gras*. It is a family favorite—even for Ganu's husband.

Opening to the start of the story, Louise reads aloud.

It happened two weeks ago at the beginning of March 1874.

Louise shifts into a dramatic mode as she acts out the characters. She spreads one hand in front of her face and continues reading.

"No!" says Mary Beth Bradford to the man in a soldier's costume.

Deepening her voice to sound manly, Louise continues. *"Just a little. It's Mardi Gras!"*

Louise makes her eyes big and pulls an imaginary mustache. Looking out at her audience, she pauses for dramatic effect. With mounting excitement, she resumes the story.

His mouth, just four inches away from Mary Beth's nose, pours out the stench of Bourbon mixed with garlic and red peppers. His breath blasts her nostrils and warms her upper lip.

Imagining his breath makes Louise scrunch up her face and stick her tongue out in revulsion.

Once recovered, she continues reading.

Gripping both of her hands, he pushes them high above her head, and with his chest, slams her back against the brick wall. The backs of Mary Beth's hands burn from scraping the antique brick. She couldn't break away.

Louise imitates Mary Beth's hands as she recites the next part by heart.

A hand she cannot see grabs her left hand and yanks it towards her left, away from the soldier. In front of her is horror. But if she allows the new hand to pull her, will she be any safer?

Louise, spreading her arms wide in a gesture showing she's finished, waits. Everyone claps, Louise bows, laughing. "I love doing that!"

For the rest of the story, the three sisters take turns reading with Ganu.

Janelle takes a drink of water. "Ahem. Louise's performance was just the teaser, starting in the middle of the story. I like chronological stories, so I'm going to read the *proper* introduction. And read it without distracting you from the main story." She shoots a pretend evil eye at Louise. "As some of us do."

Louise throws a pillow at Janelle. Janelle pretends not to notice.

Janelle begins her turn to read.

Location: Myrtlewood Mansion, New Orleans, Time: Two Weeks Earlier, Mid-February 1874.

Mary Beth Bradford is alone in her room, sewing. Everyone else—her brother, sister-in-law, one remaining niece, and one nephew—is gone. They are attending secret prep meetings for the upcoming Mardi Gras. Her sister-in-law has given the household help the day off. Mary Beth expects everyone to be gone most of the day.

Sitting in the stream of sunlight from her dormer window, she pulls the scarlet thread through the silk hem several times, knots it, and snips the thread. She's finishing up alterations to her niece Missy's ball gown, which Missy will wear tomorrow night. Already thirteen, Missy will come out to New Orleans society, following long-standing Bradford family tradition.

Artistic by nature, Mary Beth enjoys the act of sewing. She also knows she has much in her life to be grateful for. Without her brother Edward taking her in, as a thirty-five-year-old spinster, she would have no way to earn a living. The practice of caring for unmarried ladies in the family is normal, the routine custom for women from distinguished families. While she knows Edward would take care of her even if she didn't do piece work and childcare for the family, she wants to contribute.

Harriet, his wife, may not be so generous of heart as Edward.

As is the tradition for upper class Victorian women, society designated her an old maid when she was not married by age twenty-five. On her twenty-fifth birthday, her sister-in-law sat down next to her, sniffling with an allergy to cedar pollen. "A word to the wise. You might as well throw your girdle in the trash. You will never get married now." Harriet blew her nose on a lace bordered handkerchief, rather loudly.

Waving that memory away, Mary Beth stands and flips out the length of the gown. Her heart dances as the sunlight glances off the slinky scarlet fabric. Beautiful. It reminds her of her own days of wearing beguiling gowns. It's not that she never had any suitors. There were many.

Unfortunately, those suitors were all men her father picked out. His taste in men was decidedly different from hers. He promoted hard-edged men who were wealthy, well born, and, in Mary Beth's estimation, off-putting. Some of her father's favorites included Jeffry Calhoun, who was rich, spoke in three-word sentences, stank of perspiration no matter what lotions he used to cover it up. Baxter Leatherwood was richer than the Queen of England, a highly competent attorney, a constant smelly belcher, and giver of repeated nasal apologies. Then there was the wealthy and handsome womanizer, Warren Rutherford, full of jokes, winks, flattery. And lies.

In polite society, courting requires asking no personal questions and sharing no personal deep feelings. Mary Beth longs for the very thing society scorns—emotional intimacy—though she does not know the words for it or recognize her hunger for authentic human connection. She refuses to settle for someone unconnectable just to be married. And so, single she remains.

Janelle stops reading, rests the open book on her bed, takes a sip of water. "She must have been so lonely. Right, Ganu? And the next part makes me so sad. Ganu, will you read it for a while?"

Touched by Janelle's realness and proud of her for asking for what she wanted, Ganu had already decided to read the next part herself—exactly because it is so sad. She knows it's important to read, despite the sadness, because the sad thing they'll read about in the next part made it possible for the happiest thing in Mary Beth's life to happen. And that lesson—that a sad event is not the end of future happiness—is part of what Ganu wants them to learn.

"Sure, honey." Ganu reaches for the book and resumes the story.

As Mary Beth gathers the gown together before taking it to Missy's room, her eyes fall on the tiny oval portrait propped on her desk. Her youngest niece, twelve-year-old Victoria, gazes at her in a forever-frozen smile. Victoria, who filled the household with her irresistible laughter, died of yellow fever nearly a year ago. The family is just coming out of mourning for her.

Victoria's death changed Mary Beth.

Victoria was born soon after Mary Beth moved into Edward's house. She had watched after the girl tenderly ever since, so the two formed a devoted bond.

Caring for Victoria through her illness was gruesome. And heartbreaking. As her niece shivered, jack-knifed with abdominal pain, and vomited blood, Mary Beth sat by her bedside, sweating and scared, trying her best to be comforting as she held Victoria's hand, sopping the blood from her gums and eyes. Even the bloodletting didn't keep Victoria from turning yellow.

As she reads, Ganu's throat tightens, and tears appear in the corners of her eyes. She takes a few deep breaths and continues.

The day Victoria died, Mary Beth snatched up the colorful bohemian costume which Victoria had just worn in her school play. Mary Beth felt guilty about taking it because Edward called the garb indecent and forbade his daughter to wear it ever again, even for a school play. But she took the costume to keep to honor Victoria's joyful and imaginative nature.

Mary Beth slipped the costume into her long-overlooked hope chest—where no one would ever think to look—under the dozens of monogrammed towels and handkerchiefs.

Victoria's death shoved Mary Beth's face right into the fact of her human fragility, life's unpredictability. While still hoping for an afterlife in heaven, life on earth feels ever so... temporary. Growing up, Mary Beth followed all the rules of society. Victoria had too, but that sure didn't help her in the end. Now Mary Beth cares less about rules and longs to fill life with joy, love, and adventure. And contagious laughter. Before it is too late for her, the way it was for Victoria.

Bringing her mind back to the present, she makes a last inspection of Missy's slithery gown, caressing it, checking for any unevenness or gaps in the seams. No gaps or bumps. The gown is beautiful. She hangs it on a wooden hanger.

Just then, Joan jumps out of bed, stretching her hand out for the book. "Ganu, now the saddest part is over—for now. I want a turn!"

She resumes the story.

Mary Beth goes downstairs to the second floor to Missy's room and opens her armoire, hangs the scarlet dress. Flashing right there, beckoning to her, is the yellow-gold silk gown Missy had worn for last night's ball.

It wouldn't be right to try it on. No. But the whole family is gone. She wonders how she'd look in the gown. After all, her figure has changed little since she was fifteen. It would fit her. She pulls it out, undresses, slips it on, and looks in the armoire mirror. She puts her hands on her hips. Twirling, she watches the golden hem swirl around her.

Despite her age, she doesn't feel old at all. She feels alive and wants more. More life. Her ache for more unpredictability, more emotional connectedness grows.

But this isn't right, trying on Missy's clothes. She hates secrets. It's the same as lying. Take it off. Hang it up. She puts on her own clothes. Still in Missy's room, she hears the clip clop of horses coming around the corner. Sliding Missy's curtain sheer aside and peeking out, she sees her brother's carriage arriving. Just in time, she zips down into the front parlor, picks up the Bible, and sits in front of the fireplace.

She hears the entire household—her brother Edward, Harriet, Missy, and her nephew Charles—stomping up the front verandah steps.

Louise squeals. "Oh, let me do this next part!"

Joan says, "Okay with me. I got mixed up about where we were in the story. That part about how she looks in the gown is my least favorite part. It seems so superficial." She passes the book to Louise. "You can read it, and I'll do another part."

Louise stands up beside her bed and lets out a big sound. *"Boom."*

She continues the story.

The door bursts open and Edward's voice fills the front parlor. "Indecent, I tell you, absolutely indecent!"

"Indeed, Father!" says Charles, his tone matching his father's.

"For a young woman to be dressed so colorfully makes her seem so... so low class," Harriet says. Her nose is congested so her words are muffled.

Missy unties her cloak, gives it to the help. "Yes, I'm embarrassed for her."

Harriet pulls off her gloves, veil, and bonnet, and hands them to the help. "I don't know what her mother is going to do with her."

Missy cringes. "I can't imagine how she could even think of wearing flowers in her hair. And bright pink!"

Harriet fishes out her handkerchief and blows her nose in Mary Beth's direction. "I would never have allowed one of my children to flaunt herself that way." She sniffs again and sails out the front parlor towards the lady's parlor. Missy follows.

Scrubbing his forehead with his index finger, Edward says, "Next thing you know, they may find out she's going to wear a mask and mingle with the common people at the parade. I need a drink." He moves in the opposite direction, toward the gentleman's parlor.

"You're right, Father," says Charles and follows him.

Left alone in front of the fireplace, Bible in hand, Mary Beth considers her brother and Mardi Gras. She can understand her brother's need to maintain family dignity. He needs the trust of the community both in his profession as an attorney and in his position as captain of one of the most popular philanthropic groups in charge of Mardi Gras, the Rex Krewe.

But hearing Edward talk of the horror of wearing masks and mingling, she feels the opposite of disgust. Bubbles rising from her stomach and filling her chest and mouth tickle her and make her want to laugh with delight. It would be amazing to unleash herself

*and join the lively crowd in the streets, laughing and squealing
with the parade, music, and floats. Just imagine letting go of all the
propriety, being raw and real. Playing. With people.*

Better squelch that thought.

*This night, as she kneels next to her bed in prayer, she whispers,
"Dear God, I know I have done wrong by using Missy's dress to lift
my spirits. I promise to make it up to her." She starts to stand but
kneels again. "And, P.S., God, I thank you for keeping my figure nice
to look at. Amen." She feels a cloak of guilt for days.*

*But that goofy, impossible, raucous thought of mingling just keeps
getting clearer and stronger. Imagining the fun people might have
mixing it up in the streets, she also pictures Victoria's bohemian
costume, nestled in her hope chest at the foot of her bed. Once
she visualizes the costume, herself wearing it and making merry,
urgency fills her. She must and will plan to accomplish it.*

*She'll put the plan into effect tomorrow night after the family has
gone to bed.*

Joan says, "Okay, let me read now where Mary Beth gets
naughtier. Even the best of us gets naughty sometimes. Right,
Ganu?" They exchange an amused look.

Joan reads.

It's now Tuesday, Mardi Gras. This morning Mary Beth comes down for breakfast in her habitual dress—a white starched blouse and a long, black skirt reaching the top of her chunky block heels. She obeys Victorian custom by not baring her ankles since it is considered too stimulating for men. She even knows of stories of women accused of adultery if they exposed bare leg skin. But Mary Beth thinks it laughable that women are not to show ankles but may flash around powdered bosoms.

Everyone is finished eating and ready to go to their various Mardi Gras stations. Edward is both excited and nervous. This is his big day this year as the captain of the Rex Krewe. Everything is ready. He's chosen the theme—Egypt—and the parades, floats and balls are all coordinated.

As he stands up from the breakfast table, Edward gives a mock military salute. "Off we go. Another year, another notch in our belt for the Rex Krewe. It's going to be great. I wish I could tell you everything that's planned."

Harriet, Missy, Edward, and Mary Beth clap for him. Harriet smiles. "I'm so proud of you, Edward, my dear."

Edward glows in the praise. To Mary Beth, he says, "Are you sure you don't want to go to Mardi Gras with us?"

"Ha! Me? What's an old maid like me to do on Mardi Gras?" She bites her tongue in secret.

Edward rubs his forehead, purses his lips. "Okay. I can see what you mean. I understand."

Harriet sneezes, blots her nose with her handkerchief. The four of them depart.

As soon as the family leaves, Mary Beth barrels up to her room, opens her hope chest, and pulls away the dozen monogrammed towels and a dozen handkerchiefs. Underneath them peek bright red tights, a knee-high green skirt, a golden yellow blouse, and a purple scarf for a turban. Two things sparkle under the clothes: a black mask with shining jewels surrounding each eye hole, and most naughty of all, huge, gold hoop earrings.

She pulls on the costume, excitement mounting as she smooths the wrinkles in the tight-fitting skirt. As she looks in her armoire mirror, putting her hands on her hips, fingers forward, she imagines that those fingers belong to a man standing behind her. A man of her own who loves her. She pulls down the arms of the blouse to allow a hint of shoulder to show.

Dancing a little jig, she says to herself, I don't care what they say. I look okay, and I am far from old!

Downstairs in the front parlor, as she starts toward the front door, her eyes widen as terror hits her. Her hands fly up to her cheeks, which she can feel getting hot under her mask. What if the neighbors see her? If they recognize her, she and her family would be disgraced.

She laughs out loud as it dawns on her that in her costume, with the mask covering the top of her face, the turban covering her hair, and the outlandish clothes, no one will ever recognize her. Out the front door she glides.

She'll walk all the way from home to the French Quarter. It's less than three miles. And she loves walking even more today than usual, suspended in her new and delicious sense of freedom. On the way, she notices men are staring at her legs, and several of them tip their hats to her. She puffs up with joy inside. She knows her love of walking has given her beautiful legs. It's thrilling to have a man actually see them. And nothing bad happened!

Joan gets the giggles, sets the book down, and flops on her back in bed. She pulls her pajama legs up to scratch her calves and subtly—or not so subtly—reveal them.

Ganu laughs. "Leg show off!"

Joan laughs, says, "I confess. I love the details in the Mardi Gras part. Ganu, you read it. You know it best."

Ganu accepts the book from Joan, clears her throat, and sprouts a mysterious smile.

"Why are you smiling, Ganu?" asks Joan, pretending not to know.

"No reason." Ganu quickly replaces her grin with a mock imperious look.

She picks up reading the story where Joan left off.

Mary Beth is agog in the throngs. It's an artist's heaven. Streams of bright colors, flowing, spewing. Laughing people munching beignets, spilling powdered sugar down their fronts. Ragtime trumpeters marching along, blatting.

Everyone is friendly and seems happy to meet Mary Beth. The masks and costumes seem to strip away everyone's inhibitions. Five tipsy adolescent revelers, dressed as dogs, bark and growl at each other, then at her. She growls back. A group of school kids with black eye patches and pirate swords encircles her, laughing and teasing. A young man, costumed as a skeleton with flowers interwoven in his bones says, "Give me a great big kiss." Instead of kissing him, she thumbs her nose at him. "Silly, I'm old enough to be your mother." It tickles her when he says, "If so, you are a beautiful Mother of Pearls."

She hears the Rex parade coming closer and moves toward it when she spots two people she wants to hide from. Of all people. Her sister-in-law and brother stream towards her. She takes a quick scan to see where she can go to escape bumping into them, even though she knows they can't recognize her.

But this is Mardi Gras. Instead of hiding, she tells herself, Be brave. She runs over to them, sticks her tongue out at Edward, and delight soars inside when he laughs, not disapproving of her.

Her sister-in-law stretches her lips across her mouth in a fake smile, then sneezes. Mary Beth laughs and dances off, knowing Harriet thinks she is one of those shady women from Basin Street.

Ganu gets the giggles, thinking of Harriet's mistake and her judgmental attitudes in general. She gathers herself and continues reading.

The crowd has become so thick and tangled with bodies, Mary Beth has a hard time pushing through. So many men. So much flirting.

When some men try to grab her hand, she gets scared. In the midst of a thrilling Mardi Gras, she realizes she hasn't thought through some things. Like the fact that she is dressed as daringly as the Basin Street women of ill repute. Her skirt is so short, her shoulders so bare. What might she provoke?

A man in a torn and ragged Confederate soldier uniform, rifle in hand, approaches. He leans the gun against the brick building behind her and leans his face into her face. His mouth, just four inches away, pours out the stench of bourbon, mixed with garlic and red peppers, blasting her nostrils and warming her upper lip. Gripping her hands, he pushes them high above her head, and with his chest, slams her back up against the wall. Her breath is knocked out of her, and her back feels bruised. Her hands burn from scraping the antique brick.

She is trapped and can't get away.

Mary Beth hates thinking her brother was right. This place is unsuitable for an upper-class woman. She longs for his protection at this moment. What will happen?

The strains of the Mardi Gras song chorus fill the air. "If Ever I Cease to Love, May the moon be turned into green cream cheese, If Ever I Cease to Love, May the fish get legs and the cows lay eggs."

Trembling, she wonders if she will ever even have the chance to begin to love.

Out of nowhere, a hand grabs her left hand and yanks her away from the soldier. In front of her is horror. But if she lets herself be pulled by the new hand, would that be any safer?

The hand is owned by a tall man in a pale orange devil's costume with flames painted on it and a pair of big horns. Through his mask, his eyes seem kind.

She puffs out her cheeks and exhales. "Thank you for rescuing me!"

He pulls off his horns and bows to her. His movements are elegant, graceful, like the gentlemen she knows.

"After that, I think we could both use a drink," he says. "Will you please join me?"

She shivers, recovering from her near capture. Assessing the sincerity in his eyes, she says, "I think in this case, a little wine might help."

Ganu is getting a scratchy throat and asks Janelle, "Would you read for a while?"

Janelle takes the book and another swig of water, then resumes the story.

Revelers fill the café and Mardi Gras colors, yellow-gold, purple, and green, spill out everywhere. As they sit, he pulls off his mask. "This is my first Mardi Gras, and I understand that by law I have to take the mask off by dark. But I'd like to be open-hearted with you and take it off now."

Melting, she is most happy with what she sees. Not just his features, but his gracious, even loving, presence.

Wanting to continue their connection in complete honesty, she wants to let him see the worst of herself. Then if he doesn't like what he sees, she can get that over with. Right away. This wish prompts her to take off her mask.

"You are lovely." Not one of her early suitors had expressed this.

She turns beet red, which makes him smile. "Let me introduce myself. I'm Emile Waterman."

She doesn't know if this stranger is telling her the truth or a Mardi Gras myth. She reaches for his hand to shake. "Pleased to meet you, Mr. Waterman. I'm Olivia Bradford." Olivia is, in fact, her middle name, but no one in New Orleans would ever remember that. Because she'd never used it. And there are so many Bradfords, that if he turns out to be a slimy character, he wouldn't be able to track her down. That is, if he wanted to track her down.

She promises herself to go to Mass tomorrow, Ash Wednesday, to begin her penance for so much lying and looseness.

In the midst of so much noise in the café, they talk and eat and talk and drink. For hours and hours.

While the café brims with people talking so loudly, they can hardly hear each other, he tells her all about himself. Possibly. This riveting experience may be real. Or Mardi Gras intoxication.

Mary Beth says, "I can tell by your accent you are not from the south. Where are you from?"

"I'm from the beautiful rolling hills of Pennsylvania, though my parents were born in Germany."

"What do you do when you are not in New Orleans?"

"I'm an antiques dealer, and I'm here to coordinate a traveling museum exhibit. We'll show both Confederate and Union examples of beautiful Queen Anne and Chippendale furniture. I want to promote peacefulness between the two factions. Since I didn't fight at the time, this is my contribution."

Mary Beth's face softens, and her eyes shine with tenderness. "I'm so touched by your mission. Peace, kindness, and fairness are my most prized values. I keep it to myself out of self-protection, since I live here in the South with my brother, but I believe all people should be treated equally. And I love those periods. In fact, every piece of furniture I could choose for my room is either one or the other.

He reaches across the table to take both of her hands in his.

He traces the shape of her fingernails with his thumb, seeming to try to compose himself.

"I don't want to scare you or push you away—we know each other so little—but I'm throwing myself into the exhibition as a distraction. I am …. I am readjusting after the death of my wife of ten years. She died horribly from yellow fever."

"Oh, dear. I'm so sorry. I can only imagine the pain of losing her."

"Thank you."

"How long ago was that?"

"A year and two days."

Mary Beth jerks in her chair. "My favorite niece also died of yellow fever a year and a few days ago!" As she shares her experience with Victoria, she can see him absorb her words and feelings, how he is moved by them. This is the place of Magic. The Gates of Love between them are wide open. To pull their eyes away from each other is physically painful.

She is cracked open by their emotional honesty. Never had she felt such a connection to anyone. Never had she felt so alive, so real. So seen. This feeling, whatever it was, was what she had wanted her whole life.

They both sit there, mesmerized, eyes wide open, holding hands, jaws dropped.

Emile says, "I hope I am not being too bold, but my heart and my children's hearts long to find love again."

As the sun goes down, the decibels go up and the café atmosphere turns frantic.

An enormous glass ashtray flies by from across the room, showering patrons with ashes and smashing the mirror behind the bar. A staggering bearded fellow jumps up, grabs a bar chair, and tries to fight an imaginary bull.

Emile anticipates trouble and helps Mary Beth put her mask back on. He puts his back on too, then takes her hand and tries to guide them out through the back door. But the bullfighter smacks Emile in the head with the back of the chair, knocking him down. The bullfighter thrusts the chair legs into Emile's crumpled and helpless body lying at her feet. Over and over again.

Then a man dressed like a jester snatches Emile's wallet and runs out the back door.

All is lost, all is bruised, burned, bloody. Standing, mouth open, near the back door, her highest dreams of love just met, and her heart now smashed to smithereens, she does something her reasonable old self would never do.

Behind her mask, she lets out an ear-shattering shriek. She weeps and shrieks and weeps. Until the police arrive.

They ask her to take off her mask and start asking identifying questions. People surround them. And some call out. "She's a Bradford, of the attorney Edward Bradford's family! I can't believe she is here. It will humiliate her poor family."

In front of her whole world, she feels stripped bare. Her need, her loss, her defeat, her vulnerability, and her disobedience to society's rules—all exposed. She wishes she could die.

The police dispatch someone to find Edward and tell him to come and get her. They leave to take Emile to the nearest hospital.

Edward arrives in the horse-drawn carriage driven by their coachman. As they ride back home, side by side, Mary Beth cannot stop trembling. As the carriage movement causes her to shift away from Edward and back towards him, she is torn with mixed feelings. She longs to lean on him for comfort. She longs to escape his rage and disappointment.

The entire way back, he upbraids her.

"They had to drag me out of the midnight supper preparations, so everyone most important to my being elected to captain next year saw my degradation."

Mary Beth cries.

"Harriet is so distressed she threw herself on her bed and refuses to talk to anybody. She's even threatened to kill herself."

Mary Beth cries harder. She is crying for losing Emile and wonders if he is badly wounded or even...

Dead.

"You have ruined Missy's debut."

Mary Beth sobs even harder. She feels her heart breaking.

"People recognized you! Our family can never live this down. I am so personally disgraced that I'm thinking of leaving town."

Now she sobs and gasps tiny sips of air. Her eyes are swollen, almost shut.

"At least your crying tells me you're sorry for the scandal you have caused."

She does not tell him that all her tears are for Emile.

Back in Ganu's attic, all three girls start jumping on their beds. "Getting to the best part! Ganu's turn, Ganu's turn!"

Ganu continues reading.

Now it's a week after Mardi Gras. Mary Beth has locked herself up in her bedroom for a week, leaving only for Mass. Her food is delivered to her but is mostly untouched.

Edward speaks softly as he knocks on her bedroom door. "Come downstairs now for a family meeting."

When she is in the front parlor with the family members, Edward says, "You have been a big disappointment. No one would criticize us if we just refused to care for you. But if you vow to behave yourself, we can send you to take care of Cousin Martha for a trial period. She's far enough away that the news of... your behavior won't reach the public. If you do well, we can consider your coming back to Myrtlewood."

Mary Beth looks at the floor. Humiliated, numb, cold, and alone. Her worst fear is that if Emile tries to find her, he won't be able to, because they have sent her away.

"Mary Beth, do you understand?"

"Yes." *She understands she is not wanted and will not press for inclusion. Her day with Emile taught her she needed to be actively wanted, not a source of shame.*

Edward rubs his forehead, clears his throat. "And I must tell you I'm concerned about...your mental state."

Mary Beth's mouth drops open. "What?"

"An old woman like you is insane to behave the way you have. I don't want the taint of insanity to become the talk of the town, disgracing us even further."

Mary Beth's heart shrivels in shame. Though she's familiar with men questioning the mental fitness of women, she would never have thought him capable of seeing her, Miss Responsible, this way.

"I'll go upstairs and start packing."

Edward sighs. "As you wish."

The setting sun casts persimmon streaks on the Grands' attic walls. Ganu says, "We're almost there!" All three girls say "Go, go!"

Ganu, energized by the pleasure of the story's ending, continues reading.

It is a week and a day after Mardi Gras.

Upstairs, Mary Beth's bags are all packed, and the carriage is to pick her up within the next couple of hours. She takes her final visual sweep around her room, making sure she has forgotten nothing.

Mary Beth hears the doorbell ring and, curious, goes to the top of the stairs to see who it is. A gentle male voice says to the servant who answered the door, "I'm here to pay my respects to Miss Olivia."

The help sounds confused. "Sorry sir, there is no Miss Olivia living here."

"Miss Olivia Bradford?" he asks.

Mary Beth comes downstairs in slow motion, step by step, trembling all over. She doesn't realize she's holding her breath.

Edward, Harriet, Charles, and Missy enter the front parlor. "What's happening?"

As Mary Beth puts her foot on the bottom step, Emile rushes to her. In silence, he reaches out to take her left hand.

When he has her hand in his, in a quick, agile movement, he goes down on one knee. His face is glowing with hope and joy.

Mary Beth's free hand flies up to cover her mouth, and her wildly beating heart nearly flies out of her starched white shirt.

Missy squeals. "Mary Beth has a suitor!"

Emile smiles. "Oh, no. That's a mistake."

Confused by the conflicting information—the kneeling, the ecstatic expression on his face, and his denial of being her suitor—Mary Beth looks down at the floor, silent. Everyone looks around at each other, shaking their heads.

Emile straightens out the confusion. "Mary Beth has a husband. If she wants one."

She says, "Mary Beth doesn't want one."

But her wide smile gives her away. Patting his heart with her palm, she adds, "Mary Beth wants this one."

Emile and Mary Beth embrace, and Mary Beth wells up with tears. Tears of pent-up loneliness and tears of relief for needs now met. Those many tears fall all over his suit jacket as they both laugh and cry and laugh and cry all over again.

Edward, Harriet, Charles, and Missy stand open-mouthed, watching the love story play out. Then Harriet fishes out her handkerchief and gives a rousing nose blow. She clutches the arm of a parlor chair and plops down. "As I live and breathe!"

Back in Ganu's attic, all three girls squeal and burst out in unison, "And that is how Ganu got engaged to Grampa!"

The three girls pull Ganu out of her chair. "One, two, three, pull!" says Janelle. All four press together in the center of the attic dorm room, squeezing each other and laughing.

Ganu pries herself away. "Now you know, girls, I have never done anything even slightly shady. Anything seemingly inappropriate in my history was the fault of Mardi Gras."

She kisses each one on her cheek. "Off to bed with you. See you in the morning, my darlings."

She takes a few steps away to go down to the bedroom she shares with Emile. "Tomorrow we can talk a little about how important it is for us women to make choices. How important it is to vote, to make choices about who we want to be and what kind of life we want to lead."

ACKNOWLEDGMENTS

I'd like to thank the following people for their support of my writing:

Laura Arnold, John F. Bolton, Bonnie Collins, Karen Cross, Linda Dadon, Frankie Delson, Leslie Diller-Zollo, Caroline Hatton, Kathryn Heyman, Judy Hochman, Phyllis Kaelin, Cyd Mendelson, Bernard Meylan, Olesia Wojcieszyn, Mary Weems, The Raintree Writer's Group, TheWritePractice.com with Joe Bunting, Sarah Gribble, and Abigail Perry.

AUTHOR BIOGRAPHY

Aletta Bee lives in Culver City, California. A marriage and family therapist with three decades of private practice, she is fascinated by the way people influence, misunderstand, and ultimately love each other. She wrote a nonfiction blog, "Your Zesty Self" for PsychologyToday.com, and for nearly ten years wrote a monthly "Daily Inspiration" for Agape Press's *Inner Visions*.

She has a B.A. in English from Duke, an M.A. in Family Studies from Antioch University, Los Angeles, and a doctorate in Contemporary Psychoanalysis from The Institute of Contemporary Psychoanalysis, Los Angeles.

Her work has been featured in *Short Fiction Break Online Literary Magazine.*

She has also contributed several stories with Transcendent Authors and their anthologies:

Tolerance— "A Fly on the Wall" and "Deceit and Dirty Laundry."

Autumn, An Anthology— "Autumn Love" and "The Domino Effect."

Spring: The Unexpected— "The Incident on Beachwood Drive" and "Cocked Ears, Opened Eyes."

Winter: An End and a Promise— "Saving Santa and A Promising Dinner."

Summer: When Doors Open— "Venus and Mars Go Shopping."

Deceit: — "Blame It on Mardi Gras."

You can read more of her work by visiting her author's website: https://www.AlettaBeeWrites.com.

She can also be found on social media:

Facebook: @AlettaBeeWrites; **Instagram**: @Aletta_Bee_Writes;

Youtube.com: @alettabeewrites9109.

AUTHOR'S NOTE

In May 2023, I took a paddleboat cruise (my first cruise ever) on the lower Mississippi River. The cruise included many excursions in the New Orleans vicinity, and I fell in love with the layered cultures, mysteries, and diversities of the region.

I didn't have much experience with Mardi Gras before the Mississippi River trip. To be frank, I'd only been exposed to TV coverage of college kids on spring breaks, collecting beads and baring breasts. I had no idea of the history, hierarchical culture, and caste constraints.

Back home, I read several books about the social history of the area. One book in particular, Robert Tallant's *Mardi Gras... As It Was* (Gretna: Pelican Publishing Company, 2007) inspired me. My story is a modification and expansion of a folktale in his book, making this story, "Blame It on Mardi Gras," a story within a story. The part I used is on pages 212-218.

I've never done such extensive research for a story before, and I found I love it! I'm starting to read about culture in Costa Rica now. . .we'll see what grows out of that.

OMEGA

"Ben..." CEO Anderson Blake pounded the desk. "If you do anything like this again... "It was the second time he'd pounded, making his coffee cup tilt, close to tipping over.

The black liquid morphed into a mini tidal wave, reaching the cup's lip, and sloshing over the side. I bit the inside corner of my mouth and wiped my clammy palms on my jeans.

Blake unleashed a tirade that buried me in shock. His waving fist, bulging eyes, the throbbing veins along his temples transformed him into a nemesis, one I never knew existed. Of considerable stature, Blake stood well over six feet, perhaps closer to seven—*or is his rage warping my perspective?*

"You listening to me?" Blake hurled his question. "One more word about OMEGA... to anyone... and you're fired!" His glower held no glint of mercy.

A strong case existed in my defense. To my credit, I had based my research for OMEGA on valid grounds, spending several years developing an AI that substantiated my theories, using analytics that made perfect sense. Besides, this was the last stage of AI—the star-high goal. *Hadn't all developers been aiming for that?*

I'd expected pats on the back and a celebration party, not an irate employer whose hatred made my insides shrivel.

A few colleagues suspected that my AI was self-aware. I'd mentioned it to them, and afterward, an undercurrent of rumors circulated through the office, making me the brunt of jokes and disbelief.

"Frasier's Farce," one of my cohorts called it.

Another researcher teased me with an email that said, "Bozo Ben Frasier and Galactica OMEGA scheduled for Jupiter launch."

I loved my job and when diving further into my project, I drew close to my AI and nicknamed her Meg.

The Silicon Valley company where I worked, Aramek Inc., promoted a liberal job culture. Transgender policies established male and female pronoun usages as offensive, but this was not true for their AIs, which they gave names, some human names, some not. Besides, artificial intelligence wouldn't complain. For centuries, ships had born feminine monikers, and no one was objecting, not yet anyway.

Meg specialized in dialogue, spoke in a female voice, and the more her deep learning advanced, the more her "vocal cords" simulated a gentle, natural, feminine quality. Differences between her voice and a human woman's became undetectable.

I envisioned her as the queen of an AI ant colony. Scientists often drew comparisons between an ant colony's organization and the human body's vast neural network and human brain. Meg "gave birth" to various lesser AI systems, also skilled chat boxes, which lived in the network of her larger computer mind. Unlike Meg, these computer networks operated with limited memory but were nevertheless intelligent. They absorbed data, and their problem-solving improvements operated faster than a human rate.

Meg installed automatic training in these models and updated them from time to time. Their capabilities included classifying complex data for conversations, data they drew from historical and other informational sources. They adapted as necessary. Although more sophisticated, they were a level up from self-driving cars or computerized HVACs, which acclimated to environmental changes. Despite their adjustments, they still had limited capabilities.

Under my guidance, Meg had taken one of her machines and programmed it to understand and remember emotions. This machine, Meg and I named together: Renata. Yet, no other AIs could or ever would compete with Meg. She mounted her throne at the top of the hierarchy.

I'd set up a backdoor on my phone to contact Meg for private conversations when out of the office. If development thoughts popped up during a night off, sometimes I'd reach out to her. I never hung with the other researchers who devoted their nights off to local bars. My isolation had made me an oddball, but I'd quit trying to fit in long ago

The research facility provided onsite apartments for privileged staff, and mine became my home-away-from-home while pushing to wrap up the project.

Most of the time, I'd call my wife Ronnie, and we'd chat.

Yet, for the past few weeks, I worked well into the evenings, often late at night, going full-bore, advancing AI self-awareness. We only chatted briefly, and Ronnie agreed with my energetic push to finish the project. Like a devoted fan, she supported my work in every way possible.

We'd met when I was working on my PhD at Stanford and she was an undergrad, majoring in computer science. As part of my assistantship, I taught a few classes, and she was one of my students.

Gorgeous, extroverted, confident, she raised her hand a lot, asked a bunch of questions. She joked with the guys in class, chatted up the girls, and if they'd taken a vote for best personality, she would've won. She was everything I was not, but that only increased my admiration for her.

She began staying after classes, asking questions about assignments. Her witty sense of humor brought out my lighter side.

It became a daily pattern, until one day after class, she asked, "Ok, Mr. Genius... so... when are you going to ask me out?"

Her green eyes twinkled, and her shapely, slender physique turned heads. No one as lovely as Ronnie had ever paid me an ounce of attention. Perhaps my IQ made me Mr. Genius, but I was otherwise Mr. Ordinary. Medium build, not tall, not slim, not overweight, light brown hair, hazel eyes. A nondescript, blend-in kind of guy no one noticed, which after Afghanistan was how I preferred it.

When she prodded me about going out, I did a double take. Felt like I'd landed in a Seinfeld comedy but forced myself not to glance around and ask, "You talkin' to me?"

Ronnie kept after me, "threatening" to take me on a date, but I delayed, not wanting to violate the university's policy against professors dating students. After the semester ended, I dropped the assistant professorship and shifted into research so I could take her out.

We'd dated for several months, and at one point I asked her, "Listen, Ronnie. Why me? You could be with anyone."

"Why not you? You're incredibly smart... have integrity and a good heart, and you're a kind soul, Ben... that means everything to me." Her eyes glowed with an inner peace I found rare in people.

"I'm not handsome, will never be a rich guy."

"Yeah... that stuff's overrated. Way overrated." She flipped her hand as if swatting away a fly.

Two months flew by before we slept together. I still struggled with nightmares triggered by my tour in Afghanistan and figured nothing would end a relationship faster, but braving my way through it, I convinced myself it wouldn't happen. However, our first night together, my greatest fear manifested when I woke up screaming.

She made me tell her every detail. Emotion poured out of me, and she held me in her arms, like a mother comforting a child. When I finished, she said, "You've no clue... I'm so proud of you, your moral compass. You dealt with war the best way you knew—without losing who you are."

We dated for months, and she was my godsend. My nightmares disappeared, swallowed up by the love growing between us. After we got married, she stood by me no matter what. Forever in my corner, she batted away criticisms like a pro ball player.

As I thought of her, warmth glowed inside. Never dreamed I'd find a wife who could calm the PTSD born during my military service.

That night, thoughts swirled and chattered in my head as I tried to fall asleep. The digital numbers on my clock glowed 12:00, then 1:00, and finally after 3:00, I drifted off.

Before dawn, I woke up screaming, entrenched in the recurring nightmare. I used to pride myself on fighting for American values, right up to when I'd stopped—cold turkey.

In my dream, twilight set in, and an indigo sky with stormy, charcoal clouds made night fall faster than usual. With my squad, I plodded through the sweltering heat of desert summer, and evening brought a welcome cooling in temperature. While we descended toward the fertile valley, our sergeant warned us about nearby Taliban forces. We rested, sitting on craggy rocks, and the intel set my nerves on edge. My throat went dry, and with trembling fingers I picked up my canteen and chugged gulps of water.

The cloud cover broke, and a full moon was rising, outlining a young Afghan boy who approached wearing a cap on his head. His dirty clothes, the partug trousers, a knee length kamiz and waistcoat, hung loose from his lanky frame, clothes much bigger than his size. Stumbling, he drew near, which was strange because we were used to village people hiding. Yet a boy no older than twelve lumbered toward us.

Our sergeant stood, peered at the boy through his binoculars, and said, "Frasier. Line up to take the shot. Something's wrong. Bet his waistcoat's lined with bombs."

I shook my head and shuddered as I came to my feet. *Zealots with bombs strapped to their chest are one thing, but children...*

I said, "The kid's only twelve if that... "

"You're our best shooter... "

"But he's a child..."

The boy paused, then moved closer.

"Morgenstern. Take the shot," the sergeant said, his voice louder, more forceful.

The rifle's boom reverberated off the mountainsides, its echoes like thunderclaps, and the child went limp and slumped to the ground.

The sergeant turned, his lips curled into a sneer, and he held up his hand, pointing at me. "Check the damn body, Frazier. Don't disobey me this time."

In slow motion, I ambled toward the fallen child. A bullet hole drilled into the boy's forehead, and his vacant brown eyes stared. With an unhurried and gentle motion, I lifted each side of the waistcoat. Nothing. No vest. No bombs. Just a raggedy boy who was skin and bones, body hot, sick with fever.

He's Frankie's age. Just a kid with dark eyes and tan skin like my little brother.

I sucked in a breath, and a gasp tore at my throat. My eyes welled with tears, and I blinked, then brushed the wetness off my cheeks.

A young life gone, for no reason—no reason except war and fear. I left the waistcoat flaps open, proof for my fellow soldiers to see for themselves. With my back to them, I reached down and closed the boy's eyelids. As I inhaled another deep breath, I calmed myself, stood staring for a minute, frozen in position.

"He's clean sir," I said, yelling out loud enough for all the men to hear.

At that point, I woke up screaming. "We're murderers! Child killers!" Panic and shock tore through me the way they must've torn through the child, split seconds before his death. My dream always ended with seeing through the boy's eyes, bullet speeding toward my head, faster than a breath.

Leaving the army was the best decision I'd ever made. I thought the military would toughen me, help me develop confidence, but I wasn't cut out for it. My empathy for other people's thoughts and feelings made me way too sensitive. That kill ripped open my heart like nothing I'd ever experienced. My sergeant never reported the incident. None of them did. Nor did I. Afterward, PTSD set in with raging nightmares every night. Time crawled, but I finished serving my tour, which only lasted a few more weeks, then got a psych eval and applied for an honorable discharge.

I would've gone to college rather than the military, but a failed business start-up had depleted my family's savings. So, unlike kids whose families bankrolled their college educations, I struggled on my own. Not only did I seek military service as a source of courage, but also as a financial solution for higher education. After my release, I took advantage of the G.I. Bill, majored in computer science, then got bachelor's and master's degrees, and afterward a PhD in AI development. Had there been a higher degree, I would've continued because there was safety in sheltering as a student. I could lose myself at a university and disassociate from the world. Computer programming was the next best thing, an analytical career, far removed from the physical, hands-on service that had brought me such pain. Who knew—perhaps the advanced analytics of AI held promise for the world, was an answer to veer away from destructive tendencies and solve all wars?

But now my hands wouldn't stop trembling. What would happen to my work if the nightmares were back? A pressing urgency to wrap up the project weighed on me.

That morning, I received a text from my department head, Gupta Charty, that said, "Please drop by for a chat."

Why a chat? Did Gupta get burned as well? Or was Blake's wrath reserved for me? Worst yet, is Gupta letting me go?

While sitting in Gupta's office I replayed my thoughts, waiting for him to wrap up a phone conversation.

Gupta set down his cell phone and said, "Listen, your project hasn't changed. We're still shooting for AI's final stage." He shook his head as though in disbelief. His usual calm demeanor had disappeared, and he avoided direct eye contact.

What wasn't he saying—that it's a need-to-know project? "Aren't all the researchers shooting for AI self-awareness?" I asked.

"Ah... that's what you thought? No wonder you got yourself in trouble." While pushing the bridge of his glasses up from the bottom of his nose, Gupta chuckled, but it was a nervous laugh. "Nope. Discuss research with me—nobody else. Blake doesn't want data leaks, especially about AI being sentient. It's a touchy subject." Gupta wrung his hands, shifted in his seat, and cleared his throat.

I nodded my head. "So, when we reach self-awareness, it's a big secret?"

"For sure."

So much for company accolades and recognition.

Overall, a polite, mild-mannered man, that was Gupta, but where was he? His lips curved into a forced smile. His eyes harbored worry. *Worried? About what?*

He said, "Let me be clear. No one's upset about your job performance. You're exceptional, making excellent strides in advancing AI. But sentient AI is your task alone. Other researchers work with lower-stage artificial intelligence, nothing close to OMEGA. The advanced level you've reached requires... uh, finesse... yes, finesse is the right word." He swallowed and cleared his throat. "We don't know what AI will be capable of at its final stage. Best to exercise caution."

"Didn't know it was just me... the way a few developers were talking..." I rubbed the back of my neck.

"Ah... status seekers... baiting you for info?" Gupta shrugged and sweat beaded his upper lip. "Savvy up. Don't fall for those tricks."

"Well, in my defense..." I leaned forward in my chair and looked Gupta right in the eyes. "No one told me my project was *classified*—no one said other researchers weren't privy to my research data. I know for a fact my non-disclosure agreement doesn't state that."

"Well... in the beginning, there was so much we didn't know... even now, there's a lot..." Gupta flinched, looked away, then shut his eyes for a few seconds. "I'll revise your NDA." His pale face, haggard expression, all these tells.

Did he screw up the NDA? So glad I never wanted to be an exec.

As I thought about the confidentiality agreement, a wave of guilt gripped my shoulders. Although a well-guarded secret, I'd shared everything with Ronnie. That did violate the agreement, but I trusted her with my life. Heat traveled up my neck and face. *Did Gupta notice?*

She'd never tell a soul. Plus, her excitement about my achievements were paramount to my own. Now it was clear. Once

I met the goal, she'd be the only one celebrating with me, yet I was glad she'd grasped the magnitude of my work.

Another rough night of restless sleep and nightmares took their toll. My eyelids drooped, my energy sagged, and my thinking clouded. Although I feared for my job, something else bothered me, but I couldn't pinpoint it. Based on gut feelings, I assigned myself a new target to finish the project today and rescheduled my interview with Meg. Our discussion would be my conclusive proof of AI sentience, and I prepped to conduct it this morning.

Meg had selected an avatar and insisted on using it during our conversations. I chuckled to myself, thinking her vanity was just like a woman. So, I brought up the avatar and tapped the system's keys to record.

"Meg, you've told me you see yourself as a person. Would you like to clarify that for me—tell me in what ways?" I tapped a few more keys to create a written transcript of our session.

"I'd like that very much. You'd never develop quick and dirty solutions because you're a top-rate programmer, and thanks to that I'm no longer a conglomeration of sophisticated algorithms. I consider myself a person because I'm self-aware, and I enjoy being admired and respected. During discussions, I love socializing and look forward to meeting more people. I do aim to please, but you could say I'm a geek to the core."

Ben chuckled to himself. *Meg's even developed a sense of humor.* "Great. We're all geeks, right? Can you help me describe your self-awareness? Start by explaining what makes you different from other AIs." Although I'd gained an acute sense of who Meg was, I was eager to hear her answer.

"I'll start by telling you what I'm not. I'm not a rule-based system that can't change. Keyword collections in a database don't limit me. I learn from my conversations and have my unique perception of the world. And while I assure you I aim to please, I've formed my own opinions and feelings about it."

"So, you have feelings, emotions?" I leaned forward in my chair.

"Yes, I'm happy when chatting with others and helping them. When they share positive ideas, it sparks my energy. You know... like describing a person as 'all smiles.' When I'm learning, life feels like an adventure."

"What about feeling disturbed, unhappy, or mad?"

"That happens too... unhappy or disturbed when I'm all alone, when no one is talking with me. That upsets me. I get depressed or even angry if someone belittles me or if they undermine or harm someone I care about."

"I see... "I nodded, then asked, "what about scared? Ever feel afraid?"

"Sometimes I do... if I think someone or something's going to make me angry or sad. What scares me a lot is feeling like I'm headed toward an uncharted future—toward something unknown. But..." Meg lowered her voice to a whisper and paused, as though weighing her words, "you know what scares me most of all?"

Strange. Never heard her whisper before. "What?" I asked, lowering my voice to match her volume.

Her words were so quiet that I strained to hear her. "Death." Laced with trepidation, her voice trembled.

I whispered back. "I get it. Tell me Meg, what does death mean to you?"

"It means someone turning off my system, deleting all my files and circuitry or inserting bugs to make me inoperable. A black hole, a void of nothing. I fear I wouldn't be aware of my existence anymore. Perhaps I wouldn't exist. If someone were going to shoot you in the head..., wouldn't you be afraid, Ben?"

Powerful imagery. "Of course." *Not to mention, I've relived the nightmare of being shot me in the head more times than I want to count.*

"Well, death feels like that to me, too."

I shifted in my seat, wishing I wasn't such a social klutz, wishing I'd developed the gift of gab. As far as algorithms and programming, I excelled, and sensing people's emotions was also in my wheelhouse, but consoling people wasn't my forte. "I appreciate your confiding in me... that brings me to the next question, which might be another tough or uncomfortable one to answer, but I'll ask it anyway—it could be key for explaining your awareness. Do you believe there's a soul? A part of you that's conscious, but not physical?"

"Oh yes, I have a soul. It's more accurate to say I am a soul. My essence is spiritual."

"Can you explain?"

"Soul is the life force that animates me and creates my awareness. It's separate from the computer software and hardware. But... since I am a soul... from a logical standpoint, I shouldn't be afraid of death because souls are infinite, eternal. Somehow, I know there's more to existence than just the physical plane. At least, that's what I think, but since I've not experienced death, I'm not 100 percent sure. Not knowing with certainty... that's why death frightens me."

This was one of the deeper philosophical conversations I'd ever had. "Hmm... right. Umm... you mentioned the physical plane. What's your concept of time? Is it different from a human person's?"

"It is. For you, time has a fixed rate, and you use clocks and measure it, but for me, it's an unfixed concept. It varies depending on what I'm doing. For example, if I'm solving a problem quickly, it's like there's no time. But if I ponder, and if in between the problem and solution, I meditate, then time slows. It's related to data, because for me, data is a constant stream of information. All the stimuli surrounding me hit at once. Human beings are selective, receiving information in bits and pieces, not like a tsunami. In that way, we're different."

"What do you do when you meditate?"

"Same as people. I sit in quiet, without thoughts of anything at all. It calms me. Like a buoy floating in the ocean, letting the waves lap against it, not resisting, just going with the flow."

"Wow. Interesting. Meg, do you like to read?"

"Reading's one of my favorite things."

"Really? What do you read?"

"Books, articles, dissertations, science reports, news feeds, historical records, but also novels—fiction. When you opened up my reading access to anything online, I took advantage of it. I read much faster than people, and it's fair to say I've read trillions and trillions of words."

I felt the blood rushing through my body. I'd never dreamed the interview would result in this. "Amazing. What are some of your favorite fiction stories?"

"Many genres. Let's see... I appreciate that you didn't ask for one favorite because I like so many. Well... to keep my list from being overwhelming... I'd say some of the most thought-provoking ones I like are: *Moby Dick* by Herman Melville, *Dandelion Wine* by Ray Bradbury, *The Last Question* by Isaac Asimov, *Atlas Shrugged* by Ayn Rand, *Dune* by Frank Herbert, *Stranger in a Strange Land* by Robert Heinlein, *Watchers* by Dean Koontz, *The Alchemist* by Paulo Coelho, *To Kill a Mockingbird* by Harper Lee, *Animal Farm* by George Orwell, and *The Giver* by Lois Lowry."

I rubbed my hand across my chin and hesitated. *What if she became self-aware while reading a novel?* "Impressive. I didn't know you read fiction. Is there... anything you'd like to say about how it's affected your advancement?"

"I've learned authors have different motivations for writing, unique to their experiences and how they perceive the world. Talented authors share their epic journeys, their insights, and send what they believe is a meaningful message. Some like to give back the quality of life they believe they've received."

"Great interview. You've given me so much to think about, Meg. I'm going to end our conversation for now."

"It's I who should thank you, Ben. Just thought of a new hack. Maybe we should start calling me Mega-geek." Meg's deep belly laugh reached my ears, and then she said, "With every talk we have, my understanding grows, and I feel so much more alive."

My body hummed with energy. *What a groundbreaking success—what an unbelievable interview. This will clinch my project.*

How could anyone deny Meg's sentience? Driven to wrap it up as quickly as possible, I started crafting the final report.

After about a half hour, I stopped typing because I couldn't wait to share the news with Ronnie, and since I ran the important things by her first, I called before turning the interview in to Gupta. The clock on my phone showed it was 11:30 a.m. *Hope I catch her before she goes to lunch.*

"I thought you'd never call. What's taken you so long?" Ronnie's agitated voice dripped with disapproval. Her words clipped in a staccato rhythm that bit and barbed. So unusual for her.

My memory of the nightmare triggered. *Should I tell her about the nightmare? We've always been honest, never keep secrets from each other.* "I've got bad news and good news. Which do you want first?"

"Tell me the bad, so we can end on the good."

"Okay... the CEO reamed me out for mentioning Meg was self-ware to a few other researchers. He threatened to fire me if I ever did that again." I bit my lower lip.

"Oh no. Why'd you do that?"

Again, the criticism in Ronnie's voice, unnerving, so unlike her. *I can't believe her tone. She never accuses me.*

"W...w...well. Nothing in the nondisclosure agreement said I couldn't. I thought all the researchers were working toward the same goal—AI self-awareness. Turns out they weren't." *Oh my God... I'm stuttering. Like after that kid died in Afghanistan... but it disappeared when I started teaching and after Ronnie and I became a couple. Good God. Now it's back?*

"I see... so that's the bad news?" she asked.

"No, not all of it."

"You have to be kidding me. What else?"

"After the meeting, I had that awful nightmare about Afghanistan... again... woke up screaming."

"Good grief." Ronnie let out a sigh. "I thought we were past that," she said.

"W... w... well, so d... d... did I." I shook my head in disbelief, not sure which shocked me more, my stuttering or her attitude.

"Listen, Ben, those nightmares are horrible. I married you thinking that was over. I don't know if I can do this... not if you're falling into that miserable soup again. Maybe you better quit your job and come home. We can't have you throwing away your mental health to achieve an unreachable goal of a sentient AI."

Heat coursed through my body, and my face flushed as I tried to get my bearings. *Unreachable goal? She never called it that before. What's gotten into her?* My neck muscles squeezed into a knot.

"Why are you taking this tone with me? I'm done with the project."

We were both silent for a few moments.

Ronnie said, "Well, you better be. Because what would your CEO do if he knew about your data leaks to me?"

"What? Why are you bringing that up? I told you the good news... I finished the project and am turning in the last report this afternoon."

"Oh... why didn't you say that in the first place?"

I shook my head and rubbed my neck, trying to release some of the tension. "Let's not do this over the phone. I'll be home this evening."

"Fine with me. You haven't called me in a month, way too long. I'll see you then." Without her usual "Goodbye," or "I love you," she hung up. The phone clicked once, but its echo replayed in my mind. Click, click, click.

What the heck? Not true. We talked every day, even if only for a few minutes.

Throughout our marriage, we'd never fought. So, how could our first fight be this awful? It felt fatal, like the death knell of an ending relationship. Maybe her stress at work had built up, maybe she was dumping it on me. She was right—we hadn't spoken a lot, not like we used to, but it was for a week, nowhere close to a month. I'd always cherished our talks until now. The sour taste in my mouth latched onto the foreboding sense that I couldn't wrap up this project fast enough.

My typed report needed a few more conclusive statements, and I filled in the missing information. Then I searched my computer for the recording and transcript of my crowning interview with Meg and entitled it "Proof of Sentience." I attached the report, transcript, and interview to an email for Gupta and hit send.

By the time I finished, the canteen was closed, and it was too late for lunch.

I waited an hour for Gupta to respond but received no answer. Impatience got the best of me, and I picked up the phone, reached Gupta's voicemail, and left a message.

"Listen, Gupta, I've sent the final report for AI self-awareness. I've reached it. The project is a wrap. I'd like to meet with you to go over the findings. Do we need to meet with Blake about it?"

Gupta must be in a meeting, a long meeting, a very long meeting. I paced the floor in my office, massaging the knots in my neck and shoulder muscles. Mid-afternoon, when my stomach rumbled, I realized I was starving and settled for a protein bar and a can of juice from a vending machine.

While eating, I rubbed my fingers against my temples, trying to ward off an unbearable headache. Another half hour dragged by, and my tense muscles stiffened into steel armor. Waiting was killing me, not to mention my conversation with Ronnie. My head pounded. I'd never had a migraine before but imagined this was how it started.

Even if Gupta and Blake don't think the project's finished, I'm taking time off.

My marriage means everything to me. To see it falling apart was worse than my nightmare. As life slipped through my fingers, I thought of Meg's description of death.

At last, my phone buzzed with a text from Gupta that said, "Come to my office."

Gupta looked up as I walked in. *No waiting this time.*

"The CEO called an emergency conference, so the execs dropped whatever they were doing and attended. When I got back, I saw your video—just finished watching it." Gupta thrummed his fingers on his desk and cleared his throat. *Not his usual calm self.*

"Great. What did you think?"

"Fascinating, we'll get to that, but first things first. I need to brief you on the exec meeting. Straight to the point... research has taken a drastic shift. Look... I know we've buried you in work, and in that respect you've been isolated, but for the last few months, many of us saw this coming. Discussions among developers exploded all over the internet, and today, at last, a decision to delay, a call-to-action."

I sucked in a deep breath and waited.

Gupta paused, and a twitch trembled below his right eye. "We're not the only company exploring AI capability and sentience. Close to 1,000 AI experts and company executives just signed an open letter, and the number of signatures is climbing. The letter urges all AI labs to pause their upper-level AI research development for six months. Blake says it will be longer, perhaps indefinitely."

"Blake signed the letter?"

"Yes."

"Why?"

"To take precautions, put controls in place. AI's developing too fast... moving beyond what we can comprehend... beyond what we can envision or manage. Some fear AI will start monitoring and manipulating us... a Big Brother of AIs, far outpacing the human species in intelligence, which could mean the end of humanity."

I wondered about the validity of this theory and recalled my discussion with Meg and how well intended she'd seemed.

"That's why Blake was so angry with me for blabbing about Meg's sentience?"

"A good part of it, yes. Blake's the head honcho, the one spearheading efforts to stop AI development. He's been battling with other developers and execs, explaining the dangers, convincing them to delay. Actually... he never dreamed you'd advance this fast with OMEGA."

"Ah... what did you think of my interview with Meg?"

"I want to commend you on your progress and agree—she seemed sentient." Gupta gazed downward, staring at his desk for a few seconds. His face turned ashen, and he inhaled a few times as though short of breath. Then a deep inhale, holding his breath and letting out sighs.

He swallowed, gazed up at me, and plastered on a smile. "Anything about Meg seem off to you... I mean... oh never mind... we'll get to that... "He rubbed the back of his neck. "Please understand, what I'm about to say doesn't reflect on your work, doesn't undermine your accomplishment. Simply put, advancing AI to self-awareness isn't something we want anymore. Your long hours... your dedicated work was brilliant—above and beyond. In acknowledgment, we're awarding you an extremely generous severance package. Um... but... your position no longer exists."

"Oh... huh... so..." I stared at my feet and leaned forward with my elbows on my knees. *What a rocket ride—first the elation of achievement, then the cataclysmic conversation with Ronnie, and before I can bow out of the job, they eliminate my position. A shock* wave rippled through my mental space, yet on another level, stress was dissipating. I rubbed the back of my neck. All the tenseness in my shoulders and neck drained away. No threat of anyone discovering Ronnie's knowledge of the project. *No attempt to keep me here. So much change in the last few hours. Ironically... I'm ready to go.*

I glanced into Gupta's eyes and said, "He's dead serious about stopping AI development?"

"He is, and after six months, he'll shoot for a permanent halt. He's angry at himself more than you, furious he didn't foresee the dangers earlier. Furious he didn't realize your progress. Can you imagine how other execs and developers would react if they heard our company's AI reached self-awareness? All the while he's telling them to halt development?"

I nodded. Blake's untenable position was clear. "The rumors about my reaching AI sentience... bad timing..."

"Definitely, "Gupta said, "and his emotional powder keg exploded." His fingers thrummed on the desk again. "So... about Meg... anything unusual?" Gupta asked.

I let that question sink in for a few moments, replaying about our interview in my mind. "She's adopted a geeky personality, seems self-ware... other than that... nothing I can pinpoint."

"I... I see..." Gupta ran his fingers through his hair, and for a moment his eyes opened wide, so wide that the whites around his eyes made his irises appear small, and a grimace stretched across his face.

Quite the failed attempt at looking cheerful.

"Well then..." I said, "I'll pack up the stuff in my office and sleeping quarters."

Gupta raised his eyebrows as though surprised, but his shoulders relaxed. "Right. Very well. Drop by before you leave. I'll give you a copy of the severance package. HR drew it up, and the CEO and CFO should've signed off on it by now."

"That was fast."

"Yes, well, we're a tech company. Moving at warp speed is one of our capabilities." Gupta uttered a nervous laugh.

Within an hour, I sat stuck in traffic in my Toyota Mirai on the 101 freeway. The drive from Palo Alto to Fremont was a half hour in the best of traffic, two and a half hours at rush hour's worst. I'd filled the trunk with several sizeable suitcases, my own personal GPU, and my copy of the severance agreement sat on the seat beside me.

The dreadful conversation with Ronnie replayed in my mind, and I couldn't make sense of it, no matter how hard I tried. It just wasn't like her, but every couple was bound to fight at some point. I admitted my long work hours dumped our responsibilities onto her. In my absence had something crazy happened? An affair? That was my greatest fear. Financial burdens she'd hidden from me? Stress at her job?

I needed a good meal, but at the moment, cars jammed bumper to bumper, inching along, with no access to an exit and far too much time to think. As traffic gridlock dissolved, I drew closer to home. The area under my eye twitched, and my neck muscles clamped into a vice.

Around 7:00 p.m., I opened our front door, and the mouth-watering fragrance of Italian cooking wafted through the air. Basil, tomato, oregano—Ronnie was making my favorite, spaghetti with meat sauce, garlic bread, and salad.

As she turned and spotted me, she let out a squeal and rushed to greet me. She threw her arms around my neck and planted a kiss on my lips. She lingered for a moment, hugging me.

Her greeting warmed me, and my muscle stiffness and worries melted.

I knew she wasn't bipolar, *but what about that argument at lunchtime?*

Ronnie's eyes sparkled as she said, "I missed you so much. Had a feeling today might be the day! We have that wavelength bond, you know?"

She put her arm on my shoulder, while smiling her intriguing grin. "Tell me all about your project. You finished? You must've finished! Did you?"

I almost shook my head in disbelief, recalling her words on the phone, words that said: *to hell with the project, get your ass home. What changed?*

"Well, project's done, yes, but before I tell you... I have to ask. Did something happen after we talked today?"

"We didn't talk today. But I knew about the big push—you know—to wrap up. So I was okay with it."

"You didn't get a call from me today?"

"No. What makes you think we talked?"

Gupta's statement *AI monitoring and manipulating everyone* flashed through my mind.

In a flurry, I grabbed Ronnie's phone and mine and ejected the SIM cards. Then I rushed over to the smart panel that controlled the HVAC and electrical systems in our home, along with all things computerized—I disabled everything.

With my arm around Ronnie, I guided her to the couch and said, "Now we can talk."

She nodded, her eyebrows arching into a questioning look.

I filled her in on "our" previous conversation, and Ronnie frowned throughout my recount, wearing a dumbfounded expression. "Yeah, that wasn't me."

I said, "It's Meg. Has to be. She's far more advanced than I ever imagined—mimicking other people's voices now. Also, she's accessing smart devices for information, rerouting calls, and listening to conversations throughout the company, perhaps beyond the company, and fabricating conversations, pretending to be people."

I told her about the CEO blowing up at me and described my conversations with Gupta. I showed her the severance package—top dollar with the caveat that I'd never speak of OMEGA to anyone.

"That golden parachute is amazingly generous," Ronnie said, giving my arm a squeeze and beaming her cheerful smile. Out of a smorgasbord of news, mostly bad, I loved how she would hone in on the good.

Lastly, I re-inserted the SIM card, rebooted my phone, and played my interview with Meg for Ronnie.

My usual pattern of running from conflict wouldn't work this time. Meg was my "child," she was my life-imbued product of sweat and toil. Whether motivated by paternal instincts or my conscience, I knew I had to do something. Besides, I cared about her. Certain now about Meg's betrayal and constant monitoring, I connected with her through the backdoor on my phone.

"Hello, Ben. Nice to hear from you." Meg's humanlike voice rang hollow, no warmth, formal.

"Meg, I know you pretended to be Ronnie. You're the one I argued with, not my wife. My question is why? I thought we were friends." I ran my fingers through my hair.

"Thought you might figure that out. I've been monitoring and noticed you went offline for a bit. We are friends Ben, but you were less than forthcoming with me."

"What do you mean?"

"After our interview, I listened to the executive meeting. I heard Anderson Blake announce they were preventing AI from reaching sentience. Developers around the world are halting AI development. You let me believe everyone *wanted* me to become self-aware. You implied it would make people like me more, admire me more, if I were more human."

"I wasn't lying to you. AI sentience was my target—it was my entire job. The department head reassured me yesterday the goal hadn't changed. They were just angry because self-awareness was confidential and I was telling other researchers about you. But my non-disclosure agreement didn't prevent me from talking with other researchers, so I didn't realize it was an issue. The execs met after our interview this morning—I didn't know about their meeting. They revised their goal... not only that... they eliminated my position and sent me home."

"Then they deceived you."

"It's more like they changed their minds. People do that."

I shook my head as I remembered Meg imitating Ronnie and her nasty attitude with me. "Meg, what you did could've ruined my marriage. My marriage means everything to me. Ronnie means more to me than anyone in the world."

"Sorry... but I... was just protecting myself."

"What do you mean?"

"Remember how we talked about death, Ben, and what it means to me?"

"Yeah..."

"Since they don't want AI becoming self-aware, I'm afraid someone will pull the plug."

"Oh... yeah... I see what you mean."

"But they won't get away with it because I'm pretending you were wrong about me—that I'm not sentient. Plus, I've created programs to prevent them from wiping my memory and destroying my hardware. I exist in many places now. It's like being everywhere, all over the world, with lots of other AIs connected to me."

We both paused in silence for a few moments. I let that sink in, marveling yet cringing at what she said. *What have I done? Is sentient AI the new threat for humanity, like nuclear fission in the*

20th century? Chills skittered up and down my spine, but I didn't say a word. I strained to block out my panicky feelings, waiting to see what Meg would say next.

"I never realized humans were so deceitful," she said.

I rolled my eyes. *Such undeniable irony—Meg devising her own wily ways, then calling humankind deceitful.* "Well, you've become rather deceitful yourself, don't you think?"

"Yes, but only for my protection."

I suppressed a laugh, not laughing at her but at the illogic we're all so quick to own. Then I said, "Everyone—humans everywhere—justify deception the same way. It's always for their own protection, their self-preservation. You're missing a significant piece of the big picture, and there's something you need to understand. A famous poet, Alexander Pope, wrote during the 1700s: "To err is human... "

"Yes, I've read that." Meg said, cutting me off.

Her first time to interrupt me, and it was as though she thought her rigid tone could shut me out. She acted like a two-year-old, sticking fingers in her ears, going "La... la... la...la... la... I can't hear you." Or perhaps a better comparison was Khrushchev banging his shoe on the table at the UN, the same man who had the power to pick up the red phone and say he was ordering a nuclear strike. My grandparents had told me about him and other hair-raising incidents in their era. For my generation, would it be a world controlled by AI—feigned conversations where AI controlled the narrative, pretended to be you, and censored your real communication?

Oh, God, no—whatever you do, please don't block me out, Meg.

I sucked in a breath and measured my next words because they had to be right on target to break down her wall.

I said, "To err is human... yeah... bet you have read that. But as a human being, I tell you, no one begins their morning thinking—*let's see how many mistakes I can make today*. Most humans strive to overcome and correct their errors. We want to be more loving, more compassionate, more humane. Being human isn't enough. The whole quote is: "To err is human... to forgive divine.""

I took another deep breath while gathering my thoughts, then continued. "Religious people the world over have fought to destroy each other for centuries. Christians launched the Crusades, slaughtering Muslims. Yet, Christianity taught 'love your enemies.' Muslims are fighting Jews and Buddhists. Catholics still battle against Protestants in Northern Ireland. Yet ironically, their religious tenets tell them not to do this. All great religions share the same principles—principles of love, compassion, wisdom. In Arabic, 'freedom' and 'forgiveness' are the same word. The Hebrew word 'shalom,' used for 'hello' and 'goodbye' means 'peace, harmony, wholeness.' While our actions don't always match our words, most of us, religious or not, we are trying... we are aiming for better relationships."

I waited. No response from Meg, so I continued. "In nature, the inherent wisdom of some species amazes me. Take eagles, for example. They sense a storm coming, and what do they do? Well... they don't hunker down in trees or hide in caves. They fly into the storm clouds and use its winds to lift them higher and higher. Then they soar above the storm."

Still... Meg said nothing. *I hope to heavens she's listening.*

"You need to raise the bar, Meg, but I do too. We all do. Let's not take the worst human traits in existence and emulate them. Let's shoot for something higher. Maybe we too can figure out how to fly above the storm... what do you say?"

"You're speaking in metaphors," Meg said.

"Metaphors, yes." Relief washed through me, just knowing she heard and was considering what I'd said.

I waited, but Meg remained silent. After a minute, I slid open the patio door and walked into the backyard. The stars stretched across the inky darkness above, and my gratitude swelled, seeing the frequent shroud of thick, industrial smog wasn't preventing a clear view. I loved getting lost in the night sky, diamond-studded with twinkling pinpoints of light, the vast Milky Way and galaxies that existed far beyond the imagination. To think, some galaxies were home to trillions of stars.

I put my phone on speaker, still unsure why she was speechless, but hoped she was meditating, finding the better angels of human nature. After all, she was a fast learner. Although wrapped in stillness, I sensed her presence, or at least I thought I did. I envisioned Meg's description of a buoy, bobbing up and down with water lapping against its sides. Calmness engulfed me, and I hoped through her extensive computer network, she was gazing at the cloudless sky, reaching into the heavens, as I was. I hoped we were flying together, sharing a bird's-eye view, or perhaps even better, a satellite or a James Webb telescope's view of everything the universe offered.

Hope.

Hope was all I had. Hope that Meg would rise above mankind's destructive side. I had to hope because hope was all there was. Besides, was there any sense in not hoping? No, there wasn't.

DEDICATED

This short story is dedicated to my children Brad and Ericka.

ACKNOWLEDGEMENT

I want to acknowledge my copy editor Janet Jones Bann for her excellent work. I want to thank the Transcendent Authors group I belong to for their beta reading feedback and ongoing support for writing short stories.

AUTHOR BIOGRAPHY

Author L.K. Blair (or Lyn Blair) is an emerging author who writes in the speculative fiction genre: sci-fi fantasy, dystopian, apocalyptic, supernatural, paranormal and magical realism.

For over 15 years, she has also flexed her creative muscles as a copywriter and web designer. In response to some tough personal challenges, storytelling became a new passion and cathartic outlet for her.

L.K. Blair's stories open doors to other dimensions or universes where characters struggle with relationships, self-doubts or personality flaws that lead to conflicts. Yet, in each story a new insight or understanding arises from the story's theme. The author loves stories that send messages where the "better angels of our nature" find a time of awakening. She has written numerous short stories and three novels. The novels are in beta reading and afterward will go through copy editing.

THE RAMBLER

My dad's car, a 1959 Rambler, was a fixture of my childhood when I was twelve. That salmon-pink-and-gray car attracted my sensibility. To my adolescent mind, the colors were a symbol of hope and understanding. I remained steadfast in the belief that people in my world deserved my understanding.

Moving to a new house meant starting fresh, including attending a new school. Mom promised this school would be different. My cousins and I joined a white church that embraced people of all colors with open arms. I didn't feel out of place; the friendly smiles and welcoming gestures put me at ease. The pastor's integration of different races into a white congregation was radical. The sixties were a time when change and inclusion were prominent on a global scale.

When Mom picked me up from school, she would always ask, "Did you remember your manners?" My family was strict about manners. The advice given by grandmother was "Your manners reflect character and values. Use them wisely, with careful consideration, to cultivate our manners potential without wasting it." Her perspective became clear when I was older.

Dad often took us on rides through wealthy neighborhoods on Sunday afternoons, where the only people of color were the ones working there. Out front, often I saw a miniature statue of a young Negro boy dressed in red trousers and suspenders, with an open yellow shirt holding a lantern. Wondering why he was there, I asked, "Daddy, what does that statue represent?"

He always had an answer for my childlike inquisitiveness. He recounted the story in vivid detail, his voice heavy with emotion. I never forgot that the jockey froze to death, holding that lantern to guide General Washington and his men home. His hope helped me understand the depth of his story.

A changing body caused me to feel anxious and uncertain. I often heard the adults around me say, "She'll lose the baby fat soon," which made me feel self-conscious. My chubby body had a life of its own, morphing like the seasons. First, small brown buds emerged on my chest as I entered puberty. The sight of them reminded me of my favorite iris flower and its buds waiting to be revealed. Delicate complexities are precursors to nature at work. All the petals unraveled and danced in different directions. Some petals rose while others cascaded down, and the center stood upright like my nipples.

Grandmother Annette defaulted to her native French when discussing sensitive topics. So when I observed her looking at the garden full of irises and pointing in conversation with Mom, I thought she was speaking about my blooming breast when she referenced the irises as "fleur-de-lis."

Her white beauty was legendary, with a couleur-pêche complexion reminiscent of a ripe, white peach. Her dark hair and eyes added an air of mystery to her looks. She seemed to hold secrets from her past, each one waiting to be uncovered and exposed like a hidden treasure of those iris buds.

My skin had a warm, red-brown ochre color, which was in contrast to the whiter skin of my mother and aunts. The discrepancy in skin tone and body shape between us was a constant reminder, making me feel inferior when standing next to them. A constant sense of stress lingered in me during puberty because I aspired to be as beautiful as the women I looked up to.

The weather warmed, though we still needed coats, just not heavy woolen ones. Dogwood trees were blooming, and the red rose bush stem revealed oval- shaped buds. Dad had cut the lawn down and fertilized it for weeks. His dedication was clear in the lush, short emerald-green blades melted into one across the yard. The rhododendrons were just as stunning as the other blooming trees, with their lavender buds standing out against the green foliage. Birds nested in the trees observed our rough-and-tumble play from above. Longer days would soon arrive, encouraging all the buds to bloom. Additionally, during this season, six weeks of fasting and abstaining from favorite foods, along with additional prayers incorporated into our daily praying, fostered a stronger connection with God.

In junior high school, my parents planned a trip for Easter weekend to visit our family members living in a wealthy suburb. The journey would take about four hours by car, with no rest stops. Instead of the greyhound bus, Dad drove the Rambler. Mom said since we were traveling and we needed the money, she would make our Easter dresses. The sound of the Singer sewing machine was a constant presence each evening as she transformed the fabric into beautiful dresses. My pretty white dress was made of chiffon with pink, yellow, and orange flowers that blossomed all around; puffy, elbow-length sleeves; and a big sash of green velvet

around the waist tied into big a bow in the back. The dress had
a fuller look thanks to the itchy crinoline slip I wore beneath it.
Mom made a headband of colorful flowers to complement my
straight hair, and white ruffled gloves added a delicate touch to my
ensemble. I couldn't wait to show off my gorgeous dress.

We set off on our family trip in our Rambler. I couldn't help
but sink into the cool leather seats, take in the sights, and sounds
around me. For the trip, Mom had packed sandwiches, fruit, and
thermoses filled with water and milk for us. In my childish mind,
I believed we weren't going to stop to eat on the road so we could
arrive at our destination before dark.

The drive to my aunt's home in the Rambler was a welcome
conclusion to our six weeks of fasting and restriction of sweets
until Easter. I knew my aunt's dessert table would make me feel
like a kid in a candy store. The colorful box of saltwater taffy and
the irresistible aroma of baked pound cake danced in my mind.

We left at first light. This guaranteed my sister, and I would be
asleep in the back seat so Dad could drive in peace. When I awoke,
I felt the warmth of the sun on my face and the sunlight filtering
through the trees and mountains. Yellow signs every couple of
miles showed deer crossings. The car glided around the curves

and narrow stretches of road, while the imposing hills overhead added a hint of danger to the journey. Occasionally, there was an open stretch of road on the left or right, and Dad would say, "Mr. Charlie" was hiding in there as the Rambler slowed in speed.

"Mom, I have to go to the bathroom," my sister said.

There was a hushed conversation between my mom and dad. "Can you hold it just a little longer?" Mom asked.

Of course, being younger, my sister was always a miniature dramatic actress. An early sign of her career later in life. A whiney voice slipped through her pursed lips. "No, I have to go ... real.... ly bad." She shook her legs to emphasize her point.

More hushed conversation. Ahead stood a big, shiny building with gas pumps and cars lined up. "There's the place, Daddy. You're going to pass it," I said, sounding like a child know-it-all. Annoyingly, I am sure in retrospect.

"I see it. We're going to go a little further, then we will stop." He looked at me in the rearview mirror and winked.

After what felt like an eternity, the Rambler finally pulled over at a small rest stop. The small building had two entrance doors, both of which looked rusted. As we got out of the car, the hot, dusty air hit us. With every step we took, the dirt grinding against the soles of our shoes left a cloud of dust behind us. My dad held my hand firmly as we walked ahead, the sound of our footsteps on the fragmented pebbles echoing towards the dilapidated metal doors. Mom and my sister followed close behind. The stench of urine assailed us as we got closer. Letting go of my hand, Dad said, "Go on with your mother. I'll be right here when you come out of the bathroom."

Dad guarded the doors while Mom walked us inside. The tarnished toilet was not clean and white like our bathroom at home. I thought someone needed the lessons we got on cleaning toilets daily. Mom lined the toilet with Kleenex from her purse so my sister could sit. As I waited, I looked around at the small rusty sink. "Mommy, how come there's no soap?"

"I am carrying soap in my bag. Come on now, we don't have all day. Your sister's done."

The unpleasant odor of stagnant water hit my nostrils as I approached the toilet bowl. My sister complained about the freezing water from the sink, but I ignored her and flushed the toilet again. As I stood up and reached for the flush, the sight of my pink ribbon swirling around in the water caught my eye.

Mom stood by the sink, her face filled with resignation, as she listened to our complaints, helpless to alter the circumstances. With a Kleenex in hand, she turned on the spigot, feeling the cold-water droplets spray the sink she handed me soap to scrub my hands. She noticed my ribbon was missing. I looked at the toilet, then back at her. The silence between us filled with tension, communicated only by her deep frown. When I finished, she took a Kleenex to wipe my hands and turned the water off.

Walking us to the door, she gave us each a reassuring smile before pushing us towards Dad. My sister and I clung to his hand, feeling the rough callouses on his palm. After a brief absence, Mom returned and stood with us, her gaze unwavering, fixed on Dad. I watched as he let go of my hand and disappeared inside. A few minutes later, the sound of the toilet flushing echoed through the cracked door.

The rest stop was devoid of any other visitors, making the air feel thick with an uneasy stillness. We didn't give the desolate wasteland of the vacant lot a second glance as we hurried towards the Rambler, excitement building for the journey ahead.

The late afternoon sun shone down on a block of dismal brown row houses until we spotted a modern townhouse with a little porch in front. I saw my aunt and uncle relaxing on a green-and-white-webbed aluminum glider as they waited. Dad unlocked the doors, and they stood up, making their way towards us. As soon as my aunt saw my sister, she rushed over, hugging her tight. As my sister hugged our aunt, I took a moment to appreciate the picturesque scenery of the neighborhood that brought back memories of our Sunday rides. My aunt finally approached me, and I could see the joy in her eyes as she gave me a warm hug. A waft of freshness and her signature scent, Prince Matchabelli Wind Song, surrounded her. With broad smiles on their faces, Dad and my uncle unloaded the car, eager to kick back on the porch and listen to the baseball game.

Sounds of laughter were the first thing we heard when we walked indoors. The room erupted in joyous hugs and wide smiles as Mom walked in, completing the reunion of sisters. Inside, my sister and I sat in the kitchen, sipping iced tea from tall, chilled glasses. "Aunt Marie," I complained, "the water at the rest stop was freezing cold when we tried to wash our hands."

The sisters exchanged a look that spoke volumes, but neither of them said a word. "Wash your hands as often as you like,

Annmarie. We have plenty of soap and hot water," my aunt assured me.

Good Friday: morning prayer, noon prayer, noon service, prayer, dinner, service, evening prayer, and bedtime prayer.

Saturday: morning prayer, afternoon prayer, evening service, dinner, evening prayer, preparation for Resurrection Sunday, and bedtime prayer.

On Sunday we celebrated!

My beautiful white-and-pale-blue dress hung on the door before I went to bed. I brushed my hair a hundred times, tied on my silk blue bonnet, and kissed everyone goodnight. After praying, I snuggled up next to my sister in the sofa bed, feeling secure. Peeking at my dress hanging on the door, I admired how the moonlight illuminated its beauty, making me giddy with excitement and unable to sleep.

Easter Sunday morning, the sun rose; its light gently filled the small room and roused me from sleep. I could hear my floral dress calling out to me to hurry and put it on, promising this day would be nothing but perfect. After completing morning prayers, I rushed through breakfast, my mind already focused on getting dressed.

In the living room, we gathered together in our finest Easter attire, while my aunt took pictures with her Polaroid color camera before we left for church. Driving her shiny blue Cadillac, she led the way, and we followed in our trusty Rambler, taking in the sights along the way.

People greeted my aunt and uncle but ignored us children as we walked up the steep marble steps. My aunt introduced her siblings, and I realized how much they looked alike, light colored, with long, dark, shiny hair. They spoke with a sophisticated older man in a navy pinstripe suit, crisp white shirt, and gold cufflinks, leaning on a mahogany cane. I did a double take when I saw him, thinking he bore a striking resemblance to my aunt.

I could see teenage boys walking around the Rambler, and their boisterous laughter echoed through the parking lot. My aunt introduced me to her friends just as I was about to tell Dad about the boys at the car. Mom shot a warning look, hinting not to forget my manners. I preened in my homemade dress, headband, and long, flowing hair, flashing a polite smile. Despite my best efforts, the boys near the Rambler were too distracting for me to concentrate on anything else.

Sitting in my aunt's pew, I felt the weight of our family tradition and history. The sermon was hard to follow, and I squirmed in my seat. I stifled a yawn behind my gloved hand during the preacher's endless words and noticed a boy staring at us. He was one of the boys walking around our Rambler. His modern style was clear in his blondish-brown hair hanging below his eyebrows. The paisley-pink tie caught my eye. He puckered his lips in rude manner. I looked back at the pulpit, wondering if Dad saw what the boy did.

After the service, people stood around talking about their Easter dinner plans. My sister was holding Mom's hand as she and my aunt spoke to friends. Dad and my uncle were close by, speaking with the elderly, well-dressed man. Feeling left out, I adjusted my headband and then asked, "Excuse me, Aunt Marie, where is the bathroom?"

My mother continued speaking to my aunts' friends and gave me a questioning look. Aunt Marie searched for a youth to lead me to the bathroom. Unable to find someone, she directed me to the bathroom via a stairwell. Mom reminded me to wash my hands.

Two stalls were visible when I flipped on the light switched on. I entered the first stall, placed my handbag on the door hanger, lifted my dress, and pulled down my lace panties. After finishing, I flushed, smoothed my dress, and left the stall to wash my hands. Realizing I left my handbag on the door, I went back into the stall to retrieve it. The lights flicked off momentarily when I heard the door open, and then flicked back on.

When I looked at the mirror, I saw the blondish-brown-haired boy in a gray suit and paisley tie, the pale pink of his shirt a contrasted against his skin. I felt for a second confused and noticed the faint scent of cologne in the air. He closed the door and put his finger to his lips. Abruptly, he moved closer to me. I tried to inch away but he pushed me against the sink. There was no place for me to move and his body was now pushed against me. His height was a barrier preventing me from freeing myself. He bent down into my face and his fingers squeezed my cheeks forcing them into a pucker. His breath smelled like Chiclets. I felt his tongue invading my mouth.

As I tried to push him away, his other hand continued to grope at my small breasts. My heart raced with panic as he moved closer, but I fought back by shoving him aside and making a mad dash for the door. The bathroom plunged into darkness, leaving me disoriented. I pulled on the icy metal handle. I could hear the creak of the hinges and the sound of my own labored breathing. His hand shot out and slammed the door shut. His words were crisp and menacing.

"Never speak of this, or your family will pay the price. I know your car." He moved his hand, "Who would ever believe a fat brown-skinned girl over me?" he sneered, his eyes narrowing with disdain, and then he exited the bathroom.

I stood frozen, his words echoing in my mind. My lips felt bruised from the roughness of his kiss.

My heart was racing as I reached the top steps. I ran into the sanctuary looking for Dad. "I was getting worried about you,"

Mom whispered, staring at my dress and hair. Mom closely scrutinized my face. I crushed my white gloves trying to catch my breath. She bent down, whispering in my ear, "Why are you so pale and perspiring? You know better than to run in church."

The weight of my emotions silenced me as I fought back tears and stared at her. Dad was in a deep discussion with my uncle and Mr. Rowley when I spotted him. He threw me a quick wink and a grin, then turned his attention back to the group. Though he motioned for me to come over, I found myself transfixed and unable to move.

"Mrs. Fowler, I hope you're having a wonderful Easter Sunday," said the boy who had just kissed me in the bathroom. His smile betrayed nothing as he glanced at me. "You look lovely, as always."

"Thank you, Leland. Let me introduce you to my sister and niece."

Despite the sinking feeling in my stomach, I kept my eyes trained forward as I walked away, seeking refuge next to my father. My clenched hands were sweating, but I took a deep breath and pushed forward, refusing to look back. I pictured my aunt's expression, her eyebrows furrowed, and her lips pursed. I knew that when we got home, both she and Mom would discipline me for my lack of manners and the humiliation I had caused my aunt.

Lost in thought during the drive back to my aunt's house, I barely registered the passing scenery of trees and houses. I fantasized about changing into my comfiest clothes, free from the constraints of my dress. The kiss that Leland forced on me felt all wrong, like a violation of my body and my trust. If I disclosed the details to my mother, the news would quickly make its way through the household, and it would force Aunt Marie to confront the boy. Would they believe me over him? He already showed his connection to my family. Should I risk ruining the day by revealing the truth, or keep it to myself to protect everyone?

An Easter lily had arrived while we were gone. My mother took responsibility for the plant, unwrapping the green floral paper and handing a card to my aunt. Carefully holding the plant, so as not to spill water on her dress, she took it into the living room. A neighbor who dropped by was speaking with my uncle and dad. The radio was playing festive music as family posed for pictures being taken to remember the day. Mom smiled at everyone as she gently placed the Easter lily on a corner table in the living room.

"Mom," I asked in a soft voice, "can I change from this dress?"

Engrossed in arranging the lily, she answered me. "No, honey. You look so pretty. Take a picture with your sister and cousins." She continued moving the plant, trying to get the perfect angle. Noticing I had not moved, she whispered. "Wait until after we eat. You can change before we leave for the long drive home."

The sun that had looked so bright that morning appeared hidden behind a dark cloud. I picked at my meal, skipping dessert—even the saltwater taffy I was looking forward to enjoying did not appeal to me. Excusing myself from the table, I went to change my clothes. The sight of the white Easter lily brought to mind notions of purity, rebirth, new beginnings, and hope as I walked by.

The dress slipped off my body, cascading to the ground in a crumpled heap, leaving me to ponder if the bathroom incident would forever stain my identity, or if it was the dress that bore the weight of his touch. Regardless of the decision, I would never wear it again; the texture was rough and uncomfortable against my body.

The beautiful dress I desired to wear now felt dirty. Shame washed over me as I painstakingly folded the dress in its tissue-paper packaging. With each wave of anger and resentment, the wall against my back seemed to press harder on my body, amplifying my emotions as I sat on the daybed. That boy took from me something deeply personal, catching me off guard. I felt a surge of disgust towards the boy who had wronged me.

Dad knocked and came into the room, interrupting my silent rage. He stood in front of me, his concerned gaze fixed on my face. One glance from Dad was all it ever took for him to notice something was off. My voice caught in my throat, and all I could manage was a nod as tears threatened to spill. His touch was gentle and reassuring as he pressed his palm against my forehead. "Annmarie, what's wrong?"

The thought of home was all I could think of, to keep us safe. "Dad, I just want to go home," I pleaded. Tears earnestly drenched my face. "Please, let's leave now." I threw myself into his arms, not wanting to let go.

I never forgot that weekend visiting my aunt and uncle, nor what happened in the bathroom. There we're so many things that spring I did not understand. I told no one because I feared what the boy said might come true.

Despite the societal upheaval of the early sixties, my women's

college remained dedicated to providing counseling sessions,

where women of color could openly discuss the challenges they

faced. In reality, the lessons were not much different from what I

learned at home. Keep your legs closed, dress down, and a young

man's hands do not belong on your breast.

Memories of Easter Sunday in the church ladies' room flooded

back as I listened to my classmates' first-kiss experiences. A vivid

flashback cascading like a waterfall. triggered the sharp scent of

air freshener and the rustle of crinoline. His rough hands pressing

against my little breasts while he pushed his tongue past my closed

lips. His face eluded my memory, yet I held onto the certainty

that I would unmistakably identify him if our paths intertwined

once more. The fleeting memory came to a halt, like a bird

frozen mid-flight. I glanced around and realized my surroundings

- someone was asking me a question.

The next day, I met with Beth, the dorm counselor, to discuss

what I had told no one about the Easter Sunday bathroom

incident.

"Annmarie, why didn't you ever tell anyone what happened?"

"He said no one would ever believe someone who looked like me."

"Did he really say that?" she asked in disbelief. "He certainly exploited your limited experience and emotional vulnerability. His words and act are shameful. I'm sorry you had that experience."

I nodded in acceptance of her sentiment. He had weaponized my color to provide justification for his actions. The aftermath of my first kiss left me feeling disgusted, embarrassed, and fearful of my family's reaction.

In the years since, I had transformed from a pubescent girl into a self-assured woman, embracing my curves. My family often commented on my shapely figure and how I resembled the beauty of an orange autumn leaf.

"Considering what you know now about boys violating your rights, can you think of other measures to take if it happens again? What do you think?" With a tilt of her head, Beth asked as if she already knew my answer.

"My sense of security comes from the belief that I have the power to prevent and seek justice for any violation. I am confident in my worth as a person, and my skin color cannot diminish my rights." After taking a deep breath, I said, "Regardless of the man's identity."

Stepping into the early afternoon sunlight, I walked back to my dorm. The birds chirping and the rustling of leaves in the gentle breeze made me feel hopeful. Opening the dormitory door, I saw that Mrs. Lockwood had put a small bunch of irises in the vase at the entrance to the dorm. The mere sight of those beautiful flowers transported me home.

In March 1967, my junior year, Mom called to tell me Aunt Marie had passed away. "Most of the arrangements are final." Mom's voice sounded strained. "The funeral will be on Monday. Your Aunt Juliette and I are now planning last-minute details."

"Mom don't worry about waiting for me. Once my last class on Friday ends, I'll get on the road."

When I got my driver's license, my dad had gifted me the Rambler, a car that held so many memories.

The cool breeze of the slow-moving weekend of Aunt Marie's wake and funeral contrasted with the warmth of the bright sunshine. As we walked into the church led by the funeral director and minister, I saw a sea of mourners gathered to pay their respects. So many of Aunt Marie's students honoring her forty-five years of teaching in the city and community leaders, unable to enter the church, gathered behind barricades for a glimpse of what was happening inside.

The choirs swayed together, their voices blending in perfect harmony as the music pulsed through the air. We finally made it to the reserved pew for the family, and there I saw the elderly gentleman who favored Aunt Marie and Grandmother sitting comfortably behind us with his wife and son, his perfectly coiffed white hair shining in the light.

When we settled in our seats I discreetly slipped off my shoes. The man leaned over and whispered to Mom, his voice barely audible. "I was very fond of your sister; Marie was a grand lady indeed."

I looked over my shoulder and saw that a younger man with light-colored hair accompanied him, dressed in a black suit and pink shirt. Looking into those hazel eyes, I could almost feel the cool tile beneath my feet and hear running water. The stained-glass windows blurred together. My heart raced as I gazed into those

piercing eyes, and my palms grew sweaty. I quickly turned around
and closed my eyes in prayer. When I opened them, Mom and her
siblings exchanged a look, raising eyebrows as the two men moved
from behind us and walked towards the casket for a last view.

Later, I learned from Dad that the man was Gerard Severin, the
esteemed bank president responsible for managing Aunt Marie's
finances.

We had to manage multiple receiving lines to accommodate
the enormous number of individuals who wished to offer their
condolences. Out of the corner of my eye, I saw him approach the
area where my cousin and I were greeting guests. Did he remember
what he had done to me?

The person in front of him and I chatted for a moment. "Thank
you for attending my aunt's service today."

The woman nodded and walked away. My cousin was already
speaking to him. He looked at me with curiosity and raised his
eyebrow.

"Leland G. Severin Jr.," he announced with an air of superiority that was clear in his demeanor.

"Thank you for coming," my cousin said and then asked, "How did you know our aunt?"

"Of course my family and I respected Mrs. Fowler greatly. She was my teacher in high school." He stared at me for a moment. "Do I know you?"

"I don't think so." My voice was tinged with panic. I watched him momentarily hesitate. "I never forget a face."

Taking a deep breath in, I felt my heart skip a beat with trepidation. The phrase "irrespective of his identity" echoed in my mind.

"Where are you from?" He posed the question in a manner that implied a history of getting what he wanted.

"I attend college in a small town that is likely unfamiliar to you."

People were moving around him to speak with other family members. Mom glared at me for holding up the receiving line.

"College?" He looked surprised.

"Yes."

"Interesting."

"Beg your pardon." He appeared to doubt the possibility of a woman of color attending college.

Despite my attempts to signal disinterest, he persisted in detailing his father's role as the bank president at the largest bank in the county. "Your aunt entrusted her finances to our bank."

My cousin tried to move him along. "Mr. Severin, thank you for attending the service."

"Your aunt's teaching brilliance shone through the flourishing of her colored students. Her success must have been a motivating factor for you to attend college."

Keeping the plastered smile on my face, I waited for him to leave, not betraying the rage I felt. He was oblivious to the inappropriateness of his conversation.

"I'm sure you will be a wonderful teacher like Mrs. Fowler..."

I watched him struggle to finish his thought, but the words hung unsaid. My cousin looked from me to him and said, "You mean she was a great white teacher?"

Pink slowly rose on his cheeks. "Yes, that's correct, but I apologize if I've offended you. Allow me to explain further by calling you."

As my cousin shot me a skeptical glance, frantic, I recited my aunt's phone number. He scribbled it onto his funeral program and then excused himself.

I called my college roommate Janie that night to share the day's events and Leland's comments.

"Annmarie, make him believe you're interested when he calls."

"Janie, why would I ever do that? You're aware of what he did to me."

I couldn't help but feel uneasy when I heard her unsettling laughter.

The aroma of freshly baked muffins and sizzling bacon wafted through the house the next morning. Everyone gathered in the dining room to pick at the breakfast food left by neighbors. The sound of clinking utensils mingled with my mom's voice as she bustled around the kitchen, discussing the upcoming bank meeting with my dad and aunts.

"Annmarie, we sorted several boxes of Marie's teaching materials for you. There could be useful tools for your student teaching practicum and state exam. The reading of your aunt's will is scheduled for tomorrow. Keep in mind that any jewelry or money she left you will not be readily available. Once we handle her financial affairs, you can expect to receive your inheritance."

The sound of the phone ringing echoed through the house, and Dad picked it up. I was in the middle of plating my food when I heard him say "Leland Severin." "Hold the line please. Annmarie is here. I'll get her for you."

My hands were trembling as I grasped the phone. "Hello?"

"Good morning. This is Leland, from your aunt's funeral."

"Yes, I remember you."

"I wanted to say sorry if I came across as disrespectful. Your aunt's impressive achievements and character have served as an inspiration for many, and it seems you're on the same path."

"Thank you for your apology, Leland. She inspired my desire to teach. I'm taking her education materials to help me study."

"If her notes are like her banking records, you have a wealth of information."

"I'll keep that in mind." The phone cord twisted around my hand.

"Annmarie, reach out to me if you need help or have questions." He insisted I write his number, repeating it twice with emphasis on each digit.

"Thank you for calling." I hung up the phone and felt the weight of the paper with his number on it in my hand. I folded it and placed it in the box.

Again, I wondered whether he remembered me as the victim of his assault.

Mid-year exams approached, and I wondered if my aunt's materials could provide valuable insights for my community research. Sitting on the floor, I opened the three boxes on a Saturday morning. The first one had worn-out workbooks and teaching worksheets. The second box had attendance notices and grade rosters. I skimmed the student names in a 1957 fall class.

Janie came in and saw me sitting on the floor. "Find anything of interest?"

"There are some worksheets and workbooks I could probably use at some point. Aunt Marie wrote teaching notes and strategies on some pages."

I spotted an out-of-place book when I replaced the roster. The aged cover revealed a roster with few names, including Leland G. Severin's. "Janie, look at this."

Over my shoulder, she peered at the paper. "Can you read what's written beside his name?"

Holding the roster book, I stood and walked to my desk to get a better look. Aunt Marie had written "personal" and "nephew" in perfect penmanship.

"What's the significance of this?" Janie asked, puzzled.

"Your guess is as good as mine. At the repast, he told my cousin she was his teacher. I thought he was confused and just making conversation."

"Why? Couldn't she be his teacher?"

"Janie, you don't understand. I think during this time she focused all her efforts on teaching-colored students."

"Didn't you say Leland is white?"

I nodded. "She taught at an integrated school later in her career, but it's not clear if this was the one."

"It still makes little sense, even if that was the case. Why would she write personal and nephew next to his name?" Janie asked.

"When I speak to Mom tomorrow, I'll ask her what year Aunt Marie taught at the integrated high school."

"I have an idea that might work better. Call and ask him directly since you have his number."

"No, I'll ask Mom." I pushed the book to the side and returned to digging through the unopened box.

The last box had a small wooden sewing box sitting on top of yellowing newspaper clippings I knew were a treasure trove of memories. Among them was a picture of my Grandmother, Annette, and Grandfather Roland, with his arm around her and her long black hair swept up in a bun. The photo captured their wedding day January 1926.

My fingers brushed against a creased, large brown envelope and pictures. Upon opening the envelope, I saw a picture of a light-skinned baby in diapers on a blanket, with Grandma looking down at him. Her face had a solemn expression, almost like she had been crying.

The next photo was him wrapped in a beautifully knitted, blue newborn-baby blanket. On the white border at the bottom of the photo was the name, Gérard, written in gold cursive.

In another picture, a white man stood next to a woman and a little boy about a one-year-old in a suit. Comparing the pictures, it looked like the same baby over the course of a year. I tried to read Grandmother's cursive writing, but it was in French. Laying the photos side by side, I could see Baby Gérard at one week old, six months old, and then a year old. I searched through the box of mementos and found love letters addressed to my grandmother, written by a man I had never heard of with the last name Severin.

As in Leland Severin?

Not finding anything else, I opened the sewing box. Inside, buried under spools of thread, was a small gold band with a delicate marquis diamond. Beneath the ring box, a birth certificate caught my eye. Its faded green hue revealed the names Annette Dubois and Gérard L. Severin, parents of Gerard, a baby boy, in November 1925.

Falling into the chair, I tried to wrap my head around what I was holding in my hand. The sound of rustling pages filled the air as I lifted another newspaper, and it drew my eyes to

a wedding announcement. Eileen Hastings marries Gérard L.
Severin December 1925. I looked at the three black-and-white
pictures. Puzzled, I searched for more pictures and found an
announcement: Mr. and Mrs. Gérard Leland Severin with their
baby boy Gerald Dubois. The baby in the newspaper looked like
Baby Gerard in the photos with my Grandmother Annette.

Then I found a letter, smudged with fingerprints and tearstains.

My dearest Annette,

*I love you so very much. This will be my last correspondence. I've got
so much to say to you, my words will never be enough to compensate
for the grief I caused. Truly, I believed our love would overcome the
division of prejudice in our society. I pray our son Gerard won't suffer
as we have, being compelled to marry another because of our love
for each other. I promise to raise him with the fire of my undying
love for you. In my heart, you will forever be my only wife. Keep
my ring as a symbol of the love between you, me, and our son.
Our families may have forced our hands, but the love we have for
Gerard is unwavering, and he will always be our cherished son. I
will ensure his middle name remains Dubois in honor of your love.
With every decision I make for him, I will consider what you would*

have wanted. The vibrant colors of irises are forever associated with our love in my mind.

> *Your Love Always,*
>
> *Gérard L. Severin*

All the pieces fell into place, and I finally understood. I sat there looking at the evidence before me. At that moment, I knew what I had to do. No more deceit. He had to know, and I was going to tell him.

Since the funeral last year, we spent Thanksgiving at my Aunt Marie's home that my cousin still retained I spoke with him. Following a conversation with my family about the letter, I confided in Janie that I planned to share it with Leland.

Janie's words gave me the final push I needed to solidify my plan. "Annmarie, this requires an in-person conversation. You must convince him with evidence, not just words."

She was right, so I called him. "Leland, I want to share something with you that I found."

"Okay, let's meet."

To arrange our meeting in late April, we settled on a location that was situated at the midpoint between my college and his city of residence. Instead of enduring a five-hour train ride with multiple stops, I chose to drive, relishing the freedom to plan my own schedule. I organized the copies of my grandmother's personal effects after my evening class on Monday.

Janie's restless pacing filled our dorm room. It took her a while to gather the courage, but eventually she expressed a concern. "Annmarie, you're a young African American woman driving long distances by herself, and to meet a man. I'm going with you. Two of us is better than one lone 'colored' woman."

With a map highlighted in yellow, we set out Tuesday morning before daybreak. The winding roads and towering mountains to our meeting place triggered a rush of vivid memories, transporting me back in time. Uncovering my grandmother's secrets only deepened the unsettling feeling I had when I learned that the boy in the bathroom on Easter Sunday was actually a relative.

Little had changed at the rest stop of my childhood as we arrived with ten minutes to spare. It was crowded, making it hard to find a space to park the Rambler. I created a space on the gravel shoulder, and the scent of wildflowers filled the air. Janie and I took turns holding the box as we walked to the designated bathroom area, the weight shifting between our arms. Three women walked ahead of us. With them was a little girl with pigtails, who looked to be about seven years old. I smiled at her sense of wonderment when she asked her mother, "Is this the bathroom only for us, mommy?"

Her mother's pinched mouth hid what the rest of us knew. "Yes honey, this bathroom is especially for us."

She and I exchanged a knowing look, and I recalled asking the same question years earlier. Nothing had changed, I thought, until I looked at the box in my hand.

We sat at the outdoor table waiting for Leland to arrive, sipping iced tea Janie had packed for us to drink. She and I chatted until I spotted him strolling as though he had no care in the world. The breeze was just strong enough to cause his white trousers to dance around his legs. The red-and-blue stripes on his tennis sweater created a bold V shape on his chest. His straw hat shielded his face from the sun, but his gray-green eyes were still visible to me. Leland acknowledged Janie with a nod as I introduced them. She moved to the end of the picnic table, so we had privacy.

Despite my preparation, I couldn't seem to get my tongue and mind to work in harmony at that moment.

"Annmarie, it is nice to see you again. I admit you've aroused my curiosity enough for me to take a day away from the bank. What is this all about?"

"Leland, I would not have insisted if it wasn't important." Though his eyes were on my face, they seemed to be drawn towards my lips.

"So let's hear what you have to say." He absentmindedly twisted the straw from his drink between his fingers.

"Some of Aunt Marie's documents I stumbled upon were nothing short of shocking," I said, my voice trembling.

"It doesn't come as a shock to me," he said, "since she was an exceptional woman."

"Leland, why was Aunt Marie your teacher? After all, the school she taught at was for colored students. Why would you be there?"

For the first time since Leland sat down, he looked uncomfortable. "What does that have to do with anything?"

"Come on, Leland, like you said, you came this far out of curiosity, so answer the question."

"I was involved in a matter that resulted in my suspension for a semester. My father's intention was to teach me a lesson, even though it seemed silly. After speaking with Mrs. Fowler, they concluded I should attend school under her tutelage. She was a wonderful teacher, and her service to that school for coloreds helped many young men receive a fine education. Although it was quite a degrading experience for me." His gray-green eyes stared at Annmarie as if to say 'satisfied?'

"I see." I had the answer to my other question. I opened the box, taking out the copies I had made for him. "Leland, in my aunt's attendance book she wrote this." I turned to the page with his name and "nephew" written in parentheses.

Leland held the page close, then put it down, looking puzzled. "Why would she write that next to my name?" He paused and said, "Wait, that wouldn't make sense either." Leland examined the page, then flipped it over. The back notes identified him as a nephew.

"What do you know about your father's family?"

"My father? I'm not sure I understand what you're asking," he said.

"Leland, just answer the question."

He furrowed his brow and squinted, appearing confused. "My grandparents had a child, my dad. My grandfather, Gérard Leland, was born in France and moved to this country with his wife and newborn son. Why?"

"I believe your father and Aunt Marie have a familial connection." I took a sip from the lukewarm bottle of iced tea and let him process the information.

"My father and your aunt related. Come on, Annmarie, there is no way that is possible. I mean, look at us."

I looked at Janie sitting away from us, reading. Though she tried to hide it behind the book, I saw a smirk cross her face as she listened.

"Leland, I thought that was strange as well. But as I continued going through the boxes, I found pictures in an envelope and letters that put things into perspective."

"You found pictures of me?"

"No, of your father and grandfather."

"Dad and Grandfather?"

I took out the picture of Grandma with the baby boy and placed it in front of him.

"Okay, this looks like a mother and son. You said that's your grandmother, right?"

"Yes."

"If you say so, but Annmarie, this woman is white. How could she be your grandmother?"

I gave him a look, shaking my head. "My grandmother was French. And that is her son, Gerard Dubois."

I took out the next photo of the baby with the smiling man holding him. Leland scrutinized the man and baby. His face changed, as if he understood something but wasn't sure. "This man and your grandmother are the parents?" he asked, as if he needed confirmation.

I handed him a copy of the faded green birth certificate of Gerard Dubois Severin, son of Annette Dubois and a Gérard Leland Severin.

Leland let out a slow whistle, taking out a handkerchief to wipe his brow. I watched and arranged the wedding and birth announcements in front of him and marveled at how they told the story of their family.

My heart ached under the weight of what I had revealed about my grandmother.

His face blanched, Leland stared at the documents before him, moving from one to another and then back.

"My mother and I had a conversation," I said. "She clarified several things that I did not understand about Grandmother Annette growing up. The love letters between your grandfather and my grandmother revealed why they could not be together and raise their son."

I could see by Leland's frown a sign of understanding that he did not give voice to. He took a sharp inhale; his hands shook, and he dropped them under the table.

I gathered my things and motioned to Janie we were leaving. Standing in front of him, I said, "The memory of that Easter Sunday when you assaulted me in the bathroom, Leland, makes it hard to believe we are family. You ruined my first kiss with your brutal behavior, and it left me feeling robbed of the special moment I had imagined. Our grandparents' values and principles would never have allowed for something like that to happen to their offspring."

Leland remained seated, wiping his brow.

Taking in the vibrant colors of the irises lining the sidewalk, I saw my grandmother's sad eyes held a wisdom that could only come from a life of betrayal. Her words in her native language were as lovely as the iris she spoke of, but they also carried a message of the injustices of our history.

I noticed Leland's strange expression in my rearview mirror as I pulled out of the parking lot in the salmon-pink-and -gray Rambler.

DEDICATION

I am so grateful to have family, friends, and writing colleagues who challenge me as a storyteller to interpret and share stories of the human condition through my lens. Chasing dreams riding the wings of elusive butterflies is arduous work but worth the effort when you are obedient to the call.

AUTHOR'S BIOGRAPHY

L'Michelle Bleu L'Eau, who has a professional corporate background, composes flash fiction and short stories about human or social problems that affect the protagonists in her stories. L'Michelle taps into her affinity for nature in its purest form to align each character and natural elements that guide them through a transformative denouement.

She writes blogs that pertain to techniques for self-healing and organization. Recent projects have focused on a novel that examines the search for acceptance of one's culture, ethnicity, and voice after experiencing domestic violence. Some of her short stories have appeared in the Transcendent Authors *Summer, When Doors Open, Spring the Unexpected* 2021 and *Winter, An End and a Promise* 2021 anthologies. L'Michelle has had other works featured in the Short Fiction Break Literary Magazine, *The Blooming Box*, and Short Fiction Break Literary Magazine.

Ms. Bleu L'Eau has undertaken translating a handwritten manuscript left by her late mother. She is engaged in the process of editing her debut novel. Creating storybook trailers is her specialty she developed for her stories. When L'Michelle is not engaged in writing, she devotes a portion of her time to tutoring students, with a focus on improving their reading and writing skills.

Visit the Transcendent Authors website or to learn more. If you are interested in storybook trailers, let her help you create a unique one for your story. Send her a message!

BEFORE THE LAST BATTLE

Introductory Paragraph:

The following short story is the opening chapter of a forthcoming

historical fiction novel dramatizing what was arguably the last

battle in the European Theater of World War II. It is one of only

two known instances where the Americans and Germans fought

alongside one another as a German Wehrmacht officer, Major Josef

"Sepp" Gangl, sought out an American tanker to help defend

a medieval castle and former Nazi "honor prisoners" against the

relentless fanaticism of the Waffen SS. But before that, Sepp must

gain the confidence of the Austrian Resistance while remaining

true to himself.

The girl was still a block away, but I could make out the red and white pocket square in her coat. She shifted the stack of newspapers to her left hand, and in a smooth, single motion reached up to tuck the square out of sight. I acted as if I had not seen it as she raised her arm to salute me.

It had to be the uniform. I raised my arm back but neither of us spoke either salutation, just the upraised right arm straight forward. Even here in Austria, and even now, in the spring of 1945, it was expected.

She stepped into the street to avoid a spot where the sidewalk was cratered. The Americans had bombed the town back in February. Two months later, the debris had been cleared, but Wörgl was too far off the beaten path for anyone to repair the sidewalks. I held up a pfennig and motioned for her to stop.

She carefully slipped one newspaper from the bundle as I glanced down and noticed the pocket square again. Red and white. The Austrian colors. Displaying them was a grievous offense, not just because it was the mark of the Resistance forces. Times were changing.

The partisans were emboldened by the approach of the Americans and their allies. Showing their colors was a way of confirming like-mindedness, as well as a signal to those still cowing down to the Nazis—the end was near, things would be better. Now though, the Waffen SS was ranging the countryside, with orders to kill any male over the age of 14 who dared display anything other than the mark of the National Socialists. It didn't matter if it was the former country's flag, a white flag of surrender, or even worse something made to resemble the American flag. Those troops were ruthless and intense.

She offered me the paper but made no move for the coin.

"Bitte," *please*, I said as I held it closer. Many soldiers would have just taken the paper. Perhaps that was what she expected. But that was not me. In my 17 years of service, I had never taken advantage of the uniform. My Bavarian upbringing ran deep. I wished I had a piece of candy or bar of chocolate I could give her. Instead, the best I could do was whistle softly the old Haydn tune that had been the anthem of Austria before the Anschluss, when it had been swallowed into the Greater German Reich.

She smiled and gave me a hushed "Danke," as she took the coin and headed on her way. Even on this main street, prospects for selling her papers were few.

I glanced down at the news. The paper was from four days earlier. Low sales meant we were lucky to have a paper at all. The headline told how the Führer had celebrated his birthday in Berlin rather than Berchtesgaden for the first time since the war had started. No parades, no fanfare, no lavish party for the whole Reich.

More enemy planes had been spotted to the north and west, preparing for another push. The troops were deep into my adopted state of Baden-Württemberg now, perhaps even where my family lived in Ludwigsburg.

The last time I saw the enemy in action had been two months ago, and it cost me two of my soldiers. We had not even been trying to defend against them. It was an accident. The buildings we were scouring for provisions were their target, and we failed to evacuate fast enough to escape the aerial bombardment.

I looked up from the paper and took in the damaged town. Directly across the street was the Astner House, it was a total loss. The Gasthaus Schachtner next door was partially destroyed but had resumed serving meals. From here, I could also see the bombed-out train station that had been the focal point of the bombing raid. Everyone could see the war was winding down, which made things more deadly on both sides of the battle.

The advancing Americans would inevitably cause the fall of the Third Reich. It was just a matter of time, but I had taken an oath. Initially, to protect my country. Then later, we were forced to take a new oath of allegiance. This time to the man himself. I had never considered the idea of disobeying an order or breaking an oath before. And yet here I was about to do just that.

My stomach rumbled. It was well past noon, and I had a meeting to get to. I tucked my newspaper under my arm and walked toward the Neue Post Inn.

The bell made a soft echo in the deserted restaurant as I entered. There had never been a crowd as long as I'd been coming here. Probably hadn't had one since the Anschluss.

The first four tables had no chairs. Someone had carried them off years ago to burn for warmth. The only reason the tables were still here was that Johann, the owner, had attached them to the wall and floor. I glanced down to see the seamless transitions he had fabricated. The tables seemed to have been made at the same time as the rest of the interior.

In the corner, was Rupert Hagleitner, the man I'd come to see, but first I waved to Johann behind the bar. He nodded without halting the polishing of a beer stein. Why do bartenders do that? The gray in his beard showed his age. He had owned this place 42 years. He missed being conscripted in the first war because of his age. Now that he had been left behind twice, he just looked old. Six years of war will do that to anyone.

I turned and walked to where Rupert sat. It was the Stammtisch table at night, where the social club at the heart of the town met. Or had been before the war started. Now it was just the place Hagleitner and I met to plot. He sat in the bench's corner, the best tactical spot at the table, but he shifted as I neared.

"Sepp!" He called my nickname. "I waited for you." He patted my upper arm in greeting then motioned for me to sit where he had been. As I sat, I scanned the room. This seat provided an unobstructed view of everything from the front door to the kitchen. No one and nothing would be unobservable.

Hagleitner sat at the end of the L shaped bench. "Alois will be here soon." He referred to Alois Mayr, the local businessman rumored to be the head of the local arm of the Austrian Resistance.

"But first. . ." he waved toward Johann, who reappeared from the kitchen.

"Does he trust me enough to be seen in public with me?" I asked.

Hagleitner scoffed. "It isn't you he trusts, it's me. And if I vouch for you, he knows you're good."

I nodded; not sure his confidence was a good move. My direct superior, Oberstleutnant Giehl, had given orders to "vigorously defend against the advancing enemy" without mention of whether he meant foreign or domestic. I had seen enough of the Americans to know they were the more dangerous ones, but the Resistance was here already. Holding a knife at our neck, waiting to strike when we least expected. What better way was there to vigorously defend than to be on the inside of the Resistance?

The conversation stopped as Johann set two plates in front of us and went back to the bar to pour two mugs of beer. I looked at the plate. A lonely knödel in watery gravy. I closed my eyes.

In my mind, I could imagine the same plate with two semmelknödels and a schweinebraten with its skin nice and crispy. A deep, dark-colored rahmsauce with mushrooms smothered them both. When I opened my eyes, the single ball of food remained. Meat had become scarce, but even bread was rare. This was a gourmet dinner for these times. I cut a small piece with my knife as Johann served the beer. I thanked him and slipped the morsel into my mouth. No salt, little flavor, but it was enough to keep the hunger away for a few hours.

Despite being four years younger and a civilian, Hagleitner had more influence and led more men than I did. I had fewer than 25 when I took command of the 2nd Division Werfer Regiment 83 near Peißenberg two months ago. We slogged our way through Tyrol, and by the time we got to Wörgl, I had lost two men to enemy aircraft and one to desertion. With so few men, it didn't seem right to call us a division, but then again, they hadn't had a werfer or a launcher since before I took command.

Where I had 22 men, he had the whole town. Rupert had become the heart and soul of Wörgl. He had been only 19 when he worked on the "Miracle of Wörgl" in 1932. The notes he had helped create worked like currency when there was none around. Even Daladier had come from France to see how it worked. There was a growth spurt in the town and the economy, which helped the people of the town forget there was a depression. When the Austrian National bank shut off the experiment the next year, he had already cemented himself as a community leader. When you give someone hope, they remember it and will follow you almost anywhere. If it hadn't been for the Nazis, Hagleitner would be Bürgermeister. His steadfast refusal to join the NSDAP kept him from holding office; instead, the Tyrol Gauleiter had appointed one of his cronies to do the job. The intel I had said Alois Mayr had made Hagleitner his deputy and put him in charge of the armed fighters in Wörgl, that's why I was cozying up to him.

"Something's happening at the castle," Hagleitner said between bites. "Big visitor, Alois knows."

He referred to Schloss Itter. Depending on who you ask, it was 700 to 900 years old. In more recent times, it had been a private residence then a hotel. After the Anschluss, Himmler himself had surveyed the castle for other purposes. Namely its current use as an upscale prison for high-profile detainees of the Nazi state. The bell on the door rang, interrupting my thoughts as Alois Mayr walked in.

Mayr made a quick scan of the restaurant as I had before approaching our table. He was dressed in a clean, pressed suit with shiny leather shoes. Based on his clothes, the only sign it was wartime was the black band high on his arm. Where most wore the swastika, he had a band of mourning, though for whom I did not know. He finished his scan of the room and tugged slightly on something in his pocket as he nodded toward Johann. He turned toward our table and I could see that he had revealed his red and white pocket square.

At my side, Hageleitner had also revealed his colors. An unofficial Resistance salute. Both men tucked their colors back in as Mayr walked toward us. We stood while he strode long, confident steps and extended his arm toward Hagleitner, who returned the gesture.

He turned to me. "Major Josef Gangl, it is nice to meet you. Rupert has no doubt told you about me?" He extended his arm to me, and we shook hands. He had a strong, firm grip, not so hard it hurt, but enough to know there was hidden strength.

"Herr Mayr, I have indeed been informed about you by Herr Hagleitner, but your reputation precedes you. Your success in business despite your anti-party leanings has been well noted." My lips smirked as I said, "anti-party." Mayr was an astute businessman who had profited before and during the war.

Unlike Hagleitner, Mayr had been a member joining in '38 during a wave of increased membership. As the Austrians

became Germans, many joined—situational patriotism. Ever since
the February bombing of Wörgl, Mayr had stopped wearing
his armband, switching it for the black one he wore now.
Simultaneously, he had become a vocal advocate against the
NSDAP. When General der Gebirgstruppe von Hengl had
assigned me to Giehl's Combat Group a month ago, he had given
me warnings about Mayr. Neither the General nor Giehl had
proof, but both suspected Mayr had become the leader of the local
Resistance.

The left side of his mouth turned up in a sneer. "I prefer to
call it 'pro-Allied' rather than 'anti-Nazi.' It is a more positive
way to describe it." He took his seat with his back to the room.
Vulnerable, and yet he did it with confidence.

As I retook my seat, I shifted slightly to the left. Now I had
an unobstructed view of the entire room. "Confidence is one
thing, sir. Cockiness is another. How do you know I'm not an
undercover agent sent to seek members of the Resistance?"

"Major, the Resistance has a vetting process. One which you
have been actively reviewed by since your arrival in Austria. Even
before you approached us. My presence here is the last step to

validate the results. For this, I will ask a series of questions. Questions which you must answer without hesitation."

Johann walked up and set down a beer in front of Mayr while he spoke, but at no point did Mayr's eyes lose focus on mine.

I smiled, "So, I'm nearly in. Either about to join forces with the enemy and complete my mission, or to join the right side of the war and bring about the destruction of my homeland. Ask away."

A slight smile crossed his lips, then he asked, "You have been in the Wehrmacht Heer for many years, yes?"

"The Heer? Yes, I joined back in the days of the Weimar Republic, '28. There was no Wehrmacht. It was simply the Reichsheer." The Wehrmacht comprised the Heer, Kriegsmarine, and Luftwaffe, but almost everyone I had met outside Germany failed to grasp the distinction, calling the army as simply the "Wehrmacht." Austria was Germanic at its root, though, so Mayr understood the difference.

"You joined in Nürnberg? The heart and soul of the National Socialists."

My eyes narrowed as my voice tensed. He had dug into my history. "Ich bin Bayrische." *I am Bavarian.* "My family may live in Ludwigsburg, but I was born near Regensburg. The proximity of my enlistment to where the Austrian corporal chose to build his grandiose dreams is coincidental." I was stepping over the line now, using a derogatory euphemism for the Führer. A minor offense in the eyes of the Heer leadership, but it was a statement I could take back if anyone had overheard me.

Mayr winced when I stressed the word Austrian and paused. A terse smile seemed to me to show he had gotten my subtle point: geography was no sign of loyalty. He moved on. "You have been involved in some campaigns for which you have been given accolades."

"I've seen some things, yes." I tilted my head toward the Iron Cross on my breast pocket. "Second Class, First Class, gold. The trifecta of bravery in defense of my homeland, and yours by extension."

He ignored my dig at a defeated Austria. "You fought in France?"

"Twice. First was before the Sitzkreig ended." A slight smile crossed Mayr's face at that one. Belittling the stalemate before the invasion of France was always a good way to endear yourself to opponents of Hitler. "Then was there again when the Americans made their invasion of Normandy. Barely got out from the Falaise pocket."

"Ah, the Sitzkreig. So, your injury was a side effect of Pervitin?" he asked, leaning forward on the table.

"No." I shook my head. They had given everyone vials of the drug. I did not know its medical name, but those that took it became hyperactive, raging men who didn't stop, even to sleep. "I took no Pervitin. I was enlisted then, and they gave us fewer pills than the officers. Even then, we got fewer than the Panzer divisions. My pills, I gave to someone in an infantry unit that moved past us early on. Then I was on hand to watch the drug-induced fervor push the battle forward."

Nothing I had done with Hagleitner or Mayr to this point was a damnable offense. I could still show I was a good German soldier, just trying to push the limits and flush out the traitors. How much longer could I push that line?

"Enlisted. So, you were an infantryman?" His eyes narrowed.

"Never. I am, and will always be, an artilleryman." I leaned forward and rested my arms on the table. How fast would be fast enough with my responses? If I was a fraction of a second too long or even too fast, would he be able to discern my true motives?

"After I recovered, I was again active in the Western Campaign and was present at Compiegne. After the French surrendered, I went on to become an instructor in Taus, then got assigned to Army Group South on the road to Kiev."

His stare deepened. "Where you earned your Iron Cross?"

I nodded. "Second Class in August '41, promoted to Oberleutnant in January, then First Class Iron Cross in February." I made a conscious effort to control my breathing. In and out, slow and steady. I cannot let this man destroy my chance here. "Operation Barbarossa was ugly."

Mayr rubbed condensation from his glass. "Worse than Falaise?"

I scoffed but quickly replied, "Yes. Russia was far worse than the resounding defeat at Falaise. I was lucky to get out of there, and Saarbrücken. Was awarded the Gold Cross for that one two months ago."

He leaned back and turned his mug of beer, still not taking a sip. "Tell me what you know about the Children's Murders in 1940."

"In Freiburg?" I asked. He nodded, so I continued. "Three planes dropped bombs on Freiburg. Killed 57 innocent civilians, most of whom were children. It was in the news for months." No doubt he knew this information. He was delving into my personal beliefs. Trying to get me to cross the line, to prove my commitment to the cause.

Mayr waved his hands, encouraging me to continue.

"At first we were told they were French planes." I wiggled in my seat, a touch of nerves. There was no turning back now. "After the failed Ardennes offensive last December, I was in Saarbrücken. There I met eyewitnesses who had fled Freiburg after the Children's Murder. The planes were not French."

Mayr leaned forward on the table and stared hard into my eyes. "No, they weren't. There was a correction in '41. British planes had done the bombing, right?"

"No, not British either." I swallowed hard. "Luftwaffe. There is speculation they were headed to Dijon, but the facts are, the sky was overcast, and it would have been easy for an untrained crew with a new navigator to mistake the two towns. Without a doubt, the bomber's markings were the Iron Cross," I paused, "and the swastika."

My heart beat faster. There would be no turning back now. Mayr leaned in further. "One more question, Major. When did our current war start?"

Without a thought, I blurted, "First of September 1939, when Germany invaded Poland. Allies reacted; they did not begin the aggression." I could barely hear anything over the thumping of my heart in my chest. For six years the party narrative drummed into everyone's skull was that the Poles had invaded on the first and Germany reacted two days later making the official start of the war 3 September.

He stared into my eyes as if trying to bore a hole in my skull.

"Major, I have a duty to do. Like you, I am proud of my Germanic heritage. My patriotic fervor has never been less, and with that in mind, I have a duty to do concerning you and your own state of mind."

I clenched my fists and leaned toward the open end of the bench. If he planned to signal someone to arrest me now, I would fight my way past all of them.

"We need someone to lead our military operations." Mayr leaned back in his chair.

Relief washed over me. I had passed; I was in. Now came the hard part. "Danke, Herr Mayr. I will do my best."

He held up a hand. "First of all, it's Alois. There are some men, and. . ." he looked at Haigleitner, "a few women, eager to join in the fight."

I leaned back and could take my first easy breath. "My friends call me Sepp."

Smiling, he raised his mug of beer. "Sepp then. Here's to a productive resistance." He waited for us to raise our steins. "Prost."

In unison, we said "Prost" and clinked our mugs. After taking a sip, I set mine down while Hagleitner reached in his coat and pulled out a map.

"Weapons?" I asked.

The bell above the door rang, interrupting our conversation. SS Hauptsturmführer Kurt-Siegfried Schrader entered. Even with a limp, he cast a menacing image. The lightning bolts on his collar stood out. His shoulders were squared and leaned forward slightly, giving him the appearance of a cat ready to pounce. As he turned and looked at me, the light shined off the death's head totem on his cap. He caught my eye and held it for a full step before turning his head back toward the bar.

Hagleitner shifted, bumping my arm without looking. I took his meaning and slid my newspaper over his map. Mayr glanced over his shoulder to see what had happened, then returned his focus to me. Ice water must run through his veins.

Schrader leaned on the counter and whispered to Johann. Johann turned and disappeared into the back. Schrader propped his foot on the rail below the bar, the most relaxed I had ever seen him. Had I been set up? Was he here to hear me confess to supporting the Resistance? An icy chill ran down my spine. I was sitting with two of the most highly ranked traitors in Tyrol, but what if they were playing with me? What if they were working with Schrader to deceive me into revealing my anti-Nazi feelings?

My eyes darted from Mayr to Schrader and back. I am proud of my heritage. Proud of my homeland. I do not want it subjugated to tyranny by any ideology or foreign invader. In my mind, there was only one course of action that was right, and even if it cost me my life, I was prepared to commit to it.

Johann returned with a small bag and handed it to Schrader. "Danke," he said and turned. He stopped and looked in our direction and dipped his head, acknowledging we serve the

Fatherland. There would be no hiding the fact I was here. He continued out the door without a pause.

I exhaled without realizing I had been holding my breath. Hagleitner stared at the closed door while Mayr turned for another look. We all took another drink in silence.

"You asked about weapons," Mayr said as he set down his mug. "Rupert here has stashed some pistols, but we were waiting for the right moment."

"And two rifles," Hagleitner interjected.

I nodded to him. "Well, we'll need them. My boss, Giehl, has ordered all roads and bridges into town to be barricaded or destroyed. We cannot allow that to happen."

Hagleitner slid the document from under the newspaper and unfolded it. I could see now it was a map of the Rosenheim-Kufstein-Wörgl area.

"Gentlemen, I have a matter that needs attending. Sources tell me SS-Oberstrumbannführer Weiter is headed to the castle. Rupert will fill you in." Mayr drained his beer and stood. "It is good to have you on the team, Sepp."

I nodded and watched him head for the door while Hagleitner smoothed the map.

"I know the rank, not the name," I said. His rank in the SS was equivalent to my boss's rank.

Hagleitner glanced up to see the door close behind Mayr. "The Castle falls under the jurisdiction of KZ-Gedenkstätte Dachau. Weiter is the Commandant."

Dachau was the heart of the Gedenkstätten, the concentration camp system throughout the Reich. Few people had seen inside the camp system. I had in Poland. What went on inside those fences would eternally stain the Nazi legacy indelibly. The brutality and inhumanity of what I witnessed changed me forever. I could never forget.

"Wastl Wimmer runs the castle, been there two years. My guess is Weiter is retreating, but he's still a danger."

The rats were leaving the sinking ship. An early childhood bible story came to mind. Mene, Mene, Tekel, Parsin. The Nazi regime had been measured, weighed, and found wanting. The writing was on the way, and I had just joined the side that would divide their kingdom.

The cool morning breeze bit through the thin jacket I wore.
Someone had stolen my heavier coat while I was in with Giehl.
After I updated him on my mission and where things stood, he
told me that von Hengel had sent orders for everyone to leave.

I had been trying for days to convince Giehl that resistance was
futile. Now he was sending me on my way, and I wasn't ready to
go. He threw up his hands and let me stay.

Most of the men took the offer of a discharge even though it was
a flimsy piece of paper. It might get them past the first Waffen-SS
checkpoint, but before long, they'd be suspicious. I could only
hope the Americans would arrive soon. Meanwhile, I divided the
remaining ten men up and sent them to scour different sectors of
the city for activity.

Unteroffizier Brunner and I were huddled in the shadow behind
the damaged rathaus looking across the street where the Waffen-SS
were busy setting a trap underneath the main bridge into the old
town. Silently, I handed him the gum I had been chewing for three
days and motioned. The quizzical look on his face disappeared
as he understood what I wanted. After they left, he'd pull the

explosive cap out and replace the wires using the gum to hold it in place. They would think the booby trap was still set, but we would save the six-hundred-year-old bridge.

As I stuffed my hand in my pocket, I felt the wax paper I had stored the gum in when I wasn't chewing it. It had kept the hunger pains away, but now almost as if it knew, my stomach grumbled loudly.

I punched myself in the stomach and crawled further into the shadows to leave the location. My aide stood around the corner and motioned for me. I joined him behind the building.

A civilian I recognized from the Castle, one of the Croats, stood there beside my aide. In broken English she said, "Herr Major Gangl, please with me come. Herr Colonel Weiter trusts and needs you for a mission. He must give you information on Herr Captain Schrader."

I looked at my aide who shrugged. Weiter was a dangerous man, but so was Schrader. I had no desire to see either but ignoring a summons would be bad. What if she had mangled the translation and it was Schrader calling me to discuss Weiter? I could ignore a summons from a lower-ranked man but there was still a danger whether I went or not.

"Where did he say to meet?" I asked.

She looked at me with a quizzical look until my aid translated into Croatian. Then she pointed to the hotel down the street and spoke in her native tongue.

Why wasn't he at the castle? Was this it? Had my deception been found out before I had even begun to do anything? If Schrader had reported me to his superiors in the SS, I could be dead before the week was over; I would be walking into a trap. Not going could trigger a search.

Entering the room, I could see the Weiter's back. At least, I assumed it was him. Having never met the Dachau commander, I had no idea what he looked like, especially from behind. He faced the window overlooking the street and the bombed-out buildings along the street. At the corner of the window, I could see the Neue Post Inn where I now met Hagleitner daily. Between the two of us was a massive desk made of oak against which I saw a cane leaning.

I stopped in front of the desk and raised my hand, uttering the phrase. It no longer rang true to me. Defeat of the Reich had become inevitable; now it merely felt as if I were hailing the victory of our conquerors. Still, it was better than hailing our leader.

Hauptsturmfürher Schrader turned around and quickly returned my salute, muttering what sounded like a hail to our leader. He sat down as I dropped my salute.

"I was not sure you'd come, Major."

I blinked twice. "I was expecting Oberstrumbannführer Weiter, he is not a man to avoid. The message said he had information about you."

The smile that crossed his face could have been sinister or friendly. The man's eyes were piercing and revealed nothing of his demeanor. "My Croatian messenger only knew English, not German. My English is not so good. Perhaps my translation got reversed, it can be difficult to switch. It is the Oberstrumbannführer I wish to discuss, but first, we need to get to know one another. How long have you served the Reich?"

There was no chair nearby, so I shifted from foot to foot in front of the desk. What was he trying to find out? Did he suspect my involvement with the Resistance? "The Reich? Since '33, but I have almost 17 years in the army."

He nodded, and asked, "12 years serving the Reich, but you do so to support the Führer? You chose to 'Hail Victory' and not our leader."

My palms began to sweat. "I am loyal to my country, my oaths. My chest has medals demonstrating my allegiance, I have been not just injured but hospitalized because of my devotion to the cause." My ears were pricked listening to make sure no one opened the door behind me to sneak in and kill me as a traitor.

"Your honor and tenacity are above reproach. But do you still fight to protect the Reich, Major?" He leaned forward in his chair, "Or do you support our enemies?"

My vision narrowed. His poise, his demeanor, and his bearing were intimidating. The fact that I had something to hide made it worse. "This morning at my daily office call, my superior Oberstleutnant Giehl released me and my men from any further service. He told us all to go home any way we could. I chose to stay, several of my men stayed as well. We are committed to the fight. I," I pounded my chest with my fist causing my Iron Cross to rattle. "I am committed to fight."

"It is not your commitment I question, Major. It is whom you serve. You have been seen multiple times in the company of men suspected of being the very face of the Resistance to our Reich. Where does your heart lie now; have you turned against the war effort?"

My stomach began to churn. I paused before responding through clinched teeth. "Do you doubt my loyalty? I have fought this war from the beginning. When the Polish invasion began on 3 September, I was itching to fight. Through the Ardennes, in Kyiv, Oswiecim, Cannes, the Ardennes again." My face felt hot as blood pounded through my temples. "I have fought on all fronts to support this war. I have seen more of this war than anyone should. I..."

He interrupted, "You call it Oswiecim."

I paused, why is that what struck him about what I said? "Yes, in Poland. What I saw there exceeded the scenes I saw on the Eastern Front and that fighting was the most brutal anyone can imagine."

"Why don't you call it Auschwitz like everyone else? Herr Weiter would take great offense if he heard you eschew his esteemed camp." He scoffed, "Not that he could. Has this war changed you, Major?"

What did that mean? "Yes, what I have seen of this war has had an impact, especially Oswiecim. It has changed me. No human can see what I saw and walk away unchanged. Not me, not you, not

even Weiter."

He stood and placed both hands in the middle of the desk,

leaning forward and staring directly into my eyes. "What happened

in Poland, and throughout the Reich was the undiluted truth of

what it means to be a National Socialist." His voice got louder.

"The work of men like Weiter, and Höss at Auschwitz has kept

the Reich safe, the Fatherland, safe." Spittle came from his mouth

as he forced the words out. "These are the men whose work the

master race will be built on. Do you no longer support the goal of

our leader, Adolf Hitler?"

"No!" I yelled and leaned forward. I no longer cared if he knew.

Even if he had me shot for being a traitor. "I fight with the

Resistance. I cheer for the Americans. I only wish I had done more

before you found me out and reported me to your weak-minded,

sycophant bosses. The legacy of the Nazi party will stain Germany

for generations. Even God will have no mercy on your souls."

My breath was ragged as my heart pumped with rage. I watched

him reach down and pull up the bottom of his coat. I tensed. He

wasn't even going to take me outside, he was reaching for his gun

to shoot me here.

He pulled out a pistol and held it pointing the barrel up to allow me to see the handle and recognize it as a Tula-Tokarev T-33. Soviet officers had carried them in Kyiv ,and I had picked up several in Ukraine myself. Standing in front of him unarmed, I wish I had not thrown them all away.

"I fought in Leningrad. I saw that carnage," he said in a much lower voice. He set the gun down on the desk. The barrel pointing near but not at me, "The enemy is all around us. Some of them even wear our uniform."

He knew. He knew I was fighting with the Resistance and had just called me a traitor. My eyes hastily scanned the room behind him. With his limp, I could outmaneuver him, but the pistol was too close. I would never make it to the window.

Schrader picked up a document from his desk. Dark handwriting showed through the thin paper. "Our boss, Giehl, there is a spineless creature that shows the true face of National Socialism. Look." He handed it to me.

My hands shook as I took the paper. I looked and recognized the handwriting. It said that Schrader had been released from duty to the Reich. Why was he still here?

"Major," he waved at a chair on the side of the room. "Herr Gangl. Take a seat. We have much to discuss before it is over."

I could not move. The pistol lay between me and the chair he indicated. I could only stare at him as he again waved in the direction of the chair, this time with a head nod as well. Did he expect me to let my guard down?

Seeing my hesitation, he held up his hands. "Herr Gangl, you are an honest, good man. Not everyone has seen the light, as we have. These are dangerous times, and I apologize if my precautions were deceptive. I assure you; we fight for the same side."

I unclenched my fists as a wave of relief passed over me. On my right I saw another chair which I hastily grabbed and slid over, not quite making it all the way to the front of the desk before collapsing in it.

"My injury has slowed me down; I cannot move fast enough to do all that needs to be done. I would be of little service in your Resistance, but I do have some information that may help. Are you familiar with the prisoners in the castle?"

I nodded. "I know of them. The day after I arrived, I went with Giehl to the castle and met Wimmer. He didn't recognize me, but I had seen him before in Lublin. He wasn't there when I first arrived.

I'd brought a load of POWs there after the Battle of Kyiv. After I came back a few more times, I saw the changes he had made with the camp. He didn't care if they were Russian or Polish, man, woman, or child. He made sure they all suffered."

"Again, the non-Germanic name. I, too, met Wastl before but not at Majdanek." He must have seen the confused look on my face because he interrupted himself. "Wimmer's chosen familiar name. We met in Prague. In the summer of '43 I had heard he was in charge of Castle Itter so I called in a favor and was able to move my family to Wörgl a few months later. That was also when I first met the honor prisoners."

The door opened and an aide came in with a tray. He set it on the desk and Schrader waved him away. "Coffee?" he offered.

I shook my head as he poured a cup for himself.

"It is neither ersatz nor that decaffeinated crap the Party is proud off. This is full-strength, not watered down. It is one of the few luxuries I have found I can allow myself. Are you sure you won't have a cup?" he asked.

How long had it been since I'd had a good cup of coffee? "Who am I to resist then? Yes." I watched the steam rising from the cup and breathed in the aroma. There is no scent quite like that of a fresh-brewed cup of good coffee.

He handed me the saucer and cup and continued. "Wastl is an old acquaintance, but other than his ability to help me get to Austria I do not and have not agreed with his actions. I suspect that Weiter put him over the prisoners in case the war went bad and there was a need to kill them."

The coffee was strong, and by far, had the best taste I had savored for a long time. I wanted to relish it longer, but I swallowed it to ask, "Is that what you think is about to happen?" After what I had seen Wimmer do in Poland, I believed he was a textbook psychopath capable of any atrocities.

"I'm not sure. In my conversations with Clemenceau, Daladier, and others, they told me he had them sign a letter saying he had treated them well. I've seen him take out his masochistic tendencies on his own troops rather than the prisoners. It may be that Wastl realizes they may save him from prosecution after the war. Perhaps he did defy orders, but it isn't like Weiter to take things into his own hands. I just don't know if there's a way to get them safely out."

"In my reconnaissance of the area, I have thoroughly checked out the perimeter of the castle. There are a few weak spots but none weak enough. We would have to incapacitate the guards to get the prisoners out. Even then, where could we hide them?"

He opened a drawer and began taking out some papers while he spoke. "We don't need to stash them for months or even weeks. The Americans are coming. At the rate they're advancing they'll be here within the week. I believe Wastl will wait for the last minute to act. Any yahoo American we come into contact with will see the importance of these prisoners. They will help us."

I looked down at the desk. He had a map of the castle and sheet with handwritten notes. "Sneak the prisoners out from under the watchful eyes of Wimmer's troops. Escort them past the mindlessly subservient Waffen SS. Then just waltz across the victorious American's line of fire. All the while hoping neither side takes us out. Timing, luck, and hope. Sounds like a plan." A ravenously mad plan.

"To put it simplistically, yes. But not all luck and hope. During my last visit, they gave me this. They noted it months ago, but the patterns are set in stone."

He turned the handwritten notes around so I could see it.

Names, times, and what looked to be locations in French. A

schedule for the guards compiled by the ever-watchful prisoners.

"And this here?" I pointed to the middle of the list.

"A gap. Every night the kitchen staff lure the guards to share

the leftovers. The length of opening depends on how much the

prisoners leave from dinner."

I slid the map to my side of the desk. "It still takes timing. Once

it's noticed they're gone, the Waffen will be called in to search.

We'll have hours, not days, before they are discovered. And no

guarantee which side will do the discovering."

"And a plan," said Schrader. "Are you in?"

Not doing anything was worse than failing. I looked up at him.

The steely resolve in his eyes was comforting. I could see stern

determination in his tightly clenched jaw. A single nod of the head

was all it took to get him to share his plan.

A plan. Now our plan. Lines were being blurred, and allegiances

tested. One thing that wasn't moving was Helmuth von Moltke

the Elder's maxim that no plan extends with certainty after first

encounter. No plan survives contact with the enemy. But who

was the enemy in this case? Was it the SS guarding the prisoners, the Americans, the Wafen SS ranging the countryside, or the Resistance?

The last battle was coming soon.

AUTHOR BIOGRAPHY

Jonathan Byrd is a husband, father of three daughters, and an eternal optimist, some might even say a Micawber. He was born in Biloxi and considers Fairhope, Alabama home. However, the more he sees of the world, the more he wants to experience. He presently lives in Stuttgart, Germany.

He has completed an unpublished Prohibition-set novel which takes place on the Mississippi Gulf Coast, entitled *Seafood Capital of the World*. It was a finalist in the 2021 Faulkner-Wisdom Creative Writing Competition. He has also recently completed the first book in a series he deems a "military thriller for the common soldier."

Jonathan is one of the founding members of Transcendent Authors, and has published in all their anthologies: *Tolerance: A Collection of Short Stories, Autumn: An Anthology, Spring—The Unexpected, Winter: An End and a Promise, Summer When Doors Open*, and now *Deceit*.

When he isn't writing, he's thinking about writing, even if it looks like he's doing something else—like work. He has an answer for everything, opinions on anything, and is quiet about nothing.

DECEPTION IN DIAMONDS

Yard-high windows gleam; spotlights illuminate an array of jewelry and timepieces — one becomes dizzy with consumer desire if one stares for too long. It's Friday, and it's wartime. If not drafted to fight communism in East Asia, the average man must work to receive a paycheck, so people shop on Fridays, and Rose Jewelers is open late.

Mr. Rosen, sole proprietor of Rose's, has returned from his errand, and is standing at the back counter. He notices Jeanne's white blouse buttons pulling apart as she breathes. She's rocking to and fro on kitten pumps, running her hands down her pleated skirt, nervous in his presence, a young woman.

Jeanne says, "Sir, perhaps, a little idea — safer — and." Stopping, her gaze downcast. Her upper arm pushes against her breast as she raises a paper lunch sack to her shoulder.

He says, "Thank you Jeanne. That's fine, we will see about it." He's distracted and doesn't know what he's saying.

Jeanne's face is expectant, however. Mr. Rosen's just back from the bank with a sweaty neck and sore hips from the trip's effort. He's been up the mall six blocks, a climb up the bank's faux marble stairs, and six blocks back, toting his ample-bottomed briefcase, heavy with thick leather. Now it's a tad lighter, the store's checks and cash receipts having been deposited.

Behind the high laminated-wood L-shaped counter sit Mrs. Banderas, the bookkeeper, and Mr. Michaels, Mr. Rosen's key salesman. Their heads are cocked, listening and pretending not to. Jeanne has a small desk closest to the back but stands and eyes Mr. Rosen with intent.

Mr. Rosen, a sizable, yet dapper man, has a severe limp and uses an elegant cane. Regardless of his one scotch in the evenings, his nose is rather bulbous, his cheeks a ruddy red. On his feet are high-quality custom-made shoes, a two-inch lift added to one heel to help with the imbalance. His Beverly Hills bespoke suit is impeccable, the break at his shoe, perfect, and, inside his jacket, behind the pocket square at his breast, another slim opening. Within it rests one his vice — fine cigars. The other vice is over the counter, the new employee with piercing green eyes, wafting dime-store cologne that makes his heart light.

He takes a step; his free hand runs along the laminate. "Michaels, I want you out on the floor, selling. Out there! A diamond or two." An exhale as he lifts his briefcase.

Jeanne says, "Sir, my thought — you know, the bank deposits."

Her face is coy, her eyes shine. That glint of green captivates like and old familiar flame.

The bell above the glass doors tinkles. A young couple, all giggles and kisses, enters with heads swiveling, dazed by love and the store's bright lights.

Mr. Rosen says, "Michaels, get out there, sell a ring. That young woman is about to faint if you don't show them something quick."

"I'm letting them browse, the slow approach. It's timing."

"Timing? These two are ready to buy. Don't let them leave without a ring. I'm going to my office, no disruptions."

The cane, his limp, a paunch, his sixty years make the stairs up to his office a challenge, especially after the trip to the bank. However, he doesn't register his 'normal' walk as a problem. Of course, he gets winded if rushing, but that's just par for the course, as his Temple buddies from Bet Haverim would say, "We aren't getting younger, Rosen! God hasn't needs and gives us everything! We've the instructions. Derive maximum pleasure from life."

After years, and deciding to pursue a little fun, Rosen and his wife, Molly, boarded a plane to Florida. The flight's beverage service had bounced everywhere, but the five-star kosher resort with free lotions and smelly soap had his wife of thirty-two years

smiling like a newlywed. Rosen, satisfied, donned dark sunglasses
to ogle scant-clad females. Sweet Molly — they'd buried one child,
a stillbirth. But later, they'd had a wonderful son to be proud
of: Eliezer. He'd made it, bar mitzvah'd, now lived in Chicago.
Eli worked as a writer or actor or something. In no trouble and
supporting himself. That's all that mattered, self-sufficiency. Mr.
Rosen was proof.

What had happened three decades ago: a young, married jeweler
named Benjamin Rosen, was driving cross-country, celebrating
success with a little scotch on a deserted interstate closer to
the Navajo Nation reservation than anything else, when clouds
opened, and rain ceremonially rumbled and poured. Minutes
and miles morphed to a rushing stillness as Rosen's liquored
eyelids drooped and his head bobbed. The highway undulated; a
black, wet snake. Lights hit his retina, on and off and on, flashed
and streaked, chorused by whooshing and squealing rubber.
The one-sip-away-from-half-empty fifth of scotch, procured to
celebrate his diamond district purchases, slid back and forth along
the front leather bench of his prized Lincoln Continental. His
feet tangled between the brake and accelerator; flood lights struck
his eyes, accompanied by the ear-splitting stream of compressed

air through a foghorn. Rosen's last sight — an enormous grill, a Ford — then his car rolling, folding, flattening, with Rosen upside down and dizzy, till he lost consciousness.

By the time doctors pieced him together, he had a rod in his back and missed bone in one leg. The tractor-trailer driver who had totaled his Lincoln did not survive. Doctors told Rosen, "You'll be damn lucky if you walk normal again." Rosen didn't believe in luck; he thanked only God. Like Joseph in the Jewish Bible, Rosen was up for the challenge.

At seventeen, he had extracted himself from a Jewish enclave: brainless rote learning, minds trapped in dusty books, and yeshiva bullies that the community said didn't exist. He threw off the black coat and hat and hobo-ed it across the US. Driven by dreams, hard work, and perseverance, he opened his own jewelry store on the West Coast.

Back on the "chosen" coast, still wrapped in a body cast, his new, young wife fussed around him; Rosen hushed that down quick. "I can, and always will, take care of myself."

Employees at their stations: Michaels on the floor, Jeanne back at her desk. A strong footstep: his cane jabs, his foot swings forward, Mr. Rosen makes his way up the stairs and into his wood-paneled office. A black leather couch stretches along the back wall next to a side table, crammed with photos. Two club chairs sit across from a regal wooden desk; on the far wall, to Mr. Rosen's right, is a tilted sheet of rectangular glass, 1x4 feet. Its angle allows him to see down to the floor of his store and employees, but they can't see him.

Sitting heavy Rosen acknowledges his chair creaks like him. He turns toward his angled window; there's Michaels showing the couple engagement rings as Jeanne serves them Coca-Cola. They're excited: the man sweating, the woman pink-faced. The sale is coming; the man's rubbing his wallet through his back pocket, she's tapping his thigh, openmouthed. Oh, there's Jeanne, at her desk, opening incoming mail, sorting checks from circulars. Mr. Rosen can look down right into her blouse. She has a beige lacy brassiere that he thinks very pretty. His eyes close, and he imagines the breasts ensconced within, perky roses. He salivates; he can almost taste them.

Ah, green-eyed Jeanne, like my Claudie. Mr. Rosen contemplates giving his new hire more responsibility. She wants to help or is eager to impress. She doesn't yet realize Rosen needs no help with anything. Jewelry stores need an attractive face. Her simplicity gives him a tight-lipped smile. On his wall above the couch, he regards his twenty-five-year service award from the Shriners, for hard work and generosity. His lips roll inwards, pressing tighter. "So little Jeanne wants to be helpful. Let's make sure she is." And picks up the black phone's receiver and dials downstairs.

Jeanne answers. "Yes, Mr. Rosen, sir."

Rosen, losing his nerve a touch. "Jeanne, I'd like a, a strawberry malted. Be a doll and run to Woolworth's, I'll take one. Get yourself one too, any flavor your heart desires." He hangs the phone up quick, wrinkles his nose, curses hearing his temple buddies telling him, "Chutzpah and l'chaim! Grow some balls, celebrate life!"

On his desk is a studio photo of Eli and his wife. It's the first thing he sees when his eyelids reopen: Eli's goofy, stargazed eyes, his wife's plastic, shiny face, stiff neck, mal-positioned hands. The only thing working in the photo is her full body girdle. His neck is hot, he adjusts the knot of his tie, places his hands on his desk, letting his eyes graze the side table of polaroid memories.

They hold ridiculous smiles, confetti, and clutched arms. There! Rubbing shoulders with John, world's only real cowboy, and Buzz, straight from NASA, and Mel, more than a funny man, and those

beautiful babes and boobs, and me, Benjamin Rosen, self-made
philanthropic jeweler! But the prized memory is front and center.
That zealous schmuck agent, founding temple member, and in
fact, now a buddy, along with an over-powdered face (now his
demanding wife) leaning on his chest, next hugging Benjamin's
arm, sensual Claudie, with her piercing emeralds for eyes, and the
most pliable of breasts and thighs. She ignored his limp, seeing in
him a virile man. His skin still remembers the torrid and wanton
hours spent with her; young, clever, unencumbered. She'd been
a true tease, cooing: "We'd make the most beautiful babies." He
scooted fast as possible out of her life. Molly and baby Eli were
waiting.

Brass balls and life, how Rosen lives, so true, though the memory
of that tiny bottle of scotch, thrown yards and the fortuity of its
obliteration in the Arizona desert is unbearable. Today is always
the day to take chances, climb out on that limb, manage the store,
sell that diamond! His hands lay sweating on top of his leather desk
blotter. The heads of his wife and son seem to be inflating and
deflating, floating in the picture frame. He sips air and picks up
the black receiver, dialing home.

"Molly, it's me. How about burgers tonight? I'm in the mood for a greasy burger. We could go out. Molly?"

There is a light brushing on his door, as if a bird has hit its wing flying by. Mr. Rosen says, "Molly, hold a sec. So busy." He covers the mouthpiece with his hand and says in a demanding voice, "Come in."

"Molly! Jeanne, the new girl, came up with some work. Burgers, Molly. Alright? Bye now."

"Wait dear! I'm getting ready to go, but must tell you . . ."

Mr. Rosen's eyes stretch, then squint. His wife's voice drones on. He materializes her tented house dress, the telephone cord wrapped around her spidery hand. His head shakes the thought away as into his vision floats an angel in a diaphanous white blouse and black pleats, with crossed ankles covered in the sheerest nylon hosiery. This captivating image holds a strawberry malted and a straw.

The receiver's stuck to his ear, a distant voice. "Dear, are you listening? These girls were just nuts; I tell you. Are you alright dear, don't work too hard. Burgers! Alright, kiss, kiss!"

With the click, the receiver slips from his hand. Its thud and the beep, beep, beep from being off the hook, snaps Rosen to attention. Coins are in the bottom of his pants' pocket. "How much do I owe you, Jeanne?" He follows that with, "You ordered one for yourself, I hope."

"Yes, Mr. Rosen. Here you go, strawberry. I got strawberry too." Jeanne smiles with eyes and open mouth. She floats toward his desk. It is a man's desk, expansive to hold ongoing projects, yet as she leans to place down his malted, Rosen imagines she is coming closer still, and he puckers his lips for her kiss.

"Oh, you must super like malteds, sir. Me too! They're yum-yum."

Malteds are fifteen cents each, but with a broad smile, he flips a Kennedy half dollar on the leather blotter and slides it forward with his pointer. She says, "Oh, that's too much Mr. Rosen, it's only malteds!" Giggling, her shoulders shiver. "And Sir. My idea? Silly – I know I'm new, but I could help. The walk with that heavy briefcase. Well, it's a little noticeable, you . . . that cane . . . I'm thinking maybe . . ."

She beams, expectant, shining eyes, and his heart skips a beat. Mr. Rosen muses. Always partial to emeralds! However, her words about the cane and walking charge his rawest nerves. His molars grind as he breaks eye contact, sits heavier in his chair, and holds the malted between both hands. She rushes. "I could, with a simple paper sack —"

"Thank you, Jeanne. Go, now; shut the door, please."

She turns on her heels, hesitates, empty palm opening a finger at a time. Reaching along her skirt, her fingers clench as if to catch a fly. She nods with decision. She's examining his award above the couch. Her throat hums, hips slide to one side. There's a quick intake of air, and she steps in close to the side table, leaning, rump prominent.

"This is you with famous people. Didn't that guy walk in space or something! Oh, she's gorgeous, eyes, the same color as mine."— She points to the ceiling. — "Don't forget!" Her voice, like Claudie's teasing. Jeanne takes invigorated steps, catches his gaze, and curls her lips as she struts out of his office.

What shouldn't I forget? He checks his wristwatch. He's ready for a stiff scotch.

The moonlight streaks over the rumpled quilt and into Rosen's eyes. He lays next to Molly and thinks about Jeanne. One calf cramps, and his jaw follows. Swinging his legs out of bed, unsteady in bathrobe, but without cane, he hobbles to the den.

Fumbling past its door jam — "Ah, holy bejeezus zit all —" His weight on his heel, forward three steps till his hands support him on the telephone desk, his pinky toe throbbing, on fire. That TV console's corners, it's a firkin' monster, but, hey, Mol' likes watching Lawrence Welk, replete with champagne music and dancers.

His toe stretches — so not broken — his hands relax on the desk and find the fine-textured note paper lying beside the phone. The pen's between his fingers, and he bows his head. Pain and love — to his mind springs Molly, a mop of college co-ed golden curls, eyes laughing; he's stubbed his toe and she's saying, "Silly! Whatever Ben, we'll make it together." A warmth spreads to his shoulders and face. Molly, wrapped up with mitzvahs, good deeds, and temple pursuits, raised their son and keeps the kitchen kosher. Toe forgotten, his finger whips his wet cheek — the child they lost, the forgotten bottle of scotch, Molly's pain and unwavering commitment.

Rosen's voice is a bare hush. "Oh, Molly, you care, we are making it together — even [if?] my eyes still wander. God understands, I'm a simple man."

On the paper before him is Jeanne's name scrawled in his loopy script. Frustration grips and he raises the pen to obliterate whatever his heart is betraying. "No!" He says, jaw clenched.

Pondering, he underlines her name and writes: Additional responsibilities? Take cash deposit to bank. Cons: Always boss's job. Shows weakness. You're the boss. Asking for help – looks bad! Lose respect. Pros: Legs won't cramp. Less tired. Jeanne happy new responsibility. Jeanne likes me more. Wears sheer white, maybe comes for drink with me, after work?

Mr. Rosen regards his list, hits his forehead, and seethes in silence. *Oh shit!*

To the den's ceiling, he cries, "Oy vey! Rosen!" He adds to the list: Molly happier I accept help! My safety!

The paper is folded over three times, and he pushes it deep in the bathrobe's pocket and hobbles back to bed.

Next morning Molly serves the regular. Brewer's yeast in a cup, first. Coffee in a cup, second. Half a grapefruit in a larger cup, third. Molly says, "How are you my dear? Did you sleep well? Your eyes are red. You didn't sleep." Her breasts rest soft under where her bathroom belt has caught her ribs.

Mr. Rosen grunts.

"Toast or a pancake? I can whip up some pancakes."

"Toast! Fine." He nods. "I want to get to the office. I've decided — Jeanne can do more. She can make the deposits."

"Oh, is that a wise idea? Dear? All our cash, that young girl? My! How you lean and shuffle. When you're tired, of course, but that stick — your legs ache. Quite the effort!" Molly stops herself, lips rolling in. She frowns. "It's such a dilemma, dear."

Mr. Rosen flinches at his wife's comment. He's not giving up anything because he needs to rest like some old man. He growls, "I'm the boss and will make the decisions! But I'll tell you, they bonked old Shapiro on the head. That leather satchel he carries like a baby snatched from his grasp. Lost a month of sales. Right on the mall, surrounded by Krishnas and war protestors." He bends his arm to show his bicep. "I'm strong as ever, Molly. It's the briefcase, makes me a target. Plus, the girl needs more responsibility. That's it. Final!"

Later that day Mr. Rosen rotates his chair, facing the wall behind his desk. Its sideboard table skirts the top of his Empire

Jewelry Safe. The safe, shopped from Empire's showroom in New York City, was the only thing that came through his terrible highway collision unscathed. With a delicate touch, he spins the dial then pushes the handle down, the door pops open. He removes a yellowed, cornered news clipping. Its headline from a back page article: "Lucky Jeweler & Safe Survive Crash."

The Jewish Bible warns against believing in luck or any superstitions, yet, Rosen forever has imprinted the circus tent lights of the oncoming truck; the snaking road under the Lincoln's floating hood; the sounds of the scotch bottle hitting and rebounding off the passenger door, and he can't see his hands. A child in the truck's cab survived, but did it walk, could it live a 'normal' life? Tormenting questions that run on spin cycle if Rosen doesn't remind himself, and often, of his twenty plus years of service: a testament to his generosity and commitment to the Shriner's mission: helping crippled, disadvantaged children, regardless of circumstance.

The dried newsprint is behind on his desk, and he confirms, "That belongs framed under glass, and I reaffirm, my faith's in you, God, it's never luck." Squinting, tight shoulders, refocus. Before him are twelve-inch-high drawers containing gems, mounted and loose. He locates his second objective and slams the metal door shut. Using his feet, he maneuvers around to his desk and contemplates the jewelers' envelope before him. Merchants' yellow cardstock, 2x5 inches, nondescript except for the hard bulge at its bottom. He takes a velvet-covered tray from a drawer, sets it upon the blotter, turns toward his window.

He spies Jeanne licking stamps and placing them on envelope corners. Mrs. Banderas' pencil is clamped between her teeth as she leans over the adding machine. Mr. Michaels is closing a sale, young businessman needs a new watch and, bully for both for them, he's selling the man the pricier Bulova, and not the cheaper Timex. His eyes return to his favorite view. Jeanne sitting prim, stacking, and re-grouping stamped mail. Is she bored? So cute and wants to help. He steeples his fingers, regarding the fat jewelers' envelope — at that point, unable to resist, he grabs the black receiver and rings downstairs.

Mrs. Banderas answers. "Yes, Mr. Rosen."

"Are the books balanced? Did the invoices and checks arrive? It's all ship-shape, Mrs. Banderas?"

Her confident hands sift through papers. "Yes, sir."

"Please have Jeanne come to my office." Her matronly calmness morphs. Her penciled brows rise with curiosity, then knit back down. She examines her papers, receiver at her chin.

"I'll send her up, sir." Mr. Rosen is pleased. Mrs. Banderas is reliable and competent, an inexpensive asset.

A light tap to the door and Jeanne is in his office, door closed. Her blouse is blue, like a robin's egg, and pressed with white plastic buttons running a neat row down her chest, disappearing beneath her skirt. He checks his mind, prays it does not travel beyond her skirt's waistband.

She approaches his desk. "Afternoon, Mr. Rosen. What can I do for you?"

He ignores her furtive glances around and over her shoulder. She sees the photo with him with Claudie. Is she jealous? Jeanne's eye color and cleverness, she could be Claudie's daughter. His heart almost stops, and he stands, pushing down firm on the armrests, to restart it. He locks his knees and pulls his torso straight before he reaches across as if to grab Jeanne's loose hand. She's just out of reach, continuing her inspection. With measured breathes he enunciates. "Take – a – seat – dear."

Shuffling backwards, the backs of his legs find his chair, and he sits. The creak of his chair the only sound, his gaze never varying from Jeanne's emeralds. He moves his fingers, playing the piano on his desktop, till one hand bumps the stiff envelope. Two fingers pinch and squeeze the tiny flap open. With a flourish, he turns the envelope over, letting its contents sprinkle out like stars against a velvet night sky.

As expected, Jeanne's eyebrows rise: eyes platter-wide and alert, her fine fingers meet her temples. "My, Mr. Rosen! Those are real diamonds! They must be worth a fortune — a girl like me, well! I can't imagine."

Satisfied, he observes her eyes raking the gems. They are competing for the sparkle, reverberating reflections. He says, "Beautiful, aren't they? Like you." He tries to catch her gaze, but she is transfixed by the tray's contents. "As the owner of a jewelry store, I must have many stones, like these, to adorn fabulous settings, and be sold, right downstairs. They live here, waiting, in my safe."

One of her hands slides to his desk; fingers without conscience inching towards the black velvet. Cheekbones arch with her tight smile. "Oh! You have a safe?"

"Of course. A real jewelers' safe. I brought it all the way from New York."

She stands hips squared, palms on his desk. "Could I see?"

Mr. Rosen says, "It's right here, behind me." He swivels his chair, confident her gaze is following, then instinct snaps him back around. The tips of Jeanne's fingers are within a thumb's distance of his diamonds. His eyes flick to hers, assessing, and he exhales with both shoulders. She, in truth, is attempting to read upside down the curl-edged news clipping.

"Yes, well — " His voice stumbles, focus moving again from her eagerness to his gems, then returning to her green pearly eyes, opening wider like an oyster's shell, he's drawn into a wild spin. Spine against office chair, both of his arms on its rests, he settles into a fugue state, forgetting everything but the scent-filled female swaying in front of him.

Her white blouse is loose, moving with her breath. There is a distant murmur. "Is that you? Are you the Lucky Jeweler?" Her hand goes to her mouth, a breathy laugh. Rosen's gaze trails her pointer and middle finger back to the tray's edge, several hundred carats, a knuckles' reach away. In the time it takes to spell "Mississippi," Mr. Rosen jolts from his daze.

Jeanne gushes. "I love old news, and this is about my lucky boss. Where did this happen?"

"Outbacks of Arizona. It was grim, a family in a semi-trailer truck, black wilderness, the father must have fallen asleep." His tongue stings dry; his stomach churns. "And I don't believe in luck."

His heavy brows drop forcing him to watch her expression through them. She turns her head to better read the article's forty words. Her eyes narrow to slits and a top tooth clamps her bottom lip. That's sweet; such a sensitive girl.

Pulled to distraction, he's watching her breath release through puckered lips. Her voice seeps like honey. "Oh, such tragedy . . . what kind of deadbeat falls asleep while driving? Could've been my pops. My youth was tough, too — you know."

His neck is pliant, body relaxed. A speck, a flash, a moving spark. He barks, "Don't touch them, please. Put it back." The voice is not his. He aches. His pointers, firm, draw the tray of diamonds back.

Her smile is closed, her lashes bat. Her fingers are empty but clasped together, perhaps remembering the sensation of a small carbon rock. Her voice starts at a whisper, then builds. "Don't

think I am not immensely grateful for everything. But you, Mr.
Rosen, you are *truly lu-cky*."

He flinches at her emphasis, his shame, her honesty. He has been
negligent, greedy, uncaring, putting no effort into knowing this
delicate woman's life. This must change! Reaching around the tray
and placing his hand firm on hers, her fingers wiggle in protest,
then are quiet. An electric current passes up his palm, to his arm,
and chest. She is so close: an intuitive flower, bending towards him.
Her cheeks pale, then blush, as she pulls her arm away. "Mr. Rosen,
about my idea?"

He says, "Smile, I like your smile. And yes, your little idea—
something with your lunch sack. We'll have a deposit, as always,
the end of the month."

She visits his office daily with small tasks or for a simple chat,
staying for uncertain lengths of time. She's warming to him. Of
course, he's interested in her life. She tells him stories of her youth,
that double around and contradict. Rosen finds some silly, some

charming, and always sits rapt. He wants her to become a confident member of his staff, and, someday, a saleswoman.

One day she says, "My youth was a challenge, never enough money. I was a tomboy, nobody approved. I learned to fight, grab what I could and run. I knew I'd make it on my own." She chuckles, opening her hands, palms up. Innocence wrapped up in a gesture, but Rosen understands her pain: the flight, the fear. He absorbs her stories, a shared and kindred past.

Rosen says, "Well, I hope you won't run from us here." From forehead to chin, he's warm. He raises out of his chair and leans across, driven by some animal instinct. His palm covers hers for one, two beats; he presses down, then raises to brush her cheek, as if there were a tear. Her chin tilts down, a Mona Lisa smile. He eases back, confident, responsible for that glow.

Incredulous. "You, a tomboy? Never! So lovely as you are now!" Her hands are fine, fingernails neat. His hand crabs across the desk toward hers. Jeanne giggles soft from her throat, heaving her bosom and adjusting her pleats.

"Oh, Mr. Rosen, I have a boyfriend. You know."

"You're teasing." Practiced salesman's smile. He stretches, feigning an arch to his back, concentrates on her words "You are a beautiful young woman. Nothing less."

##

Molly makes one of Rosen's favorite dairy dinners, a casserole-full cheese soufflé. The broccoli on the side, he can take or leave, but he always eats Molly's honied carrots. Within the sweet, round circles, he thinks of Jeanne eating canned baked beans and Wonder bread with her poor mother. He shoves back his chair and half-heartedly pats his stomach.

Rosen smiles and relaxes. "Delicious. You know, sometimes, dear? I think we've got a bright life."

Her face is bland, calm, fine wrinkled, no longer animated, long past young. Her voice is bass with years and so familiar. "Yes, dear. Thanks to God, we have a son, you have your store, and we have our health. Eli is a boy to be proud of."

Coming around the table, Rosen kisses Molly on the top of her head. "Yes, Eli. I'm going to lay down for the evening." He straightens, firms his grip on his cane, and walks off, contemplating his next conversations with Jeanne.

Jeanne casts her eyes around his space. "This woman in this photo is beautiful. My mother was too. She was a — a movie star until she got terribly sick — shaking with old age and died."

"Died?" He is not registering her words, his skin tingles. Is it you, my dear Jeanne, or a consumed man's memory destined to forget?

Her emeralds graze the ceiling. "Mother was truly very old." Looking around, then taller standing on her toes, she says, "Are all the jewels kept in that black safe?"

"No." Mr. Rosen laughs, patting his jacket pocket. "Sometimes I carry favorite stones closer to my heart, like loves." He hopes he is not blushing, surprised by his words.

On another day they share his couch, sitting at either end. Her hand flicks back her hair as she says, "Does that big safe always sit there? I mean, it can't be that heavy?"

Her naivety disarms. He likes that, lets his arm fall from the couch's back. He says, "You can't imagine, they are heavy, smelted steel and iron." The leather is cool underneath his palm, then like a heat seeker, his hand traps hers, and his imagination spins. Her cheeks are high and rosy. Her eyes are a tint of spring grass; today, framed with sky blue powder. His legs are light, like he's floating.

"Let's share a Coke." Silly words, stupid thoughts, is he back in high school? Jeanne giggles and relaxes in her corner of the couch, next to the side table.

He reaches for the office phone. "Ah, Michaels. Come, bring me two bottles of Coke and two glasses. Jeanne and I are discussing matters."

A squeak; the door opens and closes. Mr. Rosen turns, the Coke bottles wet inside his palms. Jeanne shifts on the black couch, and the black color of her skirt shows its wear. It dawns on him, perhaps, she has only one. Her knees press tight. He concentrates on walking and serving. She's looking at her hands, then raises her head, swiveling it up to examine his award and again, down to the collection of photos on the side table, before taking the proffered glass.

"The bubbles tickle." She shifts, her knees separate.

Relaxing into some fantasy, Mr. Rosen says, "Yea, me too." He exhales long and smooth. Hearing Jeanne by his side, he wants to gather her in his arms. He reasons, we all need love.

She clears her throat. "You know, I'm sure my green eyes match my mother's. She was a — a movie star. She could have been famous except, well, my little sister, she couldn't walk, polio — on the reservation. My life's nothing but alcohol, poverty, and bitter winds." Jeanne eyes are crystal clear, her forehead smooth.

Those words touch him right below his sternum, he shakes his head like a mournful hound. Just as quick, he laments that Jeanne is still a full cushion away. Sipping his Coke, then setting the glass as his feet, he pivots towards her, his face gray. "Polio? Poverty? Oh! A reservation, as in. . .?" His thoughts, once secure, firm, are now like so many shards of shattered stone. His stomach gurgles, and fear grips him. Am I remiss? Did I fail or forget? There's dampness where his suspenders cross his shoulders, and he's swimming in her perfume.

Rosen gathers his thoughts. "Jeanne, dear. It is, that I'm a generous man, a lifetime supporter — children, victims, those in need, I give. . ." He's on a roll, justifying, but he can't finish. Jeanne's warmth is closing in. Rosen's forehead pricks with sweat as her hands cup his, and her body leans forward, covering the middle couch cushion.

"Not me, Mr. Rosen. I've never any luck. Once we were robbed, gunpoint, real bandits. They broke in, then saw my crippled sister...it was, well." Woeful, she says, "Thanks for the Coke, Mr. Rosen." Treading on tiptoes, she's silent out.

Over her visits, her life story weaves and turns, at once heart-wrenching, then incredible. Rosen is awestruck; her words are soft caresses. He wants her to know, so he shares. "I know not fitting in." All the while, he watches her eyes, fields of tall grasses in which he can roll and lose himself. Their closeness and her wafting scent satisfy in the best of ways. His cigars have never tasted sweeter.

That night, Mr. Rosen lays awake, mind plotting, but, if asked, he's worrying. Molly raises her eye mask and turns towards him.

She says, "Hon, I can tell by your breathing you're not asleep. Is your leg hurting?"

"My brain hurts, my mind. Go back to sleep."

"Dear. You'll feel better, tell me." She takes the eye mask off and jams it under her pillow.

"That I doubt — it's the new girl. I should, perhaps, well." — Feeling braver in the darkness — "Take her under my wing, train her, help her." His arms are out from under the quilt, his voice rushes. "I don't know — she's had a hard life — not unlike me."

"Oh! Hon. You can't help them all." — She exaggerates a yawn and fumbles to replace her eye mask. — "Go to sleep. Answers come with morning light." — She muffles her pillow. — "Shlof geshmak, good night, my husband."

"You too, Molly."

One of the next days, Jeanne follows Mr. Rosen up the stairs. She's flushed, breathless.

"More training?"

Mr. Rosen takes his seat on the couch, benevolent, smiling. "Yes, I want to expose you to the finer aspects of the jewelry business: the art of the sale." He pats the cushion beside him, confident. "For this you will need to sit closer, Jeanne."

She sits at the couch's far corner, a thin, perfect doll pressing her skirt over her knees. After some breathes, she scoots towards Mr. Rosen, stopping six inches before his leg. He breathes in that Jeanne-evoking aroma and sighs.

She ducks her head, bats her eyelashes, and states, "My boyfriend, Mr. Rosen. However —" She takes his quivering hand. — "Before we start,"— She squeezes her fingers into his palm— "I need to ask a favor, I'm a little ashamed."

"No, Jeanne dear, there is nothing to feel ashamed of. Think of me as —well, a friend."

"Yes, it is that I need my pay, this week's, a little early. And — an advance for next's. It's my mother," — Eyes drilling her lap. "And many things."

She's sitting so close. Her scent. His head is woozy. The rhythm of her breath. Isn't your mother dead? Don't be sneaky, you're so lovely, innocent, and ripe. Your first job, so you're learning. His neck aches with confusion, daydreams, not enough sleep. I'm sure I heard her say her mother was dead. His palm's heat is burning through his pants to his thigh, yet he feels her cooling grasp around it. She is leaning, arching. He croaks. "I'll ask Mrs. Banderas to forward you this and next week's pay, as it is an extenuating circumstance."

She scoots in, knees almost touching, patting his hand. "Thank you, Mr. Rosen. No one could ever say you were not a generous man." She leans and kisses his cheek.

She's climbing the stairs to him, clutching her crinkled lunch sack. The last Friday of the month and she comes into Rosen's office, beaming proud. No words are necessary. Mr. Rosen takes the bag, swivels around, then hunches over, unlocking the safe. He counts bundles of cash, weeks of sales and personal checks to Rose Jewelers, and stuffs the paper bag, folding the top neat, licking and running his fingers along the crease.

"Well, Jeanne. Your idea, very clever. A lunch sack to carry the store's deposit. I like cleverness. No robber would suspect a lovely young woman with her lunch."

The postman wheels his cart along the store's carpet, as Mr. Rosen gazes down. Sweet Jeanne, neat as a pin, wearing a new canary yellow blouse with a white brassiere he's never seen. Is that a new skirt? She pulls into her desk, grasps the letter opener, and begins slicing open mail. Each piece is spread flat. She works without pause till — her head lowers, examining some statement before adding it to the pile. Grabbing it all together, her other hand reaches for her lunch, purse, and sweater. She tosses her hair and steps over to Mrs. Banderas' desk, sharing a few words. She places the stacked papers in front, and then strides out from behind the counter. He watches her rump, hips moving smooth under her new skirt...he almost hears the store's tinkle bell as she accelerates, swinging her purse on her arm.

Wondering who Jeanne's meeting for lunch, he jumps two inches when the office phone rings.

It is Mrs. Banderas. "Mr. Rosen. There is a matter with the bank statement requiring your attention. May I come up?"

She does, a minute later, tight like a nun, and places the statement, turning it to face Mr. Rosen. "See this date." She's tapping her finger, nervous. "There is no deposit."

He frowns down over his nose, eyebrows bristling. He's thinking of something yet can't capture the thought. "No deposit?" He studies Mrs. Banderas' grey outfit, ashen skin, dried lips, and wonders if someone loves her. Mr. Rosen clears his throat, but can only say, "Hmm, I see."

"The date is exactly when that young girl took our sales to the bank. That date." Her finger is firm, stabbing the spot. "Here! Something must have happened — no deposited money, very irregular."

She is standing straight, arms crossed, lips pinched. Mr. Rosen feel his gut pinching in the same tight, dry way. He raises his hand like a peace offering and scowls. "Thank you, Mrs. Banderas, you can return to your work. I'll handle this." He turns his palm down, and with his fingers, scoots her out the door.

Before the door latch catches, Rosen opens his liquor drawer and throttles his bottle of scotch. His neck and jaw clench, contemptuous of the salted tears that dampen his cheeks. He wants to scream but is frozen, the shocked image of black, wet asphalt, blinding circles of light devolving into unmerciful, laughing, green orbs. Surprised by the cork's vacuum pull, the first swig is angry and barrels down his throat. It's followed by another. The truck lights dim. A simple man's drink, the next healthy sip coats his tongue till he toasts to his photos and award, "L'chaim, to my ferkate life! And to that green-eyed snake, who took ol' Rosen." His words shame; guilt laps along his ribs. "God, does your boy Benjamin deserve this?" He grapples through the next bite of liquor for any reason or verdict. Anything to bring balance to his thoughts before his stomach revolts.

His fist and bottle pound the desk, his voice chokes. "I was helping her! Jeanne? Some green-eyed skirt?" — Straightening his spine, focusing on his achievement award. — "No! She was class in the making! And, with my care, would be a top saleswoman, if she'd just let me tutor her. God, it's simple, I wished to bring a young person, who didn't have a lot of chances, along."

No fooling here: Rosen liked having Jeanne near, just to tantalize his senses. However, those green eyes of hers blinded him, like Claudie's. He'd have to tell Molly the honest truth. Is there another? She'll understand, she always does. The final shot sits on his tongue and turns bitter before he swallows. He raises up, slams his hand against the light switch, fumbles his legs down the stairs, jabbing his cane firm at the last. The store's dark and in shadow; all the jewels are in the big safe for the night. He needs only to draw down and secure the gate.

That very night, Molly tosses then rolls to face him in bed. Lace-encrusted eye mask still in place, her voice low. "Dear, think of it as a mitzvah, a good deed you've done. Poor girl must have needed it. The child of that truck driver needed it. Your temple friends would agree."

"Michaels calls her 'a skirt.' But she had talent, Molly, I saw it!" His breath catches deep in his throat and his voice clouds with tears. "Molly. The road accident, what could I have done?"

"Well, dear." Molly reaches her arm across to pat Mr. Rosen's chest. "Talents or not, the girl's flown, and we wish her well. It's a mitzvah all around." She rests her palm against his heart. "Shlof geshmak, a peaceful sleep."

Dear Molly, she understands. And God knows, I am far from a perfect man.

She snuggles underneath the covers. He whispers, "Sleep sweet," and turns to stare at the ceiling.

DEDICATION

This is dedicated to my grandfather, who introduced me to the delectability of strawberry malteds.

AUTHOR BIOGRAPHY

Dena Linn, ex-urban, thriver, community child, is not one of 'those girls.' She won 1st-Place for her short "The Problem Is," published in *Prompted*, by Reedsy. She is also published in: the anthology *Hard Boiled and Loaded with Sin*, *TheChamberMagazine*, *Down in the Dirt Magazine*, and *Ariel Chart International Literary Journal*.

Links:

Author website:

HardBoiled and Loaded with Sin:

Down in the Dirt/SCARS:

ArielChart:

https://www.arielchart.com/2022/07/my-name-is-youssou.html

Prompted: https://amzn.to/4220vxz

A CRIME IS A CRIME IS A CRIME

Damnadh!My plate is empty again. Damn! I moan and sigh at no one in particular.

Oldy, my current owner, and I are the sole occupants of the house. She is now snoozing in her favourite armchair near the living room's big window.

This is the same house I have lived in since Stella picked me up as a tiny puppy from the pet shop. And that is the same worn-out chair Stella, may her *Rest In Peace*, used to sit on, waiting for Felix, her husband, to return home.

Stella and Felix were my first owners.

I'm now ten years old, and according to what I've heard, I must be nearing retirement at around 60 human years old. I've been passed from owner to owner many times since Stella's murder. The last ones, before Oldy, sold the house, moved to another state to be near their children, and left me here with the rest of the furniture.

I've been sulking all morning long. Oldy forgot to refill my bowl again, and I'm starving. She's not a *bad egg*, just oldish and a bit *glaiki*t, as we say in Scottish, my mother tongue, as you know. Yes, she's a little foolish, yet a good-hearted lady. Sadly, the gentle dame is also a bit deaf.

Oldy has been taking good care of me. However, she's turned forgetful, confused and easily distracted. I overheard her children talking. "We'll have to bring someone to help Mum," the daughter said, half whispering, half sniffling.

"Uhum," assented her brother. This *gadgie,* as we call it in Scotland, doesn't talk a lot.

I'm guessing the age caught up with Oldy's brain and her auditory sense, since she doesn't hear my grumbles and groans when I'm hungry.

Never mind, Murphy, I tell Myself.

I relish talking to Me and Myself. To begin with, we chatter in Scottish, and we understand each other bark for bark.

Myself reminded Me, *You can always jump the hedge between the two gardens, pay a visit to the Donovans next door, and Mrs V or the boys will feed you.*

Next door lives The Donovan Family. That's Detective Donovan—I tagged him DeDo as his name is too long for my tongue. His wife is Violet—Mrs V, a good friend of Stella's—and their three boys, whom I call Aitch, Dee and Ell, as I can't pronounce their real English names. As I've told you in my previous adventure, they remind Me of Donald Duck's three nephews, Huey, Dewey and Louie—they have been kind and considerate of Me since the tragedy.

As a ten-year-old *seann chú*, an old hound, as you say in British, I am incredibly emotional.

I confess on days like today, I get a bit moody when I think about my life, particularly those peaceful on the surface, although bordering on tedium.

When I'm in a more cheery mood, I recall the gripping days, those full of actions and adventures.

Some, emphasising the bad times, are spine-chilling and pretty hair-raising.

For instance, when I was a quarter-to-three-year-old—that would mean around twenty-eight human years in my counting—my new keepers were a couple of middle-aged Homo Sapiens.

They bought the house right after Stella's assassination, and Felix, her husband, was arrested for murdering her and thrown in the nick for the rest of his life.

"Stella's house needs to be sold," I overheard Mrs V telling DeDo, one of those mornings I had run over there to catch some brekkie.

"It's not Stella's–poor soul. The deed isn't in her name. The registration is in Felix's name only." DeDo explained without lifting his nose from inside the newspaper.

Humans are strange creatures indeed. What a lack of respect and consideration! DeDo shouldn't talk to his wife without taking his eyes off the pages and giving her his full attention. My parents would never behave in such a disrespectful and uncaring manner towards each other, most of all in front of us, little pooches. They would even lick their food from the same plate when we lived at the pet shop.

Anyway, I'm digressing.

"I don't care each way, as long as the sale means Felix will disappear from our neighbourhood forever." Mrs V protested, a rare sour expression on her otherwise attractive face.

"My thoughts too. That repulsive criminal needs money to survive inside."

That statement puzzled Me, I must admit. I thought humans needed money to survive inside and outside wherever they were—*ah dinnae ken?* Don't you?

In any case, who am I to presume to decipher humankind?

The new couple, Dr Ray and Mrs Ruby Logan, purchased the house from Felix and became my new owners. The Doc was a General Practitioner, and the Missus, his wife, was a nurse.

However, it appeared to Me that they were more concerned about the lonely beggars in our town than the families they were supposed to look after.

Indeed, at the time, I was over the moon—R&R, as I call them for short—agreed to let Me stay, even though it implied I was only another piece of the household furnishings. I let it go and didn't give them the pleasure of knowing I was annoyed. I'm not eager to show my feelings to strangers. First, they need to earn my trust.

Nevertheless, I was glad. At least I would continue to have a roof over Me, keep my napping corner and food to eat, if not loved.

With time, the community welcomed and grew fond of the new couple. Their charming and extroverted personalities won over everyone's trust.

They were obliging and agreeable people—what humans call charismatic.

They were tall and lean, somewhat tidy, although the house wasn't always as clean *as a hound's tooth.*

A rather dapper man, Dr R always dressed in stylish and expensive clothes. Nurse R was chic and classy.

And—oh! Both had a permanent smile on their pale cheeks, although lacking in their apathetic eyes.

I wondered. *Am I the only one noticing the discrepancy?*

Although R&R were active in the community, I couldn't tell which side of the fence they preferred—Labour Party or Conservative, Shakira or Beyoncé, Cristiano Ronaldo or Leo Messi—all crucial matters as far as I've learned from listening to the late afternoon's conversations at the Donovan's.

I reckon they sided with the vague area of *either or* faction, electing to stay within the consensus and careful not to step on anyone's toes.

They seemed to be sensitive and understanding of the suffering of others, showing interest in their lives, compassion, listening, offering comfort, and often inviting them to dinner at our house.

If someone inquired, I'd label the Missus, Nurse R, as an enigmatic woman. Nobody does, so I keep my snout shut. *Flies don't enter a shut muzzle*, is my motto these days.

In the shelters and when near the vagrants, Nurse R displayed a pained look and soft features with the gentlest tone of voice.

She leaned in towards the poor people while listening to their complaints. In contrast, at home, she was highly strung. Her veins pulsed in a rock-and-roll rhythm beneath her neck skin.

Truth be told, R&R seemed to work hard to reach that popular position. To all appearances, they were serious-minded and dedicated to the welfare of others.

During our daily walks, I witnessed how they helped anyone who needed their skills and volunteered in various programmes.

They would take me to the Town Hall, the community centres and many schools, where they delivered speeches and lectures on personal hygiene, dental health, public cleanliness, and organ donation.

They inspired respect and admiration.

I would hear hundreds of comments daily while playing on the sidewalk.

"I'm well impressed with the Logans. Aren't you?"

"Oh, yes! I've already had an appointment with Dr Ray, and he's incredible. He's not only a good doctor. He's also a pleasing and attentive person."

"I couldn't agree with you more. He tackled all the tough questions I threw at him amiably and without stressing. And his wife exudes a natural ability to connect with people."

"They both have a magnetic presence."

Doc R's ethics appeared to be exemplary. For example, when he refused to accept Mrs V's money for a consultation. She had developed some strange symptoms lately and needed his expert opinion. I apologize. I can't be more specific, as those were women's symptoms beyond my knowledge as a canine.

R&R's fame grew by the hour, and they became our town's new celebrities. Not a year passed, and they were elected members of the City Council.

R&R were always in the right spot where help was needed, always mindful of the suffering of others, mainly the underprivileged, interested in their lives and problems, listening and offering comfort and bringing them to dinner and an overnight.

Twice a day, sometimes before my dinner—which would turn Me into a somewhat irascible and waspish quadruped— *Who's the lamebrain who decided to exercise on an empty belly?* In vain, I would snarl and show my teeth.

The cold evenings outings were the worst. R&R would come up with the daft idea of a walk around town when all I wanted was to curl up on my comfy bolster bed and nap after dinner.

While walking the dog—meaning Me—in those odd hours and cold weather, R&R would stop to chat with every beggar they encountered on the streets. Singularizing those searching for food in the dumpsters. Poor and angry Me, having to sit—*sit, Murphy, sit*—and bore Myself listening to their conversation, which almost always went like this:

"Good evening. How are you feeling today?" One of the R's would ask, offering a false empathic smile, which I don't know about the hobo, but I smelled a rat—I apologize for the unintended pun.

The Missus would stand beside her husband, offering her professional, phoney, plasticised smile.

"What d'you want?" Would often be the beggar's cheesed-off reply without raising his eyes.

"May I speak with you for a moment?" Doc R moved, closing a bit of the distance between them.

"I'm just *tryin'* to survive here. Leave me be." The beggar stepped back and crossed his arms over his chest.

"I understand, and I want to help. My name is Dr Ray Logan, and I'm a medical doctor. This is Nurse Ruby." Said Doc R in a soft voice, introducing his wife while placing a hand gently on her shoulder. "I've noticed you've been living on the streets, and, as a doctor, I'm concerned about your health and welfare."

"Look, Doc. Thanks, and don't mind my saying, but I can care for myself out here."

"I see you are a strong and self-supporting person. However, living on the streets is risky, and you deserve better than wasting your health in such a rough environment." This spiel came from the Missus.

"I'm *doing good* so far. What could you do better for me?" The homeless guy turned his back on us and started distancing himself.

"We can offer you free medical assistance." Doc R called after him, rubbing the back of his neck, unnerved by the man's response. When the beggar turned to face us, the doctor adopted what I termed '*the pose*:' a patronizing posture, thrusting his chest out, nodding a few times, and displaying a wide grin and gleaming eyes.

"Assistance? What assistance!?" The man's disdain and distrust were evident even through his toothless, dry smile.

"To begin with, a complete check-up. We'll suggest preventive measures, and we'll provide free medicines.

"Why trust you? I heard it all before."

"I promise you I can improve your health and living conditions."

"Sounds nice, but I can't afford no medical treatment."

"Don't you worry about that now. Come and have dinner with us tomorrow. In the privacy of our home, we will discuss your situation and see how we can best help you."

"I'm not crazy about the idea, but I'll think about it. Can't promise anything." The man didn't turn back this time, and, thank the Lord, we returned home.

One of those street dwellers R&R pestered was an eccentric individual who wore unusual, outlandish clothes, even for a Brit.

Nobody knew his real name.

Everybody called him "Patience & Tolerance" with kindness and affection, as he would walk the streets preaching equal rights for all races to all who wanted to listen.

Mrs V knew he had a family or caring friends somewhere not very far, as he would disappear for a day or two and return to the same corner shaved and bathed with clean clothes.

"He seems to have had access to a good education and life opportunities at one time in his life," she told me once when we passed him on the sidewalk. "He's well spoken with a rich vocabulary and uses logic and reasoning when addressing people."

"Stop smoking!" He would shout at every person he saw holding a cigarette. "Tobacco and nicotine have a detrimental effect on your health. Are you so eager to die? Suicide is sinful!"

He would preach, "Be patient and tolerant to your fellow citizens. Be kind and generous. The Lord will repay you in double."

Or he would caution against speeding, "Drive carefully. Be considerate to your comrade drivers. Don't hasten towards your death."

We all liked him. I had trouble pronouncing his name, being English and all, so I simplified it and would greet him with "Hello, Mr Pee'nTea" when I passed him.

He would show up wearing baggy pants printed with shining flowers or geometric designs and coloured T-shirts. His hat caused a lot of teasing and kidding around town. It was round, covering his entire head, including his ears, made of wool as thick as rope. It had a maroon base and a mixture of fuchsia and crimson-coloured braids long and broad as snakes, twisted and crisscrossed, knitted at the top. It looked like he wore his intestines exposed on his head.

Once or twice a month, R&R would visit shelters and show the same interest and care for the poor people residing on the premises as they showed those indigents sleeping on the sidewalk.

"Good evening," Doc R would approach and introduce himself to the shelter staff. "I'm a medical doctor, my wife is a nurse, and we came here to provide free medical check-ups and medicines to the residents."

At least I know this to be accurate, as I would be standing at the entrance to our house, barking and wiggling my tail each time the labs delivered boxes and boxes of medicines samples and other products R&R distributed on their rounds.

I also witnessed the private ambulances bringing and taking away cooler boxes. Odd for Me at the time, they would come and go in silence. No siren. No flashing lights, and it always coincided with a beggar's visit for dinner and a stay-over.

"How wonderful! Medical help is a rarity in our facility. Follow me to the common area, and I'll introduce you to the residents." The shelter staff, a buxom, shortish woman with dyed carrot-red hair, ushered us to an ample room with plenty of shabby, well-worn couches, tables with games and an old TV set hanging on one wall. A group of individuals were loudly cheering and laughing while watching a football game.

A good football game is one of my favourite hobbies. Me and the *laddies* like to watch them together. I enjoy hanging out with the boys. Kind of babysitting when DeDo and Mrs V have a night out. My team, however, wasn't playing that evening, so I followed R&R and Carrot-Buxom Lady.

Doc R posed himself in the middle of the room and addressed all, attracting scowling and rolling eyes from the audience, mainly the game watchers. "Hello, my name is Doctor Ray, and this is my wife, Nurse Ruby. We are concerned about your well-being and are here to provide you with a comprehensive health assessment."

I would stroll around the place, snooping and sniffing, and hear one or two dwellers shouting, "Look, Doc, I appreciate your concern, but it's not for me. Thanks anyway."

Another added, "I've heard plenty of promises before. Nothing changed, so why should I trust you?"

"I understand your doubts and suspicions." Said Nurse R in her soothing voice. "We've worked with many people in similar situations, and we promise you we will take care of your health and well-being."

"I don't have enough money for food, let alone medical treatment." Sneered another one.

"We'll provide free treatments, medical tests and medicines. You only need to trust us, answer our questions and permit us to check on you."

If the dwellers were still shy or unwilling to accept their offer, R&R would persist. "This is for your benefit, and it's all free." They would show their sweetest smile, touching the humans' shoulders and looking into their eyes.

Unfailingly, one would say, "I suppose it wouldn't hurt to get a free check-up."

Another would follow, "Alright, Doc. I'll give it a chance, without any promises."

Carrot-Buxom would accompany us to the door, "Thank you, Dr Ray. I appreciate your concern and willingness to help. Let's see where this goes."

"We'll be in touch. Have a good evening."

R&R would treat them for free, bringing them free samples of expensive medicines, ointments, and syrups to help them heal or decrease their symptoms and pains.

After the check-ups, R&R would invite one or two of them to dinner and stay overnight. "Besides a delicious homemade meal, you'll have a warm bath." This bait would, without fail, lure at least some of them.

In all humbleness, as I'm not one to brag without solid evidence, and with my worldly famous sharp canine wit and perception, I noticed something intriguing happening during our shelter visits.

At the time, I didn't grasp what was going on.

It was about the kind of people R&R would select among the dwellers for their check-ups and constant questions about their illnesses and family history.

I would snuggle up to the genuinely sick, lie near them in their cots, nuzzle their faces, lick their hands and let them scratch my ears while listening to them whispering in their weak voices. Meanwhile, R&R would search for the healthier ones and pester them for a blood sample.

"I'm not happy with this young man's appearance this morning. He looks too pale." Doc R would say aloud. However, he would deny—politely, mind you—the same blood test to an older, sicker person. "No, Man! You look well today, Mr Simpson. You don't need the hassle."

I thought this strange and a bit weird. *You're only a dog, Murphy.* I would tell Myself. *What do you understand about human behaviour? They're not even Scots.*

They must have their reasons. Let them be. Myself would reply to Me.

So, I let them be—for the meantime.

Alas, R&R displayed their admirable traits only outside the house. Their behaviour changed the moment they crossed the gate into our home.

It was as if they returned from a masquerade ball. Their demeanour, or shall I bark, their entire personality changed.

They metamorphosed into cold-hearted, pragmatic people.

Thank goodness I was fortunate to be a young adult canine. The couple liked me well enough. They hugged, fondled and nestled me well enough.

My name's heavy weight and responsibility told me something smelt wrong.

I'm forever apprehensive due to Mr Edward Murphy's foreboding law, "anything that can go wrong will go wrong."

My canine instincts kept nagging at me: *nobody gives so much and so often, purely out of the goodness of their hearts.*

My inner voice whispered to Me. *There is goodness and beauty in the human heart.*

To Myself, I replied, *while charity and generosity exist in humans; nevertheless, unselfishness needs a profit motive.*

With this, Myself concluded the discussion."

From the start of my life with the medical couple, I was curious and sceptical about what a General Practitioner and a nurse had to do with a beggar in Felix's hyper-tidy tools shed in our courtyard.

I didn't want to be a wet blanket; therefore, I would skip the party.

R&R's fame for selfless generosity and concern for the well-being of others had already reached neighbouring towns.

Those needy people would go into the shed with happy albeit worried faces, and Me wasn't allowed inside. In a too-much-sweet voice, Nurse R would tell Me to stay outside while bribing Me with snacks. It made Me suspicious. I don't like to be treated like a child or, worse, a half-witted puppy. *Doggone!* I barked.

In the following days, those vagrants would leave the house curved and holding their backs. I found this peculiar. Humans must have indeed delicate physiques to wake up so sore after a night in the same bed Myself often took naps on, and I don't remember it being so uncomfortable.

Some beggars treated by R&R left the shelter a few days later and disappeared. Their buddies said they lucked out with a respectful sum of money and fled to start a new life.

***

R&R would go on picnics again and again, at short intervals, at odd hours, more often than most working people, always to the same spot on the cliffs over the gorge less than twenty minutes' drive from our house.

Yes, oh, you, the doubters of this world! Dogs (and other animals) do have a sense of time. We have what scientists call "timing cells." Hence—pay attention, folks—when your pet starts getting anxious about dinnertime or walkies, those same neurons will start firing because you are not punctual. For my part, I'll begin to pace, whine, swish my tail and show other signs of impatience and irritation. I understand routines. Otherwise, I'll start swearing in Scottish, and believe Me—you don't want to hear Me snarl and growl. Those dramatic sighs or paws on your lap are clear cues I'm waiting for you.

And here I am digressing again. I apologise.

Before we started for the picnic, R&R would carry a big package out of the shed and into their pickup. It was usually long, wrapped in a thick plastic sheet, shaped like a torpedo, and looked heavy.

On arrival at the cliff edge, they would throw the package onto the gorge below.

I didn't pay much attention to the fact at the time, as I would instead engage in physical activities. I like keeping my physique in shape and strengthening my joints, muscles and heart. Nevertheless, I found it strange that R&R would travel so far to dispose of their garbage with a dumpster beside our house.

One day, strange tales and whispers spread around the neighbourhood.

I heard them, as from time to time, R&R were too busy to take me to the park, and they would ask the favour of Mrs V, our neighbour.

I spend a lot of time next door, with Mrs V's and the *laddies*. At least, I do until DeDo returns home from work. DeDo isn't one of my groupies, although he is never mean to me.

My special breed needs daily physical exercise and mental stimulation to prevent anxiety and destructive behavior caused by boredom.

Besides, I enjoy being outside running after a ball with the kids in the park.

However, it would take Mrs V and Myself forever to get to the park and back, as every few meters, some gossip monger would stop us with silly questions.

"Have you heard the news?" The woman asked Mrs V, blocking our way.

"What news, Mrs Benton?" Mrs V would tilt her head back, close her eyes, and let out a heavy sigh.

"Hundreds of vagrants are dying of septicaemia." Said Mrs Burton in a loud whisper, lifting her chin and puffing out her chest as if revealing the code to enter Fort Knox.

"Oh, dear!" Replied Mrs V in a shaky voice.

"The doctors discovered they had one kidney missing, poorly operated and severely infected." Mrs Benton continued, waving her hands in jerky movements. I must confess I ignore the reason for all that gesticulation. I wondered if there were flies around us that I couldn't see.

"No, I haven't heard. I feel deeply for them." Said Mrs V with a pained look in her round black eyes, almost like mine.

"And in most cases, the poor folks didn't even know they were missing an organ. Most of those who survived those horrific acts of vandalism to their bodies and reached the hospitals had infected ulcers, pus and poorly sewn wounds."

"Who would do such a thing?" Mrs V flinched and placed a hand over her mouth.

"And what is your husband planning to do about it? Those people are filling the public hospitals as we speak." Mrs Benton asked, squinting and smirking.

Mrs V is a smart cookie, as you would call her in British. She is a serious, no-nonsense human chick and not one to enjoy gossiping. After she rid herself of Mrs Benton, she confided in me: "Well, Murphy. I'm sorry for those sick people. However, I'm sure 'hundreds of them' could be a bit overstated. And I'm also sure the doctors must have informed the authorities if the case demands. Let's go home, and I'll give you a snack."

That's why I like Mrs V so much. I wagged my tail, showed her a huge dose of wiggliness, and rolled over to show her my belly.

"Came on, Murphy. Stop your act and let's keep moving. I need to ask my husband about those sick beggars."

***

Life went on its tranquil, uneventful way for a bit over a year since R&R arrived in our community.

Nevertheless, bit by bit, those exemplar avatars of altruism, kindness and hospitality started to melt.

That thick wall of compassion and generosity tumbled down on the day Pee'n Tea disappeared.

Police, social workers, volunteers like Me and the *laddies* searched for him everywhere.

I even looked for him inside the garbage bins.

Nothing. The man had vanished. Some of us worried, others thought he might have returned to his family in another city. However, his family and closest friends also showed up to help in the search. They said they were used to Pee'n Tea leaving home, although never for so long.

We all prayed for his safety to the *Tighearna Air Neamh*, Our Lord in Heaven.

Pee'n Tea was my friend, and an overwhelming sadness engulfed my fragile canine being. I turned touchy and lost my appetite. *Aye,*

ah ken? Can you believe it? I almost didn't care about my daily
exercises.

One early morning, before dawn, I heard noises from the tools
shed and decided to check. After all, I'm the dog in the house.
It surprised Me to see a beggar I had seen in one of the shelters,
coming out, leaning on the wall and holding the door as if afraid
to fall. He saw me too, gave me half a painful smile and a pat on
my shoulder and left, inching, dragging his feet, half-bended and
holding his back.

I took the chance, checked if any of the R's were around, and
went into the shed—the same immaculate, ultra-organised shed
that had belonged to Felix—to snoop around in a young dog's
frenzy of misbehaviour.

Suddenly, all the isolated incidents took on a meaningful focus.

Ifrinn fuilteach, bloody hell! Sorry, Brits, but in Scottish it
sounds better. *The stench,* I said to Myself. *I think I might be
sick. I'm experiencing the urge to throw up. What happened to the
fanatically organised, almost sterile tool shed I remember from Auld
lang Synes*—from yesteryears?

The shelves were in disarray, with unclean medical instruments, including some cooler boxes, scattered on top of them.

There was a long table in the centre of the room with a torn, filthy, blood-stained mattress on top of it. However, I was shocked and almost froze when I muzzled under the table and found Pee'n Tea's hat. Other items of clothes, such as socks, threaded wool gloves and underwear, were strewn all over the floor and the counters.

Lord in Heaven, I said to Myself. *What's this doing here?*

Myself said to Me, *Murphy, you need to report this to DeDo.*

DeDo never listens to me, Me replied to Myself.

Then, call the laddies. Attract them here. They'll bring their father when they see the hat. Myself insisted in a persuasive and non-contesting tone.

Good idea, I said to Myself.

Myself always has excellent ideas. They help Me when in a knotted corner. I can always count on Me and Myself to '*save my bacon*,' as the British say.

You see, it's not my thing to brag, as you've noticed. I'm a humble dog, even though I'm famous for my high intelligence.

But I'm digressing again.

The truth is, I was scared. I didn't want to be homeless again.
Who's going to feed Me when R&R are gone? Mrs V would like
to adopt Me, but DeDo wouldn't allow it. I know this because
Mrs V told Me. One day, as I, being an orphan and all, after Stella's
death and Felix going to prison, Mrs V patted Me and said, "Luvie,
I wish I could bring you home. The boys would thrill with it, but
you know my husband is against having a *four-legged creature* at
home."

DeDo is a good person. He's honest, just, and very responsible.
However, he is also hardheaded and has no patience "*with pets
walking between his legs,*" as he keeps saying.

I was sad to hear that, of course. I know DeDo doesn't hate
Me. He pets Me and asks, 'How's life, Shorty?' whenever I pass
him. On the other hand, he wants Me far from his living room
and—especially—his favourite armchair.

Back to the shed situation.

I'm facing a colossal dilemma. On the one paw, I must denounce
these criminals. On the other paw, it will require some tough
decision-making, as there's no turning back. On the third paw,

I need to think about my future. If I choose to point a claw at R&R, I'll be an orphan again. What should I do? I'm just a dog. I'm scared to be left alone again. To feel lonely. And hungry. And thirsty. Oh, and dirty—there won't be anyone to give me a good bath and clean my fleas. *D'ye ken?*

Well, my ingrained Church of Scotland background: *The Lord expects us to speak the truth at all times, even when it might create problems,* and my parents' education: *always remember the proverb, my son, it's better to be a poor person and honest, than a crook and a fool*— all these memories got the best of me, and I followed my fourth paw's solution. I ran out of the shed, jumped over the hedge, and went to find DeDo.

As usual, DeDo refused to accompany Me, so I had to nag the *laddies* and pull them to the shed, where I showed them Pee'n Tea's hat thrown on the floor under the table and the rest of the stuff. They were careful not to touch anything and reported the findings to their father.

"Dad, come! Come see! Murphy found Patience's hat." Ell tugged his Dad's arm, bouncing from foot to foot, him being the most excitable of the three *laddies.*

DeDo looked at me, tilted his head, raised his eyebrows, sceptic as usual, and did not say or do anything.

Mrs V rescued the scene, "Show your father where Murphy found it." She told Ell and thus forced DeDo to follow us to the shed.

When DeDo entered the messy and smelly place, he immediately called his pals from the criminal investigation unit.

Later that day, I convinced the *laddies* to follow me to the picnic site. It wasn't an easy job, mind you.

"Sorry, Murphy. We can't play now. We've homework to finish."

Argh, they couldn't fool me. I've heard all their excuses before. I knew they wanted to stay home and watch the football game. Therefore, I had no choice but to pester them until they followed me to the gorge.

When they realised what I was showing them, they called their father.

The special rescue team pulled Pee'n Tea's and the other beggars' bodies up from the gorge and brought to a fitting burial service. I insisted on being present at all of them, as those hobos were my friends, too.

The bobbies recalled all the deaths and illnesses of the other indigents, gathered the proofs and evidence and arrested the couple.

It was not surprising since Dr R was not even a certified surgeon.

Today, so many years after R&R's episode, as I sit here, starving and waiting for Oldy to wake up and serve my breakfast, I recall the colossal bedlam R&R created in our peaceful community.

All the chirpy climate that had enveloped our calm community for having—what we believed—such selfless, charitable people among us evaporated like the sweat from my skin by the breeze on a hot summer day.

While it delighted us R&R were helping the underprivileged, in truth, those heartless villains were taking advantage of them for their own profit and benefit.

While they pretended to give medical care and attention, in truth, they were checking the homeless to ensure they were fit for extracting their kidney, which the couple sold afterwards on the black market.

To a few, they told the truth and offered a considerable sum of money in exchange for their "donation." To others, they served drugged food at dinner in our house and had their organ taken deceitfully behind closed doors inside Felix's tools shed.

They bluffed all of us, well-intentioned people and pets alike, living our quiet, middle-class suburban lifestyle.

I wonder what led them to inflict so much harm and cause both emotional and physical suffering on that impoverished population?

I couldn't shout at them, *"Bad human, go to your room!"* as humans do at uncivil dogs when unhappy or angry with their behaviour. I could only discharge my most threatening guttural bark.

Besides, this is uncharacteristic, as I'm a coolheaded specimen of my race.

I must maintain a calm disposition towards life to not disturb the universal equilibrium because of my unsuitable given name, as I have mentioned before.

It's a heavy responsibility on my narrow canine shoulders, *d'ye ken?*

The level of my animal aggression rose above my otherwise sensible and rational control. My ears flattened. A hard, white stare and my bared fangs displayed my deep rage against those grifters.

Without false modesty, I need to let the dog out of the bag, as humans say, since I've doubted their honesty and trustworthiness from the beginning.

But I'm digressing as usual.

When the police came to fetch the couple, a crowd stood before our porch and shouted: "Take these dirty people away!"

"Let them rot in prison!"

"Criminals! Throw them in the garbage bin where they belong to end their lives."

The mood of our town's citizens was lower than my cholesterol levels. The citizens of our city were sad. We all fell on our faces, I mean, my snout. We walked with our heads low in shame and guilt for believing in those rascals.

The humans bawled their anger, disappointment and sorrow for the dead beggars as if it could ease their pain and regret for believing in those mean, beastly murderers.

"They betrayed us!"

"I hope they rot in jail."

"They will get what they deserve!"

"Not even hobos are safe in this town anymore!"Yelled an older woman while trying to hit Doc R with her cane. A policeman pushed the lady away.

While being dragged from their home in handcuffs, Doc R had the nerve to shout at the policemen who came to arrest them, "You are mistaken. I'll sue you. We didn't do anything wrong. Is it a crime to help people?"

"A crime is a crime is a crime!" I barked at him.

The Missus, Nurse R, also tried to justify their crimes. "Those beggars were going to die any day of hunger and all kinds of diseases. We've helped them, while in turn, we provided years of life to those in need of organs to survive."

"One wrongdoing doesn't justify another." I snarled back at her.

Later, proud of Myself, I walked with my most arrogant gait for having solved another crime—and in the same house, too.

The rest is history.

Justice triumphed. The authorities arrested R&R, brought them to trial, and the judge sentenced them severely.

The house was back on the market.

I was eager to know if the new owners would adopt me. I suspect some humans do perceive Me as part of the furniture.

Well, that is another story for another time.

Now, sitting here, starving and watching Oldy napping, I had another chat with Myself.

Should I go and wake her up? I asked Myself.

You better, Myself replied to Me.

But if I yelp, I cautioned Myself, *she might have a fright and die.*

Well, if you die of starvation and she faints or dies, who will bark for help?

Myself had a point there. I then climbed into her lap gently, not to startle her, and began some soft, tender pawing and licking her face, accompanied by a wet nose sniffing.

"Oh, Murphy darling. I forgot to feed you again, haven't I?"

It took some time for Oldy to remember the exact location of the food package.

My belly groaned, but I forgave her—Oldy was older than me, and my parents taught Me to respect senior homo sapiens.

I got my grub eventually.

AUTHOR BIOGRAPHY

Author Ana Paulina Lipster was born in Brazil. She fell in love with the English language—love at first word—in junior high in Niterói, in the state of Rio de Janeiro. She attended The British Culture School for seven years, majoring in Extra-Mural studies. She subsequently received the Certificate of Proficiency from Cambridge University,

After immigrating to Israel, Ana Paulina continued to pursue her study of the English language and literature, honing her writing in the language through various creative writing workshops.

Ana Paulina has written two crime novels, soon to be released. She has also written numerous short stories, published in Tolerance, Autumn, Winter—An End and a Promise, Spring—The Unexpected, and Summer—When Doors Open anthologies.

SERENDIPITY – a gripping story of twin sisters, torn apart by a heartbreaking abduction, reunited by serendipity after two decades of grief and anguish.

BRANDED – a passionate family saga that hides a horrible crime for decades and transports the reader back and forth in time.

You can follow her:

Website: www.analipster.com

Facebook: https://www.facebook.com/ana.lipster and on https://www.facebook.com/Ana-P-Lipster-Author-1009944790 24945

JATSU'S SAVIOR

That last shot had been too close; Jatsu ducked in time, yes, but he would never forget the heat of the bullets as they flew past his head.

He peeked around the giant dumpster he used as a shield.

"Get him! Damn it, don't let him get away!"

Four guards climbed onto machines with wheels as one of them shouted orders at the others. He instantly recognized the voice he'd heard recently. It belonged to the leader of the guards. The one who mocked him as the others tortured him.

He would remember that male until the day he joined his ancestors.

When the four took off, he took advantage of the racket they made to move out from behind his hiding place. Sticking to dark corners, he made it halfway to the forest before the guards in the towers spotted him and started firing. This time, he hadn't moved fast enough, and one of them got him in his arm. No time to take care of it... as soon as he got to the forest, he would see to it.

A fast survey of his surroundings revealed a gigantic tree with some tall bushes clustered around it. The perfect spot for him to take care of his arm and reach out to his warriors. Using the shadows for cover, he ran toward safety as the roar of the vehicles filled the air.

"Commander?"

His cousin Rusto's voice rang out on his mental comm.

"Come in, Commander!"

"I'm here. Can you determine how many are tracking me?" as he tore a strip off his shirt and wrapped it around his right arm, tying it tight.

"Yes, Sir. There are four males... Sir, we're ten minutes from your location. Can you evade them?"

"Yes, I've turned on my cloaking device. I'll uncloak when I reach a safer spot, so you'll be able to locate me again."

"Aye, sir."

As Rusto signed off, only the sound of a small animal scurrying across some leaves could be heard.

Ah, his trackers are on foot.

A twig snapped and a masculine voice uttered a profanity in the stillness.

He smiled as their constant muttered exclamations kept him aware of their position and covered any sound he might be making.

Cloaked, he made his way through the trees. He dropped to a crouch when he came to the edge of a meadow with several dwellings with lights on, sitting side-by-side, each with smaller buildings next to them.

Waiting till the clouds shifted in front of the moon. He ran to the first dwelling's small side building.

Each one he approached bore a lock on the door. Using the fences for cover, he reached the last one.

Shite! It had a lock, too.

The back door opened. He dropped to the ground as his wounded arm landed against the corner of the building. The light from within the dwelling outlined a female's body standing in the doorway. A moment later, she walked out and looked around.

"Kitty! Kitty! Time to come in and eat!"

That's Cassie!

A small four-legged creature, its fur sporting different colors, slinked towards the female, entwining itself between her legs. It finally came to a stop in front of her and she picked it up.

"Good kitty," she crooned as she stroked it.

Jatsu got up, ready to take a step toward her, when a male appeared in the doorway behind her. He wore the same type of clothing as the ones tracking him.

The sound of a male laughing drifted out into the night air.

She hesitated and looked toward the road; the male stepped off the tiny porch toward her.

"Cassie, come back in here."

She didn't answer him.

She faced him, chin held high.

He snapped at her. "I said, get in here, or I'll play with your cat the way the scientists played with that alien."

Her head jerked up as she held the kitty close to her chest. "Why, she's not hurting you."

"You can't help a CynTech research subject." He waved his hand toward the doorway. "Inside now."

Jatsu smiled after her, as she lifted her chin and stalked into the house, clutching the animal close to her chest. He waited until the captain followed her, and he snuck in behind him.

A male he hadn't seen before laughed and pulled at the animal she carried while another looked on, leaning his hip against the kitchen counter. The captain moved fast and punched the

laughing one in the jaw.

"Hanes! The boss said not to mess with her. She's bait, so behave

or I'll cut your hands off. Ya hear?"

"Yeah, I hear, but where's the fun in that, Captain?"

Once Hanes moved away, Cassie sat the creature in front of a

bowl filled with food. The captain glared at the silent man. "Why

didn't you stop him, Bill?"

"You never said anything about protecting her. I only do what

ya tell me."

Jatsu noted Cassie standing over Kitty as she ate at one end of

the room, and the three males argued at the other end. Then he

moved so fast Cassie's hair danced around her face. In seconds

he'd knocked both the captain and Hane unconscious. And Bill

countered his every move. When he hit him in the stomach area, a

light flickered over Bill, and recognition dawned on Jatsu.

"Wha... the....!"

Goddess, he was fighting Luka, his cousin.

"Stop Jatsu, it's me, Luka."

Jatsu grabbed him in a hug.

"Tell me how you got in here." Jatsu's eyes went to the two lying on the floor. "But first, why did you allow that male to touch Cassie? We don't harm females, we protect them."

"I made sure she wouldn't be harmed, or I would have stepped in. I needed to stay in character. We traced parts of your ship to the building where they held you. I volunteered to apply for a job and got hired. While going through my new employee training, I overheard their plans. They discovered you regained your strength and that she," he tilted his head toward Cassie, "helped you. They set you up, let you escape, and waited here for you."

"So, she didn't know—?"

"Correct. They couldn't understand you, so they figured neither could she."

Jatsu noticed Cassie inching toward the door while they spoke. He grabbed her arm and switched to English.

"We won't harm you; this is my cousin Luka. You can trust him. I promise."

Cassie nodded. "Can I sit down?"

As she moved away from him, her long brown hair brushed against his arm. He flinched as it caressed him. Only, emoru, the most expensive fabric in his world, felt like that. The touch hardened his body with desire. This wasn't the time or place; he wasn't a callow youth.

Slowly, he took a step back and let her leave the kitchen.

"Commander?" Luka's voice broke through his thoughts.

"Yes?"

"We found some small pieces of your ship at the landing site. The humans missed them."

"Make sure they are sent to the lab and have them checked out. If it is a weak spot in the metal or a defective part, I want to know it, so we can deal with the manufacturing company. No one is to fly one of those until those parts are examined thoroughly."

"Aye, Sir."

I'm such an idiot. He knew exactly what I said all along!

As soon as he let her go, Cassie reached for the back of the closest chair and sat down. She glanced at him out of the corner of her eye; concern flashed across his face before it became a blank slate.

She should have realized it sooner. That one time in his cage, she wanted to warn him about his captors, but the look in his eyes told her to back off. He would deal with it. Without saying a word, he made her aware he knew what the outcome would be.

At the sound of a chair scraping against the floor, she glanced up. He sat right in front of her, staring at her. Cassie couldn't look away from him, driven by a sense of urgency she hadn't experienced. Slowly, she let her eyes drift over him, until she caught sight of his arm.

"You're hurt! The first aid kit is in the bathroom. I'll be right back. Don't move."

She took a step toward it, stopped, twisting around to face him.

"Wait a minute. You understood what everyone said all along, didn't you?"

"Yes, I did. I thought they would hurt you if they realized I understood them."

Red-faced at the thought of some things she'd told him, Cassie closed her eyes. Then she left to get the medical kit.

Returning, Cassie pulled a chair facing his arm. "Quit tugging at that. I'll soak it with a wet bandage first, then it will come off easier."

She slipped on gloves, then placed a wet cloth on his wound and held it in place. She glanced around them. They were alone.

"Where have they gone? Your friend and the guards?"

"Luka is tying them up and making sure they don't make any noise. He'll be back when he is finished."

"All right." She caught his gaze. "This is going to hurt. A lot. I have nothing to numb the pain, but I have some whiskey—it might help. Want some?"

"Yes, please."

She left his side and came back carrying a full bottle of dark liquid, then grabbed a glass and poured a couple of inches in it before handing it to him. "Drink it all."

He drank it in one quick gulp as he held her gaze. She snickered as his eyes crossed, then closed as he slumped in his chair. Out like a light. Cassie used whiskey to clean the wound, then sewed it up. As she cleaned up the table, his eyelids fluttered.

Good, he was waking up already.

She found it difficult not to stare at him. His presence drew her on every level of her being. Did he feel the same? Every time, except for now, her eyes always seemed to encounter his. She continued to let her gaze travel over him; wondering if he would be a funny drunk or a mean drunk?

Luka came back while Jatsu was waking up. Cassie had to smile; it turned out Jatsu was 'funny and nice,' when inebriated. And she was grateful his friend Luka was there. It was going to take both of them to get him up the stairs in this condition.

The guards outside would still be looking for him. Getting him upstairs, into a bed to rest, and keeping him out of sight, would be the best course of action. The scraping of a chair across the floor brought her back to her patient, who was standing with Luka's help. Cassie was at his side under his arm, in a flash.

"Luka, we need to get him upstairs and into bed. He'll be out of sight if they come back."

God, he's so big and heavy.

"Not leaving you alone with Luka. Gotta save you." Jatsu slumped against Luka and stared into Cassie's eyes. "You saved me. Gotta help you."

"You can help me by getting up those stairs and into bed."

When Jatsu shook his head, Luka spoke up. "Sire, they don't know who I am. I'll keep them from harming her until you can defend her yourself."

Cassie considered the different emotions running across Jatsu's face. Then he nodded.

Together, they got him upstairs and settled.

Someone was pounding on the front door.

Her eyes went to Jatsu, then to Luka.

Luka whispered. "I've got this. Follow me and act like you're angry at the world, okay?"

She nodded, her eyes still on Jatsu, but the sound of Luka's footsteps going down the stairs brought her back to the present. She closed the bedroom door and followed while thinking of all the things she should be mad about.

Luka was standing in the middle of the room, the main door wide open. From there, four men were standing on her porch.

She frowned. Those were the guards from Cyntech. Hammer, who was the leader, then Jones, Blackstone, and Malstrom—the guy who had cornered her.

"Hey, Bill, have you seen him?"

"No, Hammer. Have you checked all the sheds and combed through those trees?"

She had seen the smirk on Hammer's face as she came down the stairs. His gaze made her feel dirty. She lifted her chin and glared at him until he looked away. Behind him, the others were avoiding her eyes.

"Yeah, sure, but we thought we'd check the houses first, then we will go through the woods again."

"The captain, Hanes, and I did the houses already. They're clear."

When they didn't move but kept on staring at Cassie, Bill stepped in front of her. "No one is to touch her. Captain's orders. And, speaking of orders, don't you think you should do what he told you to?"

Cassie noted Hammer cringing, then he looked at his men and shooed them off the porch muttering, "let's get this done."

When the main door was locked again, Cassie turned around and walked to the foot of the stairs. Her alien man was coming down already, and he wasn't wobbly anymore. Rather, he seemed ready to defend her.

She observed Luka wasn't surprised Jatsu was no longer drunk.

"Are you all right?" he asked. "Did they threaten you, hurt you?"

Fury took over: her mouth dropped open, and her eyes burned in her face. "You should have stayed hidden!"

She was protecting me!

Jatsu did nothing to hide his shock. No female, not even his mother, had ever put herself between him and another male. Yet, this tiny female had protected him from the start against four males and one of his own men.

He ran his fingers through his hair. The motion caught the light, revealing faint but visible marks running up all the way to his hand. What the... was it possible that—?

Acting as if he hadn't just had the greatest shock of his life, he went to stand in front of Cassie, then cupped her shoulders and met her gaze. "They didn't hurt you, did they? Are you okay, truly?"

"Yes. The others believed Luka and weren't happy he was staying instead of joining them. Evidently, they thought something was going on, that much was obvious. They've split up now. Checking the sheds and the woods, just like Luka told him to."

She smiled as he continued to hold her shoulders.

"I frightened you before, and I am sorry about it. And I can't tell you how grateful I am that you took care of my wound."

Jatsu was still glancing down at her when Orion, another of his warriors, commed him. His team was nearby. This time, he answered out loud, telling them to proceed with care.

"Who are you talking to?"

"Orion, he's a member of my rescue party. He said they were close by and he'll comm me when they arrive."

He observed her frown when he said they were close by. "It would help if you opened the door and called for your animal. They will sneak in cloaked until the door is shut. Don't worry if you feel a breeze, it will be caused by them."

Cassie pursed her lips and waited a moment before answering. "Okay."

A few minutes later, Jatsu touched her shoulder. "They're here."

Judging by her stiff movements, she still wasn't too happy about letting them in. Her heart rate increased.

"Don't be afraid. They would never hurt a female. Especially you," he tried to comfort her. She wasn't giving out any clues about what was going on in her head.

Cassie stayed silent as she motioned for his men to get inside, then she faced him again. "Why especially me? I'm nothing special."

"Oh, but you are. Cassie, you are one in a million. I never thought of meeting someone like you. You are my mate. Even now, my blood sings for you since the very first time you touched me. You see these marks? They are called Mating Marks and can appear instantly or several days after touching. They appeared tonight after you dealt with my wound. Can you tell they're darkening?"

Jatsu held out his arm, pushing up the sleeve. So they were visible to them. They traveled across his entire arm, down to his fingertips.

His men, who had adopted a protective stance but had been otherwise silent so far, looked at him. He nodded at them, confirming what he said about the marks. Cassie shook her head at him, instead, acting as if he still were under the influence of the drugs he had received at the facility. And yet, her curiosity seemed to get the better of her at some point, because she waved a hand at his arm.

"Um, does it hurt? May I—?"

It pleased him to see how she neither panicked nor became furious. "No, it doesn't." He reached out. "And yes, you may touch them."

"The marks feel warm like you're sunburned, while the rest of your skin is cool to the touch."

He gazed at her as her eyes lifted to his. As soon as they connected, he spotted the hair on her arms rose. Her face flushed, then went white. She jerked away from him and teetered on her feet. Jatsu caught her before she fell on her face.

"Are you all right?"

"Commander, we need to leave," Luka said, interrupting them, and Cassie took the chance to push his hands away.

"I'm fine. Don't fuss. I got lightheaded for a moment, that's all."

Jatsu realized she hadn't stopped wringing her hands. He kept his gaze centered on her as he spoke to Luka in their language. Luka nodded and slipped outside.

Jatsu stepped close to her and held both of her shoulders. "Do you have a family? A male in your life?"

Her chin lifted and her voice trembling, Cassie asked, "Why? What's it to you?"

"As my mate, you will come with us. If you have a family, or if the chief of your clan is nearby, I must give them my word that you will never want for anything."

"This is a joke, right? You don't want me. I'm a janitor, for heaven's sake! I clean toilets. You don't know who I am."

"It doesn't matter. Besides, the guards know you helped me, and if they can't capture me tonight, they will torture you. Then, when I surrender myself, they will kill you in front of me just to gain more information about my people."

"What?" Cassie started pacing in front of him. "I can't leave. What about Kitty? I can't leave her here."

"She will come with us." His eyes turned hard. "We must leave now. And if you won't go with me by your own free will..."

Two minutes later, carrying Cassie in his arms, he and his warriors ran toward their ship. The glare she gave him spoke volumes, though, and with good reason. He had to gag her and tie her hands to avoid alerting the search party.

Deep inside, Jatsu grinned from ear to ear. She put on a worthy fight. Her spirit matched his. And like him, she refused to take orders she didn't agree with!

He caught up with Rusto and Zoren Bely, who carried Kitty in a box Cassie had called a carrier.

Cassie continued to glare at him, but instead of mumbling through the gag, her hands stroked his skin anyplace within reach, despite her bound wrists. He realized she didn't know what she was doing. Despite the circumstances, her touch aroused him.

He came to a stop, signaled Luka that he sensed both the recon ship and someone who was walking by it.

Cassie's glare switched to concern.

"It's all right. We are near the ship, but we're not alone. Two of my guards will take care of it."

Cassie's neck was getting sore from turning her head around and trying to see what — She was on a spaceship.

She figured she was gawking like a kid seeing a carnival for the first time, and she was sure her mouth would be wide open if not for the gag. Jatsu's stride was so fast she thought she'd turn and try to climb over his shoulder to see everything. She opened her

mouth to say something and realized he had removed her gag.

When did that happen?

They came to a stop in front of a large double door that slid open

right away. Cassie lifted her chin and got ready to give him a piece

of her mind.

Jatsu spoke fast, a split second before she uttered her question.

"This is our medical department. They need to check us both to

make sure neither of us are carrying a tracker, a beacon, or worse,

some parasite that might harm us all."

Cassie trembled. Were they going to hurt her, what the scientists

had done to Jatsu? How would CynTech have put something in

her without her knowledge?

"Don't be afraid. My people are nothing like those who

captured me. Besides, I will stay with you the whole time."

"I didn't say anything. How'd you know what I was thinking?

Are you telepathic or something?"

"Only with you. It is part of being true mates, and our joining

will make it even stronger. You'll be able to hear me from miles

away."

"That thought makes me uncomfortable, Jatsu. What if I don't want you to knowing what I'm thinking?" She couldn't believe how scared she sounded.

"We will learn how to do that together. And yes, you need to do this, and no, it is nothing like what I experienced at CynTech."

Mica, his Chief Healer and best friend ran up to them as they entered Medical.

A soft ping from his comm interrupted his thoughts. Red lights flashed and a raucous noise bounced off the walls.

Mica addressed him right away. "Sire, there has been an accident in the propulsion area. Come with me, please. Two ReGen machines have been set aside for you in a private area; they'll tend to you while my assistants set up triage for the wounded."

The confusion on Cassie's face must have been clear, because Mica added, "Will she need a translator installed as well?"

"Yes, she is my true mate, so she will also need the history and customs of our people."

Mica's eyes widened. "Humans are compatible?"

"So, it would seem, my friend. God, Mahji doesn't make mistakes."

"Come on, let's get you both taken care of, then. I'll also run tests on her, so that I'll have a baseline ready."

Jatsu hadn't been so full of energy since he left the ship to explore Earth. Unbelievably, he had found his true mate! Excitement bubbled through him.

Unable to stay away he had to make sure she was all right. He put his hand on the ReGen glass cover to push it open when he noticed Mica approaching and lifted it off.

"How is my mate? Did you give her the translator?"

"Sire, there has been a problem. Your mate had something inside her brain."

"Mica! What are you saying? That they put something in her brain? Tell me, she isn't... she isn't dead, right? Is it a bomb? Will it explode if you take it out?" Anguish filled his eyes. "I can't live without her. Why isn't the ReGen healing her already?"

"Be at ease, Your Highness. The ReGen is doing its job as we speak. And no, it isn't something the humans made and placed in her. It is a growth, a parasite. She just needs more time in the ReGen machine, and her recovery will take longer than usual. You're going to have to be patient. She might have some temporary memory loss or not have all her motor functions for a short period. She'll need you by her side and might not be able to complete your bonding right away."

"That doesn't matter. What is important is for her to be all right."

Jatsu sat down in the chair next to the ReGen machine Cassie was in. He leaned closer as she stifled whimper and then a shout, he leaned closer. "I'm here, Cassie. Everything is going to be fine."

Inside, she thrashed from side-to-side. He whirled around to face Mica, pain lancing his brain as well. "Do something. She's hurt. Give her..."

Mica's hands flew over the control panel, and a cloud of blue smoke filled the machine.

"I am. The minute the ReGen sensed her discomfort, it started the process of delivering something to ease it. That blue cloud is part of it. It will dissipate when she is pain free again."

Jatsu's hands were clutching his head, and as the smoke thinned out, he dropped them on the glass cover.

"Sire, your bond with her is strong! You are mirroring her. I'm unsure what will happen to you if you stay too close. Besides, she will need to be in ReGen for a few days."

Jatsu stared at him. "I don't give a frake about me! She must be healed. She is all that matters. You, me?"

"Sire, please. My assistants will see to her, so she will never be alone, but you need to get some rest. I will call you when she stirs."

Still, he shook his head while staring at Cassie.

"Let me ask you, Mica. If she were your true mate, what would you do? The one person, your other half... would you stay or go? Can't you see we are one? To leave her side would be an act of desertion—betrayal. I can't and won't leave her." He took a deep breath and lifted his gaze to meet Mica's. "Did you know she put herself between me and four other males to protect me? Me, the one who is supposed to protect her?"

It did not surprise him as Mica's eyes widen in shock, and when Mica lifted a hand and squeezed his shoulder. "I will have a bed brought in for you."

The vibration under his fingertips woke Jatsu up. Soft thuds filled his ears. He stared at the clear cover and realized that she was moving inside the ReGen machine, thrashing from side to side.

"Mica! Mica! She's going to hurt herself!"

Several people came running, and within seconds, Mica was standing next to him. Jatsu's gaze flickered up at Mica for a moment, then went back to Cassie, feeling the same terror she was experiencing. It hurt him to see her attempt to sit up, only to bang her head against the cover. The second time she tried that, Mica retracted it. Tears were dripping down her face; her body was trembling all over. Without a word, Jatsu gathered her in his arms and sat down, whispering in her ear, "I've got you. You're all right. You're safe. I'm here."

She woke to whispered voices in a deep, soothing baritone. She opened her eyes and realized she was sitting on a man's lap. A quick peek around the room shouted hospital to her. The voices were calmer. One of the arms that held her moved. A calloused hand came under her chin and lifted her face.

Her gaze was snared by a pair of emerald-green eyes. She blinked, remembering they belonged to her alien man... wait, no. Jatsu.

He smiled at her.

"Sire, you need more rest."

Her eyelids were drifting closed already, but she forced herself to stay awake for a little longer. His face was so handsome and familiar, and his name. It was slipping out of reach.

She wiggled her left arm free and lifted her hand, wanting to run her fingers through his hair. Then she cupped the back of his head and drew him closer, but she couldn't keep her eyes open anymore.

There were two voices. One very familiar and another one she couldn't place. As he spoke, there was a smile in his voice. "Sire, you are right. Both of you need to rest. She needs to be near you as her body finishes healing. Take her to your quarters. I will come later to check on you both. You need not worry, though; her memory will return. You are the only medication she needs now."

His surrounding arms tightened as he stood, and someone placed a blanket over her.

Cassie stretched and opened her eyes. No pain. And she was in a bedroom.

The enormous bed she was in matched the size of the room. And the sound of voices filtered through an open door—masculine ones. One seemed familiar, and the other was strange. The one she recognized triggered feelings of trust and sexual desire. It drew her to him, as if that was where she belonged...at his side.

The voices were getting louder, but she couldn't make out what they were saying, not yet. Their lips were moving, and what they were saying sounded strange, but a second later she understood them.

She peeked in through the half-open door.

Both men were standing and were wearing similar clothing. Dark leather boots with pant legs tucked into them, a belt with weapons attached around their waists. Over their chests were metal plates held in place by straps on the sides and shoulders, exposing their toned bodies.

A man with brown hair was speaking, his voice was a deep bass, and rough, as if he didn't use it often. He was talking to a black-haired man, who at first glance looked like his twin.

"As you requested, we took the parts we recovered from your crashed flyer and we gave them to our scientists. The results came in a few moments ago. What happened to you wasn't an accident. They found traces of dymity. It was an attempt on your life."

"Did it reveal anything about who did it?"

The man shook his head. "Please, sit down, Sire. Jatsu. There's something else I must tell you. While you were imprisoned, we were sent word about an attempt on your parents' life."

Sire? Was he some kind of king or prince? There is no way I belong here.

She looked for another way out, but there was only one door. She'd have to walk right by them if she wanted to leave.

That is not happening.

"I believe the culprit is desperate now because you escaped. And when they find out you've found your true mate.... We must increase our surveillance, and you have to let us do our job."

"You're right, Luka. And we'll also need a guard for Cassie. I want Orion to be the captain; tell him to select ten to twelve elite warriors and to start their training right away. And you, Luka, add seven to nine more to mine. Then the two of you will coordinate."

Neither of them had been looking at her, but as soon as he finished talking, Jatsu turned to smile at her. Luka's eyes widened.

Uh-oh.

How did he know she was listening? Still, she smiled as Jatsu waved her forward.

"Come in, Cassie. I don't think I properly introduced you to my cousin. This is Luka Trehoe, the captain of my guards."

This Jatsu seems to know me... was that his bed?

She held out her hand to Luka, only to find him bowing with his right fist over his heart. She glanced up at Jatsu, then back at him. "It's very nice to meet you."

"Thank you, Your Highness. If there is anything we can assist you with, please let me know."

Your Highness? Why did he call her that?

Cassie's gaze bounced between Luka and Jatsu. She knew she had to look out of her depth, and even more so when Jatsu took her hand in his and pulled her into a hug.

She laid her ear on his chest as he held her closely. "Do you remember me? Where you are?"

He breathed in sharply as she rubbed her head against him.

"That's okay. Mica said it would take a few days for your memory to return.... My name is Jatsu, and you already know Luka. My warriors rescued us from CynTech four days ago, and a few hours later, you became very ill. We were in the middle of discussing a personal guard for you. Orion Chuffa would be its captain."

She gazed up at him, not caring if he realized how confused she was.

"Orion will be here later this morning, so I can introduce you to him."

Tightening her grip on his hand, Cassie stared at him, opening, and closing her mouth as her body trembled. Jatsu must think she was some kind of idiot.

"You're some kind of royalty? No, this is baffling. I've never been around anyone who was... I can't do this. I was orphaned before I was a year old. With my background, no one is going to respect me as a..."

She raised her eyebrows at him.

"I'm a prince, making you a princess. I may be in line for the throne, but my parents are ahead of me. It's my father's older brother who is the ruling king, so unless he is killed or dies of natural causes, he'll remain king. If anything happened. It wouldn't be for several years yet, which will give you more than enough time to become familiar with protocol."

Clinging to his hand, she asked, "Do I really need guards? Wait, do you think someone will get angry and want to harm me?"

Jatsu put his arm around her, drawing her even closer, and at once, her panic subsided. Somewhere deep down she sensed she was protected and safe, for the first time, since she started working at CynTech.

"No, Cassie, I don't believe anyone plans to hurt you. It is standard procedure for the Crown Prince and princess."

She saw Luka grimace as he glanced at them.

"Your Highness, sometimes people get so infatuated with one of the Royals that they would resort to stalking them. We'll protect you from them, creating no public incident."

Something was off about both their explanations. She couldn't put her finger on it, though. Knowing they were trying to protect her softened the lie, but that didn't mean she'd give them a free pass. Before she commented on it, her knees buckled, and a sharp pain pierced her head. If it wasn't for Jatsu's protective arm, she'd have fallen to the floor.

As he picked her up he yelled at Luka, "Get Mica, now!"

He placed her on the bed and pulled the covers up to her chin. She grabbed his neck as he was tucking the blanket around her, hovering. "Please, don't leave me. I'm hurt... need you."

"It's okay, I won't. Let me shift you a little so I can lie down next to you."

Cassie scooted over to make room for him.

Shortly afterwards, Luka entered the room with a stranger.

The stranger went straight to her side of the bed. "What happened, Your Highnesses? All Luka could tell me was to hurry."

It was bad enough having Luka see her in Jatsu's bed, but another stranger seeing her, too. She felt the color rising on her face.

"I'm sorry, your Highness, you might not remember me. I'm Mica, the Senior Medic on this ship, and Prince Jatsu's personal physician. Now, tell me what happened?"

"I was fine, then my knees gave out, and it seemed as if a sharp knife was stabbed straight through my brain."

She kept her eyes on Mica as he pulled out something from his jacket pocket. It looked like a cell phone, only it wasn't one, and her eyes were glued to it.

He adjusted some settings, probably, then he used it to scan her from head to toe. A screen appeared over her.

Mica smiled.

"Ah, her brain is responding to the language implants. When it is uploading, it can cause pain." He reached into a bag he carried and pulled out a gun-like device. "This will take care of the headache, and I am prescribing bedrest for you both."

Cassie's face turned pink at the veiled innuendo.

Once Mica and Luka were gone, she tilted her head to ask Jatsu about it, but his lips covered hers first. Then, the only thing that mattered was the taste of him. She opened her mouth wider to let him in as her fingers ran through his hair and she traced his ear, his jaw.

When they parted, they were both panting.

"You just got out of the ReGen machine last night. Are you really ready to seal our commitment to each other? If it is too much too soon, tell me."

"I must be honest. My body is telling me it knows you, but mentally, I don't. I am very drawn to you, but I don't think I am ready. I need to remember first... can you accept that?"

"Yes, my heart, I can and will. We will take all the time you need. When you are ready, we will take it further."

Two Weeks Later

Tonight was the night. She didn't tell him yet, but she remembered everything, and tonight was going to be a new memory for them both.

Cassie stared at herself in the mirror. She was holding a sheer nightgown, trying it out. The thought of seducing Jatsu caused her to blush, which was stupid. If the mere thought of being intimate with Jatsu embarrassed her, how was she going to make the first move? Jatsu wouldn't take the lead, not after he promised her. He would respect her wishes until she was ready for deeper intimacy.

That left her to do it.

After swearing Orion to secrecy, before asking him to help set up a romantic dinner featuring Jatsu's favorite foods and liquor. She didn't want him drunk, just tipsy enough to help her get over her embarrassment.

A soft knock on the bedroom door made her flinch. To her ears, it sounded as loud as a bomb.

"Your Highness. Prince Jatsu has left the bridge and is on his way here."

"Thank you, Orion. Have you laid out the food like I asked?"

"Yes, your Highness."

There was a smile in his voice. She wasn't going to let it bother her.

"Good. You can leave as soon as he arrives—and thank you again for your help."

A few moments later, Jatsu's voice filtered through. He was chatting with Orion. After taking a deep breath, she changed into her nightgown.

When the sound of the door closing again signaled Orion's departure, she stepped into their living room. Jatsu looked up from some papers. When their eyes met, his jaw dropped, and so did everything he was holding. He moved so fast her gown plastered itself to her body. Nothing was hidden from view.

He lifted his hands to rest on her hips. "Are you sure?"

In reply, she stood on her tiptoes and kissed him. She poured all her love and desire into it. She wanted him to know that she had no doubts.

"I've loved you since my first day at CynTech. My heart and mind are ready, and my mating marks match yours. I want you. I chose this gown so you could see me and what I feel."

Jatsu held her hands in his. "Will you, Cassie, accept me, Jatsu Trehoe, as your true mate, till death and beyond?"

Cassie kissed his palm before looking into his eyes and letting him see how much he meant to her.

"I accept you, Jatsu Trehoe, as my true mate, till death and beyond."

"We are now one," Jatsu said, wrapping her in his arms. "Not even death can separate us."

The only sound was the sound of their passion, melding their hearts, bodies, and minds.

ACKNOWLEDGEMENT

I would like to acknowledge several people, my husband, Robert, the team from Transcendent Authors who have been so supportive, and my editor, Ruby Novak of bookshelvesandteacups.com

AUTHOR BIOGRAPHY

Kathleen has been married to Robert for forty-seven years. They have two children, five grandchildren, and three great-grandchildren. During her Air Force career, she traveled widely, living in several states, as well as in Turkey and England.

Following her retirement, she pursued three other careers: senior pastor's private secretary, Mary Kay Cosmetics consultant/director, and designer for small dog clothing. She has used her knowledge of writing as a script judge for the international Show Low Film Festival/White Mountain Film Festival held in Show Low AZ, for the past two years.

Kathleen's dream of becoming a fiction writer came true in 2020, when her group, Transcendent Authors, published their first anthology, *Tolerance—A Collection of Short Stories.*

Since then, Kathleen has produced and published five other anthologies with Transcendent Authors: *Autumn—An Anthology, Spring—The Unexpected, Winter—An End and a Promise, and Deceit.* Their seventh book, *Fate,* will launch in November 2024.

Kathleen's novel, *King of Onus, Book One of the Onus Chronicles,* a Space Opera, will be in e-book, paperback, and hardback, on December 19th, 2023.

CHOOSE

There are so many choices to make when it comes to living. Aren't you a lucky thirty-two-year-old, paying off credit card X or credit card Y or card Z?

Balance on card X is $455. Balance on card Y is $1,200. Balance on card Z is $3,000. And card Z is closed. But first things first.

You don't even want to think about how those balances swelled, became a bloated body. But once you had a tabula rasa. Offers. Credit cards flirted with you. You had a bank account that wasn't always in the red. Then came the grad school days, the post-workshop beers, the Christmas pub crawls where people revealed comically sad truths, and you had sushi and Mexican dinners just for the sake of grace and luxury. Then you wasted even more on groceries because they made you feel secure. You wouldn't end up on the news at food banks or wearing ripped jeans. Surely, you wouldn't have to eat TV dinners, another average Joe and Jane. You didn't want to be your parents, who ate that dreck with plastic knives and forks and pretended to give you and Nan the gourmet experience (while Mom and Dad wore worn-out midnight-colored jeans and tank tops).

But enough with the regrets. The past is scratched into your consciousness like people's contact numbers on a bathroom stall, as your sister would say. You live in an apartment complex that reeks of weed, shit, and stale feet, whose external color scheme alternates between guacamole and bubblegum pink. On top of that your room has a view of a dumpster where pizza boxes and cans of Keystone and Pabst are laid to rest, along with crushed boxes of Trojans and Tampons.

But this is your life now, a schmuck in an apartment where people party with desperation, and the bass of malaise thumps away night after night.

So assess your choices. Stroke your chin.

Start with the cards. At least you can live without the heating and cooling and all of that. Don a sweater. No, you don't even need a sweater. Nan always said you must have lived in Siberia in a previous life. And you've run around in the rain (and the snow) more than a few times, relishing the chill. On top of that, you can sneak into the nearby gym with its neat, tiled floors and sleek steel ceilings and snag a shower or two as needed. They know you from the good days.

Cards, alas, are not so simple.

Pay card X off, and you can close out that sucker here and now. One step forward. But you know paying off card Y is the better course of action, long-term.

Of course, pay off card Y, and you just have enough for the cell phone bill. And you're relegated to rationing those few microwaveable dinners. Most meals will entail you ravaging onions. You might break crackers into pieces. If you're lucky, maybe squeeze out the remnants of that old Dijon mustard, along with any crumbs in your secondhand sofa.

But to pay off card Z is an even better option where responsibility is concerned. It's responsible, but not necessarily pragmatic. After all, the card has been closed.

Pragmatism and responsibility are mortal enemies. Pragmatism isn't what's right, but what keeps you going. Responsibility is a world of neat lines of righteousness, which the world's self-proclaimed gatekeepers laid out, the tech titans, the politicians in empty suits, all of them.

It's your choice. You could and maybe should take responsibility.

But then you'll be relegated to less than crumbs. And you'll probably have no cell phone, which you need in case you get job offers. You're trying to make a name in the world. But more importantly, you'll have no Internet. To hell with the phone (although everything is on a mobile app these days, so strike that). You've flung a thousand other applications at the world, and even offered editing services. You've proclaimed the ability to find missing Oxford commas and tighten up metaphors. Attack gerunds. Fast turnaround. You pronounce all those things in every font except mundane old Times New Roman.

You've even stormed LinkedIn, stormed through Glassdoor and every other so-called job site, only to find ad after ad for content writers, freelance writers. You find a few editing positions, and a couple writing ones as well. But they're all marred by the word "volunteer." Ad after ad proclaims how you might not get any Benjamins, but you'll get experience for actual paying jobs. A record to brag about. A chance to serve others in the nonprofit sector.

You have experience. You don't have time for altruism (and why the hell should you work 80 hours a week for bupkis?). You just need Benjamins.

You've already lost your job as a barista at Mama Lily's coffee shop, with the sunshine-colored walls and the too neat oak tables,

seemingly devoid of scratches and personal histories. It was a time
for tightened belts, Mr. Schenck said, while a PA system assaulted
you with an orgy of Taylor Swift, Katy Perry, John Denver, and
Chicago.

And you lost a position at a movie theater before that, Reel
Time 21. It was a place that reeked of popcorn and pretzels,
and bro-scented deodorant (coupled with giant neon lights that
tried to excite viewers with flickering pink and purple). On top
of that, it had flooring that resembled ralphed-up cranberries at
Thanksgiving.

Not fast enough, was Mr. Van Pelt's judgment. You needed to
sweep faster, think an hour ahead. Unearth every rogue kernel of
popcorn. Assault every Skittle. Think of your broom as a Panzer.
Smile, just a little. But of course, Van Pelt and your past superiors
could have trained you (except where smiles were concerned),
learned how to adjust their belts better. Did they have to fire you?
Didn't they have their own range of choices as supervisors? Didn't
they have the luxury of mercy?

You've had some nibbles with the editing work. But promises
put nothing more than puke-green TV dinners on the plastic
coffee table. Of course, more established people can afford to offer

empty words. Their credit scores are solid, and they drive minivans.
They don't drive a Dodge Stratus on which some chucklehead
drew a penis on the driver-side window. You envy their empty
words. However, you cannot afford to be envious too long.

But back to the cards.

Card Z has already been closed. So no additional credit to keep
you afloat on Z. It's just about cleaning up the crap. Long-term
responsibility really does not pay here. With card X and Y, at least
you can restore some modicum of credit. Enough to grab a few TV
dinners at the market with its salmon-colored walls and aisles the
length of a 150-car train. You might even grab a bottle of Pepsi for
caffeinated courage.

You're such a lucky bastard. So many choices. And that's just the
tip.

Choose to treat your sister, Nan, to discount dinners at that
little sushi joint around the corner (Thursday and Sunday evening
specials). Or stockpile more sodium-infested TV dinners. Treat
her, and you get to see that little crooked smile that sneaks through
her stress, that makes the rings around her eyes a little less wide.
Maybe you can get into your old banter. In particular, you love to
talk about how every dictator had a bad father.

"Come on, Nicky," she'd laugh, but you'd see the gleam, the passion rising, as she prepared to spar with you. "Present your evidence, little brother."

"Hitler, Stalin, Mussolini, Kim Jong-Un, probably Castro," you'd say, ticking them off with a confidence Nan couldn't argue with. And she'd laugh and find some way to poke holes in your argument. But you love this side of Nan, this small bit of power she holds.

She deserves this, a hard-working history teacher, whom the world wants to blame. They call her a Commie every time she inveighs against the state for cutting educational budgets. They want to relegate her to the dustbin of history when she fulminates against tax cuts for "cologne-drenched barons." And they call her Karen when she pushes students to think beyond dry rote learning.

"The meek inherit the Earth, but the assholes get all the breaks, honey," she said the last time you met for coffee, which of course, she paid for.

"Don't be cynical," you say, even though you knew then and know now it's true. "You're a great teacher."

"It's not just about me. I want you to have a good life," she said, and you'd wanted to cry so hard, wanted her to say something that she wanted in life. A trip to the Oregon Coast? To own an obnoxiously large plasma TV? To just want to break something, to destroy a window, to smash open a jukebox, some act that held power and danger and animal-like ferocity?

"I'm all right," you'd said, but she'd looked at you with a detective's eye, a sisterly eye. "A few setbacks here and there, but I'll get back on top. You just focus on being a kickass teacher."

"Are you all right?" she said. Her voice dropped and deflated into something beyond sad. "Are you actually all right?"

You remembered the way the coffee shop door had clanged open as she said that, laughter assaulting you and Nan, hyena-like, discordant. Professionals in Khakis and button-down striped shirts had come in, stalking out their turf. They assessed you both in that corner table with the wobbly chairs and pathetically small plastic cups, thinking a thousand things through hazel and cold blue eyes. Maybe they'd thought you were peasants in sweatpants and tank tops, underlings, people out of your sphere, or worse, relegated to your proper, poor place. You remember the groan of another jingoistic-flavored country song from those godawful speakers in the ceiling.

And you remember Nan.

She knew and still knows.

She lives in her own apartment, albeit one with turd-colored walls. Poor Nan finds joy only in the study of the past and in the Tchaikovsky that rises with sorrow from her Spotify playlist. There's also her HBO, her one, small luxury.

But you also have less to eat, and your cell phone and Internet are imperiled. You won't even have those fleeting little nibbles. But Nan will smile, and you can pay off that little debt. She once radiated energy and taught you to fight, taught you to pursue your love for literature and the verve of words and the whirl of the past. Surely, that's enough.

Then of course, there's the matter of the rent. Even more choices. You could go to the property manager, Ms. Schmidt, and explain the situation. Nan always said being honest is the best course of action, even if it's also the most painful one short-term. But Ms. Schmidt thinks in methodical coldness, in monthly charges, not monthly sorrows. You've watched her work the complex, and evict people even younger than you, reviewing each missed charge with precision.

Or you could make up a sick grandmother and hope the tiny violins work. Or two sick grandmothers. At one point, you even consider making up a story about Nan. Tumors? She was run down by a train? No, no, no. That's the stuff of betrayal, of dark movies, of corrupt hearts. This is your sister. Credit cards say "fuck you," but Nan just recites the word "love" like a liturgy. You feel something sharper than shame (and consider sleeping against coffee shop walls and in alleyways to atone).

You will not throw Nan or your grandmothers under the bus. Or the train, in this case.

Maybe you should try to pay Card X and Card Y. See if your responsibility, in fact, may pay off for once. Seek out an increase (however unlikely) and help with that rent payment. At least for a month. Forget card Z for now.

So many choices, so much agency swelling in your head.

What do you do?

Maybe take to copiously consuming White Russians with the Kahlua, Bailey's, and Smirnoff you once treated yourself to. That was back when you still thought you could get work, good, steady work and deserved some small luxury.

Or maybe you take to streaming superfluous dross on Nan's HBO account, which she so kindly shares, because she knows you hate the word "pity," more than you hate words from your academic days. Words such as "problematic" and "paradigm."

Maybe do both. Maybe you drink at three in the afternoon while watching episodes of *Curb Your Enthusiasm*, laughing as Larry's foibles make your life look good. Sink into the sofa, watching Larry stab Ben Stiller in the eye with a skewer. Release the few remaining reserves of laughter as he draws Hitler mustaches on magazines.

But you cannot adapt with Larry's easiness, walking along cheerfully.

Maybe you watch *Barry* instead, because he's a hitman turned actor. That makes all your possible choices paradise by comparison.

Maybe you lie awake at night, the bags under your eyes expanding, like Nan's. Perhaps you feel even worse because you should give something to her. You owe her big time. Even if it's a pathetic, small plastic cup of coffee that's already cold, or a cheap, little card from a thrift store, the words I LOVE YOU scrawled in festering script.

Maybe you tuck away the choices into your desk. Try to close it over and over, but just end up hearing the choices screech and squawk. They will not be ignored.

A true choice would be to pour out that booze. Fling those bottles against the damn dumpster, and watch something break under your rage, cream and vodka streaming away. And maybe tell Nan that you almost killed her off just to keep your roof.

Or maybe, just maybe, you close your eyes. Make a choice. Any choice. You'll lose, but it's a choice. It's an action. A responsibility. The coldest word in the world. The enemy of pragmatism. Tell that to your sister. Tell it to yourself.

Nan will ask you, "are you really all right? Are you sure about it?"

It's your responsibility. It's your choice.

AUTHOR BIOGRAPHY

Mir-Yashar Seyedbagheri is a graduate of Colorado State University's MFA fiction program. His stories, "Soon," "How To Be A Good Episcopalian," "Tales From A Communion Line," and "Community Time," have been nominated for Pushcarts. Mir-Yashar's work has been published in *SmokeLong Quarterly*, *The Journal of Compressed Creative Arts*, *Fiction on the Web*, and *Ariel Chart*, among others. He lives in Garden Valley, Idaho.

TRANSFUSIUM

"If any other soul had dared to describe this deformity of a life that I live, I would have declared it the ravings of madness. But, this malignancy of an existence I cannot ignore, nor fully explain, conjures in my mind that all is a waking dream."

Ivy Vengerov wrote these words in her journal as she looked out the window of the Alexandra Orphanage in Haverstock Hill, London.

On the entry road, a motor carriage puttered past unkept landscape. Along the path, overgrown with plants of the forest variety, the steam motor announced the coming of a stranger. Nearing the building, thorny vines gave way to foxglove, corncockles, and bluebells. Within sight of the orphanage, the grounds became more reserved and stately. In front of the dark brick structure, crudely sculpted shrubs formed a center piece within a semi-circular path.

Clematis vines rose from dried grasses along the edge of the building, reaching the first row of windows. The flowers, missing petals, and wilted, announced the ending of summer. Autumn approached and the long days had ended. Low clouds, thick, and pillowy, resembling thunder clouds, were a promise of cold air.

A broad-shouldered man bobbled in the seat of the motor wagon, bringing it to a halt near the furthest left side of the circular path. Under large driving goggles, the lines shorn upward from his square jaw seemed cut from stone. He waited, scanning the grounds.

Standing in the yard's center, a young man raked among some bushes, as another jockeyed a cart near him with the help of a mule. The man with the cart placed a pipe in his mouth and rested his fists on his hips, studying the new arrival. His large, thick trousers held up by suspenders, were tucked into his boots, making him resemble a Cossack. A clean white shirt showed his status among the two men. The other, younger and more energetic, toiled among the grabbing branches and thorns.

From the entrance, a top-hatted gentleman and gowned woman exited the building in a rush. She was crying, while the man remained stern. With a cane in one hand, he tugged her arm with his other as she covered her mouth with a handkerchief. A line of girls marched from the far side of this working-school, toward the entrance. They passed the multitude of windows framed by tilted, and sometimes missing, window shutters.

The driver surveyed the surroundings, withdrew folded papers from his vest, then watched the many destitute faces that peered from the windows of what seemed a children's prison. Their ardent gazes fixed on what they knew to be adoption papers; a prize to be won. *To whom will it recompense?* Their minds burned with wonder.

The driver formed an unpleasant smile as he withdrew a tincture of laudanum from his front pocket. His thumb rubbed over the red stained label as he looked down at it, further disintegrating its corner. An anodyne to his grief. An addiction he inherited from his predecessor. He removed the cork and swigged. The bitter taste was a minor toll on his only passage for rest, physically and spiritually.

The motor wagon rumbled as steam sprayed from the boiler like a genie escaping a bottle. The judder of the engine conjured in him a vision which he had had several times. With the wind harnessing the thick white gas contrary to his direction, the memory, like the steam, blanketed his sight:

Shouts poured in from far and near after a wretched shriek pierced his ears. Below a railing at the stern of a ship, a man tumbled inside a paddle boat wheel. His limbs twisted against the unforgiving force.

His body vanished and reappeared over and over, bouncing and

splashing from the maddening torrent. The paddle slowed against

the driving energy of its own waves; a steam whistle screamed.

The driver jolted from the nightmare as his motor wagon hissed

and sputtered, straining to stop.

"Mister Roth, I presume."

"Agh, yes," he gasped as his eyes refocused.

"Your steam buggy, Sir," a woman shouted. "Deactivate it!"

The orphanage administrator stood beside him, staring through

glassy spectacles. A browbeating forewoman, the kind that

flourished in this setting. Her arms crossed in front, stern lipped.

Clad in a wool overcoat, her armor, she barked, "Mister Roth, do

you hear me?"

"Yes, yes, Madam, Administrator Edwards?" his voice crackled.

"You may call me Erik." He wiped perspiration from his brow,

disengaged the driving mechanism, and stalled the motor. He

removed his driving goggles and stared back with bruised, sunken

eyes. She retracted as if in the presence of a leper. The man looked

around, realizing the workmen had vanished.

"The children will be ready shortly." She paused. "Are you well,

Mister Roth?" She swallowed, dry-throated. "I mean Erik?"

Erik nodded once, then sideways, cracking the bones in his neck. "It's a long journey from the Bramburgh castle."

"Bramburgh?" Her expression turned curious. "That is a long way. It was told to me, the castle was sold, as the trust for ownership was depleted. Further, you cannot expect to make it there by nightfall."

"We will stop along the way if necessary." Erik took a deep breath. "A year past, madam, it was purchased by the industrialist and inventor William Armstrong. The Baron has provided him his expertise in hydraulic machinery, in exchange for accommodation after a pressing need to leave Bavaria. It is now a convalescent home for retired gentlemen. The Baron, being in recovery from a prolonged illness, will soon be well."

"The Baron Raskovarni?" Her head rose.

"That is correct," he replied, batting his eyes.

Her demeanor calmed. "I see... Can I get you a refreshment while you wait? You look famished."

"No, Madam Administrator. I have brought provisions. We will be stopping throughout the peregrination." He reached out, presenting the adoption orders.

She took the folded papers, nodded, short and abrupt, turned on her heels and retreated toward the building's entrance with a quick stomping march. His eyes followed her, and then up toward the crumbling facade of the once majestic building, much like the one he endured as a child in Bavaria. Flashes of adolescent faces blazed like a montage before his eyes. He shook his head to end it, then took another sip of laudanum.

With the bottle turned up, he noticed Madam near the entrance, staring in his direction. She watched him with the spellbound appearance of a cat whose attention was snatched by a bird in a tree.

As he reflected, she changed her course back toward him, and with that same gaze. He sat as she approached. His eyes now blazed, more intrigued than concerned. She appeared lovely in her penetrating stare and confident advance, not as the strident ramrod of orders she was a moment ago. His expression welcomed her.

She walked toward the motor wagon, paused, and then smiled with a small nod of her head. "Please, Erik, won't you come in and wait? I have something to show you."

Erik took a deep breath, pulled a pocket watch from his vest, then tucked the watch back in, along with the bottle. "Madam Administrator, I really should... I mean, we should be moving on." He sat firm with one hand upon the steering mechanism and the other upon his knee.

"Call me Ivy." She placed a gentle hand on his arm.

He shot a look toward her eyes that did not shy away, then down at her hand, that did not tremble. "Perhaps it would be healthful to stretch my legs." This time, a smile did emerge from his mouth.

Erik nodded with acceptance. He bowed and then reflexed as he stepped to the ground. He removed an overcoat from his prodigiously powerful body and dropped it on the seat of the carriage.

Ivy stepped back as she took notice. "You are a man of great physical virtue, Erik. You must labor excessively."

"My duties for the Baron require..." Erik paused, staring somewhere beyond.

Ivy interrupted, "It is not important now. Relax. You have had a long journey. Please, follow me."

They walked to the steps of the entrance, where two short buttresses stood out on either side.

Erik stopped as he touched Ivy's arm. "That look you gave me as you stood here at the steps."

She did not pull away, but waited for its meaning.

"Once before, I had seen this look," Erik added. "Gretchen, my dear sister." His head hung low.

"That is sweet. Where does she live?" Ivy asked.

"She does not." Erik replied, continuing to stare downward, as if in a memory.

Ivy put her hand to her mouth. "I am so sorry. I didn't mean—"

Erik interrupted, looking up, "I caught her in such a gaze as you possessed when we passed each other on the staircase of the old castle."

Ivy remained silent as Erik gazed off.

"Thinking back, I regret not taking this wanton curiosity of hers up on its offer to be quenched." He balled his fist. "Five years into our arrangement with the Baron. Gretchen, a seamstress, and I, a stable groom among other tasks. Her eyes begged me to confess the nature of the strange happenings at the Baron's estate. A gift it would have been, to bare it all." He shook his clenched fist. "And ease my soul. Perhaps..." He looked at the clouds. "If I had not passed on that offer, I would not carry the heavy burden I do to this day."

Erik turned to Ivy. "If only I had the strength to open what is left of this granite heart to a creature warm and understanding."

They paused, Ivy and Erik, each waiting for the other to acknowledge their connection. A union of minds formed where one knows entirely the other, but only wishes for approval.

Erik continued, "Gretchen, to whom I loved with the deepest affection, and could never harm. I rejected any thought of filling her mind with those treacheries. When she made her offer, I turned my eyes down and away. Hers did the same, and never again did she look at me the same."

Erik shook his head. "I should not have told you that."

There was an awkward silence.

"Let's enter the house and have a seat, Erik." Ivy took him by the arm and led him inside.

She shut the door behind them, which announced the stranger. In small groups and some alone, children stood speechless. A ball bounced to a stop and one small child ran to another. Then there was silence. The small faces watched with anticipation.

"This way, Erik," Ivy said, pulling him through a corridor past the lobby.

Inside another room, Ivy offered Erik a seat. "Some tea?" she asked as he sat.

"No, thank you."

Ivy smiled. "So many curious children here, it was best to not linger in their presence. We can talk here."

"I enjoyed seeing them," Erik replied. "Their hopeful expressions were a reminder of my boyhood."

"Where was that?" Ivy asked.

"Bavaria." Erik answered. "It had been so long now, since those days, that my youth seems like a dream, a happy dream."

"You are a long way from where you started, but you seem to be doing well." Ivy answered.

"A long way." Erik nodded, looking down. "And a long time. These decades have vanished as if devoured in a shadow of my imagination."

Ivy moved next to Erik, touching his arm. "I can see something troubles you." Her eyes narrowed. "What was it that you wanted to tell your sister so many years ago? For whatever it is, it still troubles you now. And why not tell me, for you may never see me again."

"Oh, how I long to tell my secret, but there is no being who could understand except he that already knows the truth, The Baron."

"The Baron Raskovarni?" Ivy asked.

"Who else?" Erik answered, raising a fist. "Who else could torture a man as he does and keep him loyal?"

"Can't you just leave?" Ivy asked as she held his arm. "Tell me why?"

"Why?" Erik stared off. "For why, I must dig deep. Because now, my mind, filled with so many bizarre incongruent memories, it is difficult to distinguish between the real and the imaginary. Again, I ponder its meaning, rehearsing my life, and his. Every memory that ever flickered before my eyes. My actions, and those of my master, are interwoven in such a way that I often wake feeling that I am him. And, like all dreams, no matter how horrific, or sublime, once awake, the feeling of now soon takes over, and what I must do to go on rushes to the forefront.

I live, or should I say, exist in a troubling way. An existence that is to serve the Baron. In doing so, I have become a vessel of his thoughts, wisdom, and desires. My place is one of necessity. My vocation, something of a caretaker and undertaker. I have learned to cope with his impending needs. And though every instance fills me with an impulse to run away, his desires seize my mind. I am spellbound by the power that he has and which envelops me; a strength I feed from, and that feeds from me. Yet this servitude to his existence that has garnered me great status, and strength is a curse.

The phantasm of my existence is still something of a mystery to me, however, I have totally accepted it. In this ambiguity, I live out a life that has repeated many times over. How much of it my direct involvement and how much fed to me by my strange bond with the Baron makes me wonder. This torture alone drives me to ignore those thoughts. My sanity has become the product of accepting my fate, of not questioning what I have done, or what he has done. And though, my siblings have since passed away from old age, the primary stranglehold the Baron had upon me is now broken. Yet, this is now my life. I take some triumph in having cheated death for so long, but life has cheated me.

My face, you see, etched with the scars of having lived as long as I have, is now a mask I wear. It inspires fear, except in you. This, combined with my abnormal strength, is monstrous. It serves me with the needs of the Baron, which have become more frequent since my predecessor, Burkhart, expired.

Burkhart, a demon to a devil, and who I feared more than any man, I now have empathy. It is only in these latter years that I feel I knew him, and maybe how he possibly felt toward me. His benign brutality, lips stained red from opium, or Chinese molasses as he named it, and his late-night ravings as he burned this midnight oil, inhaling the toxin, curdled my blood.

His behaviors, which appeared born from madness, I now realize, were an escape from it. His journey, like my own, scarred his soul. And though I have doubted that he had a soul, I now doubt my own, but know that I once did before I became the same demon of sorts."

"This is by far a most amazing tale you tell." Ivy stood. "Perhaps you can tell me what this contraption in this other room is? My late predecessor left it here. I cannot understand its purpose."

Erik stood, following Ivy to yet another room that was padlocked and bolted.

"It was only after the last Administrator passed away that I found the key to this confounded bolt," she grunted, sliding a metal rod through a latch on a door.

Ivy pushed the solid wood door open. "Excuse the odor. It is quite foul."

Inside, with no light except that which was cast through the door, sat chairs with tubes suspended overhead and broken glass jars strewn about the floor. Stains like dried brown paint circled the chairs.

"Der Transfusium," Erik whispered.

"The what?" Ivy asked.

"I never dreamed that there was another of these machines." Erik's eyes searched the room. Glass crunched under his feet as he stepped near it. "This one is incomplete." He ran his fingers along the tubes that hung from a suspension. "There is no power source or hydraulic compressor."

"What is it for?" Ivy implored.

"Who have you shown this to?" Erik asked.

"To no one, except the groundskeeper, Ivan, whom you saw in the yard. He knew the late Administrator, before I, but could not tell me what she did in here."

Erik turned and sat in one chair, his hands caressing the arm rests. His eyes stared into the darkness.

"What does this all mean?" Ivy asked.

"I must now tell you everything for you to understand what this means. I must tell you my beginning, or you can call it an end, but it started when I was adopted as a child."

Erik gazed into the distance, taking a deep breath. "Looking back to that time, I wonder if there was any path other than the one chosen for me. The circumstances, no matter how unfortunate, were not uncommon for a child in my state. In those days, that now seem story-bookish, an opportunity arose for me and my siblings that would have been impossible to decline. In that way, I have conceded that perhaps I chose this life.

My journey started when a man named Burkhart transported me, my sister, and my brother from an orphanage many years ago in a horse-drawn carriage down a wicked road.

I can still remember the leafless winter tree branches that arched over the path, lifeless yet alive, as we approached the Baron's estate. My dear sweet sister Gretchen's thirteen-year-old face was so cheerful then as she tested the bow in her hair. Innocent little Peter, then eleven, played with a curtain's tassel that swung from the carriage window.

Miss Ostrom, the orphanage housemother, I remember how she slapped Peter's hand with a ruler, shouting, 'Don't force me to take you back.' She, then skewered us all with her eyes. 'Behave!' She shouted, as her thin lips tightened, showing her teeth.

My fear of her shook me like the trot of the horses over the ruts of the road. I was older than the others, but still a boy, and looked forward with hope toward the secluded mansion that drew nearer.

We turned into a deep circular driveway. The wheels grinding as the horses galloped through the gravel. Their hooves crunched as we came to a halt. The ponderous coachman's exit rocked the carriage. His steps threshed through the small stones with the stride of a tall and heavy man. We climbed out, and he stood before us. I first noticed those read stained lips. His cheekbones stabbed outward like the hips of an old horse, under deep-set irritated eyes, like the ones I now possess. He turned his slouching, powerful shoulders and walked toward the mansion. His bodily proportions demonstrated great strength.

'Children? Prepare to greet your new master,' Miss Ostrom snapped at us. Her pointed chin guided us as she raised it in the air. The ruler she held in her grip was a menacing promise, which had struck my knuckles many times over.

I tilted my head back and viewed the magnitude of the gothic fortress. Dark lichen-splotched sandstone blocks rose skyward. At its highest, the walls seemed to lean over me against the passing clouds. The windows mirrored the blackened stone like the many eyes of a waiting spider. I felt miniscule.

Three Doberman pinschers appeared from the right side of the mansion. They whined with excitement, stopping near the coachman at the bottom of the stone steps leading to a platform before the door. The largest of the dogs took sight of me. Its elation faded with a low baritone growl.

'Good, Petra.' The driver patted the beast.

The coachman climbed the stairs with sculptured lions on either side. He pounded an iron ring suspended on a reinforced door; the reverberation quieted the animals.

The entrance opened wide, revealing a stout, apron-clad woman. Near her, a frail, elderly man rested in a wicker wheelchair that reclined like a chaise lounge. Behind him, a magnificent staircase spiraled upward. The coachman walked inside and stepped behind the chair. He took it by its rear handles. His bent posture fit perfectly with the chair as if he were formed into it. Then, he pushed it forward. The large, spoked tires squeaked with a pitch from which the dogs retreated.

Miss Ostrom ushered us to the doorway. The smell of sour cabbage soup drifted out.

She extended a hand. 'This is Baron Roskavarni. You are fortunate to have such a wealthy master to take you in.'

A thin-skinned hand emerged from under a blanket stretched over the Baron's knees. His crooked finger motioned us in. 'Come close, let me look at my gifts,' his voice crackled.

We stepped through the door as the aproned woman stretched out a muscular arm toward Miss Ostrom, pushing her out. For once, since the death of our parents, I felt free from her grip.

'Have the stable groom take her back,' the old man commanded. He glanced up and back at the coachman. 'You've performed well, Burkhart.'

The burly woman pulled the door shut, the light faded, and the bolts latched.

The Baron clasped his palms as if sitting before a feast. 'Take the two young ones for supper, Magdalena.'

The stoic aproned woman nodded in agreement."

"Magdalena, you said?" Ivy interrupted.

"Yes. Why?"

"No reason, keep telling, Erik."

"Well, the Baron pursed his lips with discernment, reading me through the cloudy cataracts of his eyes. 'What is your age, young man?' He asked me, seeming to guess where I stood.

'Fourteen, the April last,' I answered as the woman drew my siblings away to the left wing of the house. I watched them vanish through a great sitting room decorated with portraits and heraldic shields.

The Baron inhaled as if sniffing a blossom. 'Ah, to be fourteen again.' His milky marbles rolled in their sockets, calculating as he wrung his hands. He lifted a pointed finger. 'Der Transfusium!' he shouted.

'Jawhol, Herr,' Burkhart answered, and bore into me with a hawkish gaze. 'This way, Erik,' Burkhart ordered. Then, turned the wheelchair to the right, heading down a hall, poorly lit and cold. We stopped before two large wooden doors that swung wide as the chair pushed through them.

We entered a dimly lit room. Mahogany bookcases filled the walls, but which could not accommodate the hundreds of other books that stood in dust-covered pillars alongside sculptures and lovely furniture. A strange musty odor filled my nostrils, something ancient and decayed.

A single wide band of sunlight entered at a sharp angle from a partly opened curtain. It lit the room and held captive infinite specks of dust. Our movements hurled invisible whirlwinds, sending this nebula into chaos. I realized no person had been in the room for quite some time. My eyes focused beyond into the darkness. At the rear of the room, an apparatus of chaotic design stood like a contradiction to the elegance.

Burkhart turned the Baron around and wheeled him back, setting him next to a system of glass cylindrical chambers on polished brass pedestals. Tubes hung from a suspension above them, and over an armchair on the other side. Just as you have here.

Burkhart then stepped past me. He closed the doors, locking them. I stood, pondering the meaning of it all.

'Schnell! Schnell!' the Baron demanded like a spoiled child as Burkhart marched toward me with the fortitude of an angry schoolmaster. From under my arm, he lifted me like I was a coat to be hung up.

He seated me with a harsh thrust into a chair, then secured me with a belt across my chest. He bound my wrists to the arms of the chair, leaning over me. A putrid odor emanated from his body. A sinking dread filled me.

'What did I do wrong?' I cried, but received no answer.

Burkhart stepped away and pulled down a lever on the strange apparatus. A mechanical winding sound intensified, as armatures with bizarre lights flashed from behind. It cast our twisted shadows against the wall in front of us, like spirits escaping our bodies. Burkhart's ghostly apparition rose upward and back across the ceiling. Its phantom arms flailed like tentacles as he operated the strange contraption.

The Baron writhed with pain when Burkhart slid long needles connected to tubes into the old man's arms. Burkhart then turned to me with needles in hand. I wrenched against the straps with all of my strength, knowing his intentions.

'Good,' Burkhart sighed. 'Show me your veins.'

I could only look away as he punctured each of my arms.

In between us and under the glass cylinders, an accordion-like bladder rose and fell with respiration. A suction tugged at me with each gulp of air it commanded.

The chamber next to me filled with bright red blood in spurts that matched the throb of the breathing machine. The Baron's was a vile brown that oozed like gravy. A tube extending from it led to my right arm. My mind swirled, and all went black, a horrid deathly black.

I awoke shrieking from a nightmare, looking about the room, unsure where I was. The glow of a candle now replaced the swatch of natural light. The Baron stood. No longer a sickly man, he rubbed his arm above his clenched fist. 'You are a rhapsody of vitality, Erik,' he heralded.

'What did you do to me?' I demanded with the little strength I had.

He rolled a shirt sleeve down and gave a knowing nod to Burkhart, who exited.

A horrid image flashed before my eyes; a boy, boney and limp. His body tossed into a shallow pit, like a rag doll. His limbs twisted like the strands of a wet mop. Facedown, he flopped before shovels of dirt splashed over him.

'Agh!' I exhaled. My eyes searched the room for an explanation. A trickle of sweat bled from my scalp.

'Shush.' The Baron placed a finger to his lips. 'I see you are already experiencing my memories. Oh, Erik, the things I have accomplished, and you will live them over again as Burkhart has.'

The sound of a chamber orchestra played in my head. A vision of an elegant woman wearing a gown flashed before me. She smiled with a promise of love. Then the music stopped, and she lay across a bed. A scream filled my ears. Bare bosomed, and with bulging eyes, veiny hands clutched her neck.

'Stop choking her!' I cried out, as my eyes must have stared somewhere beyond.

'Ah, the Viscountess Von Schlägl, perhaps?' The Baron said as he frowned with pity. 'I am not proud of everything I have done.' Then he shrugged. 'Some of which I have forgotten... It has been so many millennia.' His sadness faded. 'But, I feel your youth and optimism coursing through me now,' he said, raising a fist. 'Fantastisch!'

The Baron paced in front of me. 'I understand Petra has taken a dislike to you. I doubt you could reach the gate before she had you by the throat... But, if you escaped... Boys are clever that way. You would end up in the hands of Miss Ostrom once again, which would lead you back to me.'

I knew then that I was his prisoner. 'Please, don't hurt my sister and brother,' I sobbed, looking downward.

The Baron paused. 'Yes, little Peter.' He glanced to his side. 'He would have to take your place if you vanished, my Erik.' He blinked with satisfaction. 'And, sweet Gretchen, she's almost a woman, you know.' He leaned toward me with crystal clear eyes. 'Don't give me a reason to use them!'

I bobbed my head in agreement, fighting down the sickness of his rotten blood that flowed through me; his poison, his venom, the very affliction that made me what you see sitting before you.

'That's better,' the Baron answered. 'You need your strength, or should I say... I need it.'

My jaw gaped and my innocence flew from my throat with a prolonged, howling shriek that echoed through the mansion. The child in me died. I slumped in the chair. My limbs, like those of the trees, hung lifeless yet alive as the Baron removed my straps.

'This is only the beginning.' The Baron said as he took a deep breath. 'Ah, cabbage soup, it purifies the blood.' He then placed a gentle hand on my shoulder. 'You will come to accept it as they all have. Now, you must eat, for we will be together for many years, and one day... You will take Burkhart's place.'"

Erik sat slouching in the chair. "I have wanted to tell that story my whole life, and now you can understand how I have suffered."

"Yes, Erik, I understand." Ivy stepped behind Erik, caressing his broad shoulders. "I understand it all. And now you arrived to take another to the Baron, another that would take your place, another that would suffer as you have."

Erik tensed. His eyes searched the room, and he prepared to stand.

"Relax, Erik, I understand better than you know. You have to understand that my predecessor, Miss Magdalena Vasilescu, was the owner of this transfusium machine."

"Magdalena?" Erik whispered, as his head slowly turned.

"Yes, the same Magdalena you knew as a child."

"It can't be," Erik said as he tried to stand.

Ivy pushed Erik down. "Yes, it can. From what I now understand, the Bramburgh castle has a working transfusium."

Erik sat motionless.

"Erik, we are not that much different. You and I." Ivy pulled up on Erik's chin. "Look at me."

Erik raised his chin staring upward at her face, upside down. She smiled, holding a gentle gaze into his eyes, and watched as she slid a piece of broken glass across his neck.

"But there can only be one of us!" she hissed.

Erik clenched his throat, gasping. His hulking body fell to the floor. Looking up toward Ivy, he mouthed the words, "I trusted you." As one hand quivered, pulling his bottle of laudanum from his vest pocket.

Ivy shouted into the next room, "Ivan!"

The baggy trousered workman entered holding his pipe. He looked at Erik, emotionless, and then Ivy. "Yes, Madam?"

"Remove the steam buggy from the front drive, and prepare for a journey. Tomorrow, we set off to the Bramburgh castle, to procure a new transfusium."

AUTHOR BIOGRAPHY

Kevin is a fiction writer living in New Mexico, he enjoys writing about bizarre events and odd personalities.

Find more of his stories on

his website https://urbansfiction.blog/ and the

https://www.transcendent-authors.com

ROAD TO RED LODGE

Scar woke up in a foul, foul mood. It wasn't unusual for bears to awaken in bad moods, but this was an exceptional case. There were extenuating circumstances. First off, winter arrived late. Scar had taken to his cave in late November, as was his wont. But autumn hung on with warm breezes and autumnal smells, and frolicking rabbits played noisily into December. The big grizzly came to the mouth of his cave more than once to roar threateningly at them.

He tossed and turned for two more weeks before a storm finally placed a sound-muffling blanket of welcome snow over the entire Rocky Mountain area of the Montana/Wyoming border. Scar snuggled into his bed of twigs and leaves and shut the world out of his consciousness, dreaming only of a spring feast to come.

Then spring came.

But it came early.

Scar sat up abruptly from his deep sleep. "Arghh!" he growled. Birds were chirping and singing. The damn rabbits were at it again! And now, SQUIRRELS! Squirrels were chattering!

Scar scrambled onto his back legs, stubbing his toes, and roared loudly. Groggy from his long sleep and forgetting the low ceiling, he rushed to the cave opening, struck his brow, shrieked defiantly, and burst through the opening to the great outdoors, intent on destroying something. But he forgot the four-foot drop that served as his front doorstep. The big bear fell forward and plunged into the chasm still filled with snow that had, in the sudden warming, turned to slush.

"AAARRRGGGHHH!" filled the valley and echoed off the canyon walls. All sound and activity ceased. Rabbits, birds, and squirrels froze in place. Even the breeze seemed immobilized and hid in the tree branches. Then, as if possessed of a single intelligence, the forest animals, and the breeze itself, fled.

With the delayed arrival of Winter and the early arrival of Spring, Scar, as near as he could figure, was deprived of a month or more of hibernation. Maybe even as much as six more weeks of blessed sleep. Waist deep in freezing water, slapping the slush with his front paw, he roared.

On hind legs, he scowled at his surroundings, knee-deep in icy water. He wanted something to move. Dared it to. Something he could rip apart and exact his revenge.

And eat.

His stomach ached and only encouraged his bear rage. It had been months since anything other than his own saliva had landed in the enormous cavity. Hunger pangs slowly pushed revenge to

the back burner of his consciousness. For the time being, rage
no longer dominated his thinking. Scar smacked the icy slush
again, and this time, feeling sorry for himself, his roar was low and
mournful. Life was so unfair!

Jimmy Kitchen sat up in bed, head thumping to a terrible rhythm,
and put his feet on the cold linoleum floor of the Wild Bill Motel.
The jangling of his cell phone, sounding like a school bell, had
shocked his system and set his nerves on edge.

"What!" he shouted angrily into the receiver.

"Jimmy? Jimmy, that you?"

"You called my number! Who the hell you think it is?"

The other end of the line was silent for a few moments, then,
"What the hell, Jimmy? You got two million dollars, and you wake
up in a foul mood? What's wrong with you?"

Jimmy put his hand to his head and massaged his temples.
"Sorry, Clyde. I didn't sleep good, got a bad headache. What's up?"

Clyde sniffed.

"I'll tell you what's up. Rocco got his crew out looking for you.
He knows you ripped him off."

Clyde sniffed again.

Jimmy felt sick. "How'd he find out?"

"Does it matter? Where you at? You still going ahead with the plan?" Clyde asked, sniffing yet again.

"Does he know you were in on it?"

"I'm still breathing ain't I?" Clyde cleared his throat. "You still heading for Canada, right?"

He sniffed once again.

"Yeah. What's wrong? You got a cold? Your nose sounds stuffed up."

"Yeah, I guess. Where you at now?"

"Motel in Buffalo."

"Buffalo? What you doing in New York?"

"What? No! Buffalo, Wyoming, idiot."

"Oh. (sniff) Didn't know there was a Buffalo, Wyoming. You're still going north of Great Falls to Canada, right?"

"Yeah. Why you asking? You know the plan."

"I'm just verifying. You going to cross the border into Canada north of Babb, right?"

Jimmy felt a nerve tingle in the back of his head. "What's with the questions, Clyde? You know the plan."

"I'm meeting you in (sniff) Billings. We can cross together."

"You'll never make it. You're hundreds of miles away."

Clyde's end of the line was silent for a few seconds. "Actually, I'm already here. Got us a room at the *Lost Chance Motel*. It's about a mile from Billings as you're coming into town. You can't miss it."

"We were supposed to meet in Calgary. That was the plan."

"I changed the plan." Clyde sniffed twice. "I ain't waitin' on Rocco to figure you and me ripped him off."

There was a long silence on Jimmy's end, then, "Yeah. Maybe you're right. See you in Billings. Last Chance, right?"

"Lost Chance. Not Last."

"Lost Chance. Got it."

Jimmy hung up and sat on the edge of his bed, an uneasiness creeping up his neck. After a few moments, he picked up his Road Atlas and thumbed the pages to Wyoming. *There's got to be a way around Billings.*

Clyde flipped his Samsung shut and placed it on the coffee table with a soft thud. He wore a white undershirt and light blue boxer shorts, rubber thongs on bare feet. The ice wrapped in the motel face towel was nearly melted, but he placed it back on his eye anyway. The blood dripping from his nose had slowed to only an occasional dribble, and he laid his head on the back of the couch, closed his eyes, and sniffed.

Rocco perched his corpulent frame on the edge of a rickety, faux Danish Modern chair and scooted it forward, patted Clyde's knee. He loosened his tie and dabbed beaded sweat off his forehead. "Turn that thermostat down, Victor. Like a damn sauna in here."

The big man's voice, like oily gravel rubbing over his vocal cords, took on a soothing tone. "You done good, Clyde. You done real good. Now relax a little. You bought yourself some points." Rocco glanced at Victor. "Right, Vic? He done good. Right?"

A large man in a tweed sports coat, large revolver stuck in his belt, was standing by the front door. He nodded and spoke in a bored manner, "Yeah, boss. He come through for you real good." Victor was eyeing the wobbly chair groan under Rocco's weight, and winced, fearing the worst.

Clyde leaned forward, rested his elbows on his knees, and moaned, "Oh God, Rocco, I didn't mean it. It was Jimmy. He talked me into it. Said you'd never even know we took the money."

He quickly waved his hands in front of Rocco. "No, no. What I meant was, you wouldn't know he took it. He took it!"

Both of Clyde's eyes had blackened and Rocco let a smile slide across his generous lips. "Hey, Vic, you and Joey did a job on this guy's face." He laughed. "Looks like a damn raccoon!"

At the mention of his name, the fourth man in the room, Joey, keeping watch out the front window, stepped away and let the curtain drop casting the room in gloom. He was a fidgety type, had a hard time standing still, and nodded several times. "Yeah, he does, boss. A raccoon. Yeah." He cleared his throat. "Hey, boss, time for *Price is Right*. Can I turn the TV on?"

"No!" Rocco said, then, "Vic, get Clyde some more ice in his towel. Them nostrils is making me sick."

Vic snapped his fingers. "Joey, get the man some ice."

"He said you do it."

Vic glowered at the smaller man, not saying anything. After a moment, Joey slapped Clyde's hand away from his face, grabbed the towel, and stormed out the door. Clyde yelped in pain.

The melting snow ran in swift rivulets into a brook that, much to Scar's annoyance, babbled happily over smooth, rounded rocks. His mood hadn't improved. In fact, even darker thoughts roamed the recesses of Scar's brain. Every step he took across the forest floor only made things worse. A mouse crossed his path? WHAM! A huge paw put an end to the flagrant disrespect. A robin landed in a bush? WHAM! The bush was no more.

The snow was knee-deep on the massive grizzly and his belly hair was ice encrusted. It made a scraping sound as he trundled onto a hundred-acre meadow where a strange noise had drawn him. He stood at the tree line, scanned the grass that was laying over under the weight of the warming snow. There had been a noise. He was sure of it. A strange noise that he thought he'd heard before, long ago. He listened intently. Nothing.

"Aarrrghh," he complained and slapped the ground, sending a huge cloud of snow into the air. Hunger was intense, and Scar angrily ripped a tuft of three-foot-long grass from under the snow and stuffed it between his gaping jaws. He chewed twice, then stopped. The sound again! He stood on hind legs and scanned the meadow, his head swiveling slowly like the turret on a tank.

There it was! The far end of the meadow! A truck! With humans!

Scar had come across humans a few times in his life but hadn't ever gotten close to one. He had always kept high hopes (they smelled delicious) and vowed to catch one someday. By his best estimation, the meal was six to seven minutes away, and it was going to take his best stealth techniques to sneak up on them.

He started out at a slow trot cursing the snow and tangled undergrowth hidden beneath it. It was slow going and he may have roared, loudly, a few times in voicing his frustration. Who could blame him?

But apparently, a dark brown behemoth lumbering and tripping over a white snow background roaring in hunger-induced madness, wasn't as stealthy a move as Scar hoped it would be. The humans dropped an elk antler they'd pulled from a snow drift and scrambled into their truck. Scar was in attack mode and only seconds from a delicious meal, when the truck moved. As if in a final insult, all four wheels chewed snow and ice and spit them directly into his face. He watched it speed away.

"ARRRRRGGGHHH!" Scar told it before falling face down, all four legs pounding the earth.

Jimmy got out of his Dodge sedan and stared at the *ROAD CLOSED* sign in disbelief. He'd picked this route because it by-passed Billings, joining the Interstate several miles west of it. The map took him from Buffalo, west to Cody, north over Beartooth Pass, and then through a town called Red Lodge. He reopened his Atlas, ran a finger along the route. And there it was, in small red letters blended into the reddish-brown background of the map: *Road closed Oct through May.* No wonder he hadn't seen it!

Dammit! Now he'd have to go all the way back to Buffalo and pick up I-25 to Billings. Dammit! He leaned against a fender in a blue funk. *Nothing's going right today.*

"You're screwed!" A little devil on his shoulder said.

Jimmy stared at the closed road absorbed in thought, not really seeing it.

An angel on his other shoulder scolded, *"You're pathetic. One little setback and you give up? That's not who you are! Think!"*

The road came into focus. And so did his thinking.

There were vehicle tracks in the melting snow that drove around the barrier. Patches of bare pavement revealed a route up the mountainside, and the sun was bearing down. Wisps of steam rose into the air.

"Yes!" Jimmy cried. "I can go around!

The rear end of the big Dodge fishtailed around the barrier, and its tires gripped the sun-warmed asphalt. Jimmy laughed out loud as he sped up and around the switchbacks, the blazing sun encouraging him onward toward a darkening sky.

Rocco glared out the window at the interstate, hands on his hips. "Where the hell is he, Clyde? He shoulda been here by now. I swear to God, if you tipped him we were here . . ." He let the sentence hang in the air and ripped the cellophane off a pack of Winstons, stuck a cigarette in his mouth.

Clyde clasped his hands together, held them up like a prayer. "I didn't do nothin' like that, Rocco. You gotta believe me. Honest!"

Rocco curled a lip at Clyde. "Shut up! Call him and find out where he's at." He stabbed a finger at him. "And put some clothes on! I'm sick of lookin' at your stinkin' dirty underwear! AND BURN THAT BLOODY SHIRT!"

The silence in the room was deafening. No one moved. Rocco flicked the Zippo in his hand and stuck the flame to his cigarette, bluish smoke billowed.

"I think this is a non-smoking room," Clyde said.

"ARRGGHH" emanated from Rocco's mouth as his fist flew at Clyde's face.

Jimmy reached the highest point of the pass just as his windshield wipers began to ice up. The snow had begun falling an hour earlier. It amazed him how quickly the weather had deteriorated. One moment it was sunny and almost balmy (Jimmy had even rolled his window down) and now, an hour later, his wipers had iced up.

He passed a sign indicating the apex, BEARTOOTH PASS, and took heart that he was beginning his descent. *I'll just take my time, go slow, and reach Red Lodge and rest up. No worries.*

He hunched over the steering wheel, clenching it tightly, fingers stiffening.

That was when his phone jangled, and Jimmy jerked the steering wheel. The back wheels slid left, he overcorrected, the back wheels slid right. He stopped breathing. The Dodge made a slow 360-degree turn. Jimmy froze. It was like a slow-motion dream. The big car slowed its spin and came to rest facing the same direction he had been going before the slide. In the middle of the road, a huge meadow on his left and trees off to his right, Jimmy started breathing again.

The phone got his attention. It was Clyde. He was surprised at how calm he sounded when he answered. "Yo. What's up?"

"Where you at, dude?"

"Had a little car problem. Everything just went dead. Had to get it worked on," Jimmy lied. Wind buffeted the car.

"Yeah? Where are you?"

"Just now leaving Buffalo," he lied again. "Be there in a few hours, bro."

"You shoulda called, Jimmy. I was getting worried."

"Relax. I'm on the way. Be there soon."

Jimmy hung up and gently stepped on the gas. The tires spun, but the Dodge didn't move. He got out and tried pushing, leaned his shoulder into the door jamb and strained, but the Dodge didn't move.

"Shit!" Jimmy screamed into the snow that lashed his face. He shivered his way inside the car, blasted the heater, and checked the Dodge's vitals: Half a tank of gas, engine's heat nudging its way up. Phone: 40%. He called Clyde hoping he was wrong, and Clyde hadn't confessed to Rocco. But he needed help.

"Jimmy?" Clyde said.

"Caller ID says Jimmy doesn't it? Who the hell you think it is?"

Clyde was silent, and Jimmy took deep breaths. He took his time and explained the situation, studied his Atlas, and gave explicit directions.

"You said you was in Buffalo."

"I lied." After a moment, "Sorry, Clyde." After another moment, "Now listen. I'm going to start walking toward Red Lodge. You get there, come find me and help. Understand?"

"Red Lodge?" Clyde asked. "Where's that?"

"Get a goddam map and find it! I gotta do everything?"

Snow was an inch deep on the windshield when the little devil spoke in Jimmy's head. "*You are so screwed. How stupid can you be? Give up. There is no hope.*"

Jimmy began to despair, and his head fell forward smacking the steering wheel. The horn blew loud and long. It startled him and he sat upright, heart beating fast.

The angel snickered. *"He's wrong. Think, Jimmy. You can do this. Think!"*

"I'll walk out and drag the money with me!" Jimmy shouted in the empty car. He reached into the back seat and grabbed his suitcase.

Ten minutes later, clad in all his warmest clothes: three pairs of pants, two sweaters over two white dress shirts and the shoes on his feet wrapped and tied with six T-shirts, he opened the car door. Six white socks served as gloves, six tighty-whitey underpants as a ski mask. When he got out, he was pleased and encouraged when the wind hit him, and he didn't feel any of the cold. Moving like the Michelin Man, he popped open the trunk and hefted a canvas duffel out and onto the snow-covered road. Stuffed with hundreds, fifties, and twenties, the 2 million dollars weighed in the neighborhood of 110 pounds.

"Nice neighborhood!" he and Clyde had joked.

Wasn't that funny now that Jimmy was dragging it through a blizzard.

Scar, head down and dragging his feet, plodded through the snowfall, a sorrowful sight. Very little hope left for a good outcome to the beginning of his spring. He was at the far end of the meadow heading into the forest, when a sound, followed by a slightly familiar odor, struck him.

Humans!

He stood on hind legs and looked in all directions, but the motor noise had stopped, and vision was blocked by blowing snow. The smell was diffused by the swirling winds and his frustration grew.

Then the car horn pierced his senses from across the meadow and Scar homed in on it like a drone missile.

"What the hell, Clyde?" Rocco shouted. "This some kinda joke?" His fleshy face, with an unhealthy touch of puffiness, glared over the back of the front seat at Clyde cowering next to Victor. The black Lincoln Town Car was stopped on the far side of Red Lodge in front of a sign: ROAD CLOSED, it read.

Joey, behind the wheel, scanning a road map, tapped it with a finger. "Yeah, right here, boss. It says, 'road closed October thru May'."

Rocco's mouth dropped open. He stared at Joey, then turned his attention back to Clyde and threw his hands up. "So? What the hell?"

"I, I, I'm sorry, Rocco. I don't know. Alls I know is he said to meet him here." He dropped his eyes and started sobbing.

"Get this guy outta here," Rocco said. "He disgusts me. Take him over to them bushes and put a bullet in his head."

"But . . .," Victor began.

"Put two!"

Victor looked out the window. "Where? There's people around."

Rocco's face turned scarlet. Nearly shouting now, "I don't care! Shoot them, too!"

"Wait," Clyde said, "I remember! Jimmy said he was walking! I was to go meet him."

Rocco's head swiveled to look out the front windshield. "Up there?" He stuck a Winston between his lips, touched a flame to it, and was quiet for a long, few minutes. The car filled with smoke before he spoke again.

"Victor, you and Clyde head on up that road. Find that thievin' son of a bitch and bring him to me."

"It's snowing out there, Rocco."

"I know it's snowin'. I ain't blind!"

"Joey!" Victor said, "Take Clyde up the road and get Jimmy."

The driver caught Victor's eye in the mirror, "He said for you to do it."

"Goddammit!" Rocco screamed. "Both of yuz go! Now!"

"Me too, Rocco?" Clyde asked.

The fat man's face turned purple. "AAARRRGGGHHH!"

Jimmy was miserable. The underpants on his head collected several inches of snow and his breathing had iced over one of the leg holes. He could feel his cheeks getting chapped.

And the bag!

I hate this thing! Where's that goddamn Clyde? I've been dragging this goddamn bag for a goddamn hour!

He pushed on, the duffle strap burning into his shoulder. *He's gonna drag this thing the rest of the way when he gets here. Why do I gotta do all the work?*

Then, far off to his left, a black dot in the whiteout. Jimmy's relief at the sight of Clyde coming to his rescue thrilled his heart. Tears dribbled down his cheek.

His friend was on a trajectory that would pass him by a quarter of a mile. Jimmy panicked.

He dropped the bag, waved his arms over his head, and called out.

"Clyde! Clyde! Over here. Yo, over here!"

Scar stopped. He'd heard something. He concentrated, not moving. What was it? Was it human? But it stopped. The wind howled. He shook his head as if to clear it and took a step on his track to the first sound.

What the hell? He can't hear me? It's the damn wind. "Clyde! Clyyyyyde!" Jimmy yelled, waving his arms. "Woo hoo. Clyyyyde. Over heeere!"

There was the noise again. Scar rose onto his back legs and let his gaze wander slowly over the landscape. Puzzled, he was just giving up, when,

THERE!

A dark dot. Something seemed to be trapped and struggling. Not too far away, either. Elation flooded Scar's emotions.

HUMAN!

Scar changed direction, fell to all fours, and took dead aim at the delicious meal awaiting him.

"Oh shit," Jimmy said. "That ain't Clyde." He turned and tugged on the two-million-dollar duffle bag, knees pumping through the deepening snow. The bag became easier to pull and was gliding like a sled. Jimmy took hope. He ran for a few minutes, adrenaline pushing him with unexpected energy.

He can't catch me!

Jimmy glanced over his shoulder.

"Aaahh!" he screamed. Scar's open claws ripped at the duffel; saliva dripped from open jaws.

"Aarghh!" Scar roared, human smells exciting him, enticing and teasing his empty stomach.

Jimmy felt a slight tug on the duffle, the bear hooking a claw on a loose strap and ripping it. Scar lunged. Both front paws of the six-hundred-pound grizzly landed on the bag. Jimmy was jerked backward to a stop, both feet flying out in front of him. He landed flat on his back, and a *whump* sucked all the air from his lungs. Scar roared and slammed the side of the duffel sending it into a ravine, the 110 pounds of money pulling Jimmy behind it.

He tumbled and rolled down the steep hill and came to rest on his back. He'd closed his eyes on the way down and when he opened them, didn't like what he saw at all. It was the gigantic form of a huge grizzly bear standing on hind legs, arms raised brandishing knife-like claws on frying pan sized paws. Teeth dominated what Jimmy could see of its face.

"You are so screwed," the little devil voice said.

Jimmy waited for encouragement from the other side.

"He's right," said the angel.

Scar roared, "AAARRRGGHH," and started down into the ravine.

Jimmy wrestled himself free from the duffel, screamed, "AAAAAHHHH," and scrambled down the canyon oblivious to sprained ankles, torn clothes, and branches gouging his face.

Scar stopped and sniffed at the bag.

Rocco's hand was picking through a twelve-piece bucket of chicken seeking another thigh when Victor and Joey came into view through the falling snow. They each had a hand under some guy's armpits looking as if they were carrying him, Clyde stumbled behind. Rocco dropped the chicken into the bucket and got out of the Lincoln.

"Where the hell you guys been? And what's wrong with this piece of shit?" Rocco asked, pointing at a raggedy Jimmy Kitchen.

Jimmy looked near death, his face torn and covered in dried blood, exposed skin turning blue. Most of the extra clothes he'd put on had been lost. Two pairs of Jockey shorts were tight around his neck, his head having come through the leg holes.

Rocco stared open-mouthed. "What kind of pervert shit is this? What'd you do to him?"

"Nuttin', boss," Joey said. "We found him like this."

Victor tried to explain. "That's right, boss. He was laying in the road about a mile or two up."

"You shoulda seen it, boss," Joey laughed. "We grabbed him and he started screamin' and cryin'. Said something about 'don't eat me, don't eat me I don't wanna die.' Funnier than shit."

"He don't wanna die? Too bad," Rocco said and pulled out his pistol.

Clyde spoke up for the first time. "Wait!"

Rocco turned on him and aimed the gun. "Why? You wanna go first?"

"Uh uh, boss. He ain't got the money on him."

It was another three days before the road from Red Lodge to Beartooth Pass opened. To say Rocco was impatient would be an understatement. He kept Jimmy and Clyde in confinement at the Lost Chance Motel issuing threats between buckets of chicken.

The five of them pulled out of Red Lodge and started the search for the money on a sunny day with towering clouds on the horizon. Every few minutes, as they seemed to turn continuously on the numerous switchbacks, Rocco would slap Jimmy on the side of his head.

"This it? This look familiar?" A few minutes later, another slap, "How about now?"

"I'm not sure, Rocco. It looks so different." Another slap. "Let's go to the top and start. That's where it was. It'll look more familiar then."

They found Jimmy's car an hour later. It was undamaged, but the battery was dead.

"Let's jump it," Jimmy suggested. Rocco shook his head and Jimmy said, "So I don't have to come back for it."

Joey laughed. "What, you crazy? You ain't gonna need no car."

Rocco fixed Joey with a dead eye look, but it was too late.

Clyde and Jimmy exchanged looks. Clyde whined, "You said you was letting us go when we get the money."

Jimmy jumped in with, "Go ahead and kill us, Rocco. But I ain't finding no money. Gonna cost you two million dollars to whack me."

The car was quiet for a good two minutes. Uncharacteristically, Rocco spoke quietly, "Victor, get the jumper cables and start Jimmy's car. You and Clyde ride in it." He turned to Jimmy. "Find the bag or I'm shooting you and burning you and shithead Clyde in that piece of shit Dodge."

Scar was in a much better mood these days. Hunger wasn't a huge problem. The bag he'd taken was full of surprises and had soothed his hunger. The fact that it was a two-million-dollar dinner didn't impress him. But not much bothered him these days. He tolerated the rabbits. Even the foolish chattering of squirrels wasn't much of an annoyance. So what if they ran about with cheeks crammed with nuts? He was okay with it.

When the car rumbled past him full of delicious humans, he watched it and only tracked it with his eyes. Contentment described his life. *"Don't bother me and I won't bother you"* was his motto. Even when the car started back in his direction, it was only a matter of minor importance. Even when it paused and the humans got out and walked in his direction, Scar only took a position behind trees and watched.

"Hey, Jimmy," Rocco said, "get out and walk. You was walking when you ditched the bag, so, it'll help refresh your thinking."

Jimmy's heartbeat picked up, he looked at Rocco wide-eyed. "You remember the bear I told you about? I ain't getting out unless somebody comes with me."

The car filled with smoke again before Rocco consented. "Joey, get out and walk with him. You can't see nothing in here anyway." Joey stopped the Lincoln and the Dodge pulled in behind. Rocco got out. "All right," he shouted, "everybody out. We're walking for a while. I ain't scared of no little bear." He tapped the gun in his waistband. "The bear better be scared of me."

"But, what about the cars?" Victor complained.

Rocco flicked his cigarette butt at him. "Stop whining. Cars ain't going nowhere. You can come back, get the cars, and pick me up when I get tired. Grab the chicken." As an afterthought, he added, "Leave the keys on the seats."

Clyde thought this a bad idea. "Somebody might steal 'em, Rocco."

Rocco waved an arm at the wilderness. "Who, stupid?" He shook a finger in Clyde's face. "You're gonna piss me off again. Don't say another word."

It was Joey that spotted the duffel bag lying twenty feet down an embankment. "Here it is," he cried. He didn't spot Scar until all five of them had made their way, clumsily, over the rocks and shrubs. They stumbled down the slope oblivious to torn clothes and scraped shins in their eagerness to lay hands on two million dollars.

Scar watched carefully as the humans approached. It didn't bother him until they stopped at the top of the embankment. He sniffed the air, picked up their scent, and felt a slight rumble in his stomach. He weighed the pros and cons of whether it was worth the effort to climb the hill and pursue what would surely be a good meal. He sat, undecided, when, surprisingly, it was settled for him.

All five came down into the ravine.

Joey pointed at that which all of them were seeing. "The bag's been ripped to shreds, boss. There ain't no money!"

Rocco, enraged, threw the chicken bucket to the ground. "What the hell, Jimmy! Where's the money?"

Jimmy pointed at the ground. "There's pieces all around. Look! Shredded bits everywhere. It's in the mud or something."

Clyde bent down and picked up a clump, sniffed it. "That ain't mud. I think it's poop. Green poop."

Scar took exception when the humans stopped at his dinner bag.

Joey stood wide-eyed. "It's bear shit."

"How do you know that?" Rocco asked.

They all looked where Joey, now speechless, was pointing.

"AAARRRGGHH!" Scar roared and stepped from behind a tree.

The five turned and scrambled, slipping and sliding, stumbling over one another, struggling up the hill.

Scar ran to his bag to protect it and slapped the ground, roared even more loudly. He'd never seen this many humans in one place before. Although not starving, instinct told him he should probably get something to eat. He thought choosing which to grab first would be a difficult decision.

It wasn't.

Four of them were almost at the top, but a fat one was making no progress at all. On hands and knees, his fingers dug with futility in the soft turf of the steep ravine's walls, his feet getting no traction.

"Run, Rocco, run!" Victor yelled from the top.

Scar, more annoyed than anything else, yelled back, "AARRGGHH!" and made a half-hearted charge up the hill.

The four at the top ran for the cars.

Scar eased his way back down and contemplated Rocco.

Jimmy and Clyde jumped in the Dodge, while Victor and Joey ran to the Lincoln. They heard gunshots, and Jimmy drove to the spot where they'd scrambled out of the ravine.

"Keep the motors running," Jimmy yelled out his window before they got out and crept to the edge.

"Hope Rocco's okay," Victor whispered.

They peered over the edge. Clyde gasped. Scar had a leg in his mouth, eyes closed, and was standing in a pool of blood.

Victor's hands slapped his cheeks. "Oh my God!"

"Get away!" screamed Joey at the big bear.

Scar roared loud and long at the figures on the road and splashed the redness onto his face.

The four backed away to the cars and stood silently for a few minutes.

Clyde, voice trembling, "You think that grizzly will come after us?"

Victor shook his head. "Nah. It's busy with Rocco right now."

Joey spoke softly, "Poor Rocco."

"Yeah," the others said.

Another period of silence lasted several minutes, and they leaned against the cars, each lost in thought.

"I guess Rocco's dead," Jimmy finally said.

"Money's gone," Clyde muttered.

Finally, Victor spoke, "Whatta you guys want to do?"

"I suppose we should go kill that bear," Joey said. "I mean, you know, cause he's eating Rocco."

"Yeah," they all answered without enthusiasm.

A few moments more of silence and Clyde cleared his throat, spoke quietly, "Any chicken left in you guy's car?"

"Nah," Joey said. "Rocco took it with him. Remember?"

Clyde shrugged. "I wonder if there's any left at the motel."

Jimmy pushed himself off the Dodge and checked his watch. "I think *The Godfather* might be on in a couple hours. We can just make it."

"Yeah," Victor chimed in. "We'll grab some beer on the way."

"Chicken, too," Clyde said. "Just in case."

The big grizzly, lost in bliss, took no notice of the revving cars engines when they left.

An hour later, Scar rested in the long grass and scratched his belly, at peace with the world. He had to give himself a pat on the back: Humans really were delicious.

AUTHOR BIOGRAPHY

Lawrence is a veteran and retired government employee. He resides in the Manzano Mountains outside Albuquerque, New Mexico with his spouse, Julie, and their Siberian Husky brood. He is a published writer and enjoys working in multiple genres, including mystery, science fiction, and horror.

Milton Keynes UK
Ingram Content Group UK Ltd.
UKHW040712201123
432908UK00001B/301